Little Red

Little Red Lies

JULIE JOHNSTON

TUNDRA BOOKS

Published in Canada by Tundra Books, a division of Random House of Canada Limited,
One Toronto Street, Suite 300, Toronto, Ontario M5C 2V6

Published in the United States by Tundra Books of Northern New York,
P.O. Box 1030, Plattsburgh, New York 12901

Library of Congress Control Number: 2012947608

Library and Archives Canada Cataloguing in Publication

Johnston, Julie, 1941-
Little red lies / Julie Johnston.

ISBN 978-1-77049-313-1. – ISBN 978-1-77049-314-8 (epub)

I. Title.

PS8569.O387L58 2013   jC813'.54   C2012-905815-7

We acknowledge the financial support of the Government of Canada through the Canada
Book Fund and that of the Government of Ontario through the Ontario Media Development
Corporation's Ontario Book Initiative. We further acknowledge the support of the Canada
Council for the Arts and the Ontario Arts Council for our publishing program.

Edited by Kathy Lowinger and Sue Tate
Designed by Rachel Cooper

www.tundrabooks.com

Printed and bound in the United States of America

1 2 3 4 5 6   18 17 16 15 14 13

For Diane

ACKNOWLEDGMENTS

I am grateful to Kathy Lowinger for coming out of retirement to edit my manuscript and to offer her unfailing support and spot-on comments. I also want to thank Kathryn Cole, who, early on, gave me invaluable advice and encouragement. Many thanks, also, to Sue Tate for her fine-tooth copyediting and for her inestimable help and insightful suggestions. Also, I am indebted to Doctor Arthur Turner for his medical advice concerning the treatment of leukemia in the late 1940s. As always, a heartfelt thank-you to my writing sisterhood for their advice, encouragement, comfort and cheer, and to my family, close and extended, for their much-appreciated support.

CHAPTER

1

"Rachel! Come along."

"In a sec."

"The train will be here any minute."

"Coming!"

Nag, nag! My parents dash away, my mother clutching my father's arm, his coattails flapping.

I take a bright shiny lipstick from my pocket. Don't want to rush this job of sophisticating myself, but the train wails in the distance, distracting me. I wrench the rearview mirror around for a closer look. Where my mouth should be, there's an uneven gash, the color of fresh blood. I do look older, though. I leer happily into the mirror. Slamming the car door behind me, I race to the station platform.

My parents are near the front of the crowd with, *oh rats*, Mary Foley. I inch my way through and say hi to her with my hand over my mouth. She's eyeing my plaid skirt and the baggy knees of my stockings.

Folding my lips in, I slouch and plunge my hands deep into my pockets to make my coat longer. The pockets rip a little bit, but who cares? It's all part of turning into a classy woman of the world.

The steam engine wails. The line of dark red coaches snaking behind it sways as it rounds the long curve before the station. For a brief second, I have an eerie feeling that the train is taking Jamie far away instead of bringing him home. The bell clangs, the moment passes, and I have goose bumps up and down my arms.

Aha! The good old days are on their way back. Can't wait—sunshine, fishing with Jamie at Granny's farm, cloudless nights in our backyard searching out the Dippers and Orion and Betelgeuse. He has a map of the night skies, both northern and southern constellations. Once he said, *We are just tiny specks!*

I'm not, I said. I remember being soaked from the dew, from lying in the grass looking up. *I'm huge.* I meant *tall.* I was only about eight at the time, so what would you expect? Not only that, I was the tallest, skinniest person in my class. Still am, pretty much.

As my mother eyes my Hollywood lips, her jaw drops in surprise. Actually, it's more like horror. Like a peevish hen, she makes a clucking sound and rummages through her handbag for a handkerchief to wipe them off. The engine steams to a halt before she finds one. Forgetting me, she peers through the crowd, watching for Jamie to emerge through the billowing steam. I tower over her by almost an inch and a half, winner of the first round of the Lipstick Battle. I'm practicing my knock-'em-dead smile.

The war has been over for ten months, but, like many over there, Jamie's just returning, now. A boy of eighteen when he left, he's finally coming home a man, a soldier, a conqueror.

And what have I conquered? I curl my fingers around the lipstick. Childhood. Gone. Finished. The lipstick shade is *Little Red Lies*.

The coach doors open. I can't stop trying to scratch the insides of my elbows through my coat. I have eczema, which gets worse when I'm excited. So here I am, bouncing up and down, trying to see, scratching like mad, and worried that I won't recognize Jamie.

Taking time out from her own excitement, my mother frowns at me. "Do you have to go to the bathroom, Rachel?"

"I'm just trying to see!" Up on my toes, back on my heels. She puts a heavy hand on my shoulder, but I squirm out from under it and skirt behind her to wait beside my glowing father. Everyone around me is eager, too, including the passengers, as they step down to the platform and search the crowd for a familiar face.

"The two biggest disappointments of my life," Dad says, removing his hat and smoothing back his thinning

hair. "Too young for the First World War and too old for
the Second." He says this a lot, so I can ignore him. I just
hope he won't find it necessary to salute anyone. He puts
his hat back on, stares at my glorious lips, then looks away
quickly. He's not one to make comments of a personal
nature. I scratch my arms.

Jamie wrote to us while he was overseas, but I could
count the letters directed to me on two hands with all my
fingers sawed off. They all started *Dear Family* and ended
Yours truly, James H. McLaren, as if he were president of
a large corporation. I always checked the back of the last
page to see if there was a *Hi, Rachel, I miss you.* But there
never was. Not even a *Hi, Rachel, I sometimes think about
you.* Too sentimental, too personal for my brother. *Hi
there, old Rache.* Would that have been too much for him?
I wrote scads of letters to him, but did he write back to
share a single thought? Not once.

Letters not sent.

You may never get a chance to read this, Rachel,
but I hope you will. They censor everything over
here, so I'm not too keen to put it in the mail.
I was going to keep a diary but decided I needed
a face in my mind, a personality whose reaction
I could imagine. So I'm directing this to you.
    It's quiet here tonight. I can't sleep. In

*about five hours, some of us new guys are being
shipped out for our first real taste of war. I
guess I'm a bit scared.*

*For some reason, tonight I've been thinking
about home, about lying on the dewy grass at
night searching out constellations. Remember the
sky map? Once you said you wouldn't want to live
in Australia because you'd be looking at the
stars upside down.*

*Another time you asked me what God looked
like, and I said, like a lit-up lightbulb, and
you said, how many watts?*

*I think about you a lot, especially when I
need to bring my deepest thoughts to the surface, the ones you always tried to drag out of
me, whether I wanted them out or not.*

I watch the soldiers closely. Some who have farther to go
wave through the train's open windows, yelling garbled
toasts and nonsense advice to their buddies getting off.
One of the smart alecks snatches the cap from the head of
a handsome young guy with a slight limp, but he jumps
for it and gets it back with a wince of pain.

"It's Jamie!"

It really is. His hair's shorter, he's favoring one leg,
but he hasn't changed all that much. Edging through
the crowd, Mother gets to him first, grabbing him amid

a fluster of tears and yelps. "Oh, my boy!" she shrieks. "You're limping. You didn't write home about a limp. My poor darling! What happened? Show me where it hurts."

"All over," he says, laughing at her.

She leans away from him to take a good look, then grabs him again, nearly squeezing the breath out of him. She looks young and pretty in her wild enthusiasm, even with a few strands of gray in her dark hair.

Jamie shrugs and cocks an eyebrow over her shoulder at our beaming father, who has removed his fedora again. His high forehead glows like a sunrise.

"Careful, Dora," he says. "You'll break his ribs with those bear hugs."

I keep bobbing beside him, trying to get a piece of him, and at last he grins at me. But then his eyes move to Mary and his smile broadens. He grabs Mary Foley by her coat lapels and plants a great smacking kiss right on her lips, a decorous pink, I can't help noticing. I am shocked.

At last, it's my turn. His khaki uniform is rough against my cheek and smells of sweat and grown-up boy and the world. He peels me away from him, finally, and says, "So how's the old skinny-minny?"

I hang on to his wrists, not ready to release him until I can give him full benefit of the debonair look I've been rehearsing. I stretch my Joan-Crawford lips, sling out my jaw, and bat my eyelashes for all I'm worth, but he just laughs.

"Yikes!" He tries to shake free. "Get her away! What's that red stuff on your mouth? War paint?"

"It's called *Little Red Lies*."

"Are you sure it isn't called *Big Red Lips*?"

I let him go. How embarrassing! I'm such an overboard person!

No, I'm not.

I'm Pathetic with a capital P.

No. Magnificent. Capital M!

By the time I finish arguing with myself, Jamie and Dad are shaking hands and giving each other hearty pats on the back.

Jamie keeps glancing at each of us in turn, looking a little dazed. "Instead of only three years, I feel as if I've been away for ten!"

In the car, squashed between Mary Foley and me, Jamie tries to hold Mary's hand, but she glances shyly at the backs of our parents' heads and tucks her hands between her knees.

"What's the best thing about being home, son?" Dad asks.

"No one's in uniform," he says. "I can't wait to shed mine."

On the short drive home, no one can think of anything momentous to say. Jamie was the one off firing guns and throwing grenades. All we did was cope with ration tickets and a shortage of gasoline.

I sneak a sideways glance at Jamie while he looks out the window for changes on the streets of Middleborough. *Is this really Jamie?* I have a vague sense that the boy I grew up with isn't the one who got off the train. I keep taking peeks to catch him off guard, hoping the authentic Jamie will show up.

He does for a moment, when he turns suddenly and catches me staring. I bite my lip, trying to look innocent. "Pow!" he says with a pretend punch to my jaw. The real Jamie's there, lurking just below the surface.

"The best thing about Jamie being home," I say, "is that now we can go right back to where we left off before he went away."

"That would certainly be nice," Dad says.

"It's so good to have you back!" Mother repeats at least three times, twisting around to make sure he's still there.

Dad keeps saying, "Quite a change in the weather, yes siree. It's what we expect in early March, though, isn't it?"

A little chorus of agreement rises from the backseat, as if we are all strangers.

"They're calling for snow this evening," Dad says.

"Gosh," Jamie says. "What next?" Briefly, he eyes the ceiling.

"By the way, Jamie," Dad says, "I saved some newspaper clippings about the Invasion of Normandy and about our troops in Belgium and Holland. Maps, too. I'll give them to you."

"Oh, swell." Jamie is kind of slumping now.

"Oh, Howard, I would think he'd want to forget the war," Mother says.

"Not at all. Am I right, son? Sometime down the road, you might want to talk about . . ."

"You never know. Hey, any word about Coop?" His best friend Coop's plane was shot down over Germany three months before the war ended.

"Nothing," Mother says. "His parents were told to contact the International Red Cross, but they haven't heard anything."

"He'll turn up," I say. "He has to." Jamie looks at me as if he isn't all that sure. "You know Coop," I say, "usually late, but he always shows up in the end."

He grins. "The teachers used to call him the late Mr. Cooper. I'll go visit his family. They might know something by now."

Granny arrives just before we sit down to dinner. "You're all out of breath," I tell her.

"You would be, too, if you'd driven that blasted truck as fast as I did all the way in from the farm. Where's my boy? Let me get my hands on him." She gives Jamie a good hard Granny hug and says, "You're not so big that we can't still make you mind." She holds on to his shoulders and blesses him with her fierce loving gaze until he has to look away.

"Jeez, Granny," he says.

"I'd have got here sooner," she says, "if it hadn't been for that new vet, who takes off early on Friday as if nobody's cattle get the bloat on a Friday. I had to hunt him down at home."

We're standing around the kitchen leaning against things, watching Mother take the roast out of the oven, watching her make gravy.

"That's what the world's come to," Granny says. "Nobody wants to work. That's what a war does for you."

Granny's eyes are on my lips. *Here it comes*, I think. A war paint crack, or raspberry jam, or here's a hankie, wipe it off. But, no. She grins at me and winks.

Mary Foley has been asked to stay for dinner. "Sit down, please," Mother says, bustling us ahead of her into the dining room, "before everything gets cold."

We bow our heads while Dad, from his end of the table, disposes of the blessing: "GraciousHeavenlyFather-grantusthyblessingonthesemerciesforChrist'ssakeamen."

I keep my eyes open to see if Mary will cross herself. She does. In this town, almost half the people are Catholic and the rest are Protestant. A lot of petty rivalries go on because of it. Not much here in the way of any more exotic religions, though.

As Dad carves the roast in thin slices, the way Mother likes it, plates are passed down to her for helpings of roast potatoes, carrots, and canned peas from the matching china serving dishes. "Now, Mary," she says, "I know your religion dictates fish on Friday. I'm sorry you won't be able to enjoy roast beef with the rest of us, but I've made you a little tuna casserole."

"Ugh!" I say. "Poor Mary. She's probably missing out on good old macaroni and cheese at home." Mary turns red and scowls at me.

Mother plops a beige dollop, the consistency of porridge, onto her plate. "May I give you carrots and peas with your casserole, Mary?"

"No, thank you, Mrs. McLaren." She has good manners and says thank you a second time. Again her cheeks turn pink.

I can tell by the dainty bites she takes that she hates tuna casserole. Jamie frowns down at *his* plate. "I'd like some of that, too, Mother, if there's enough. I've gone off roast beef a bit."

"Now, don't be silly, Jamie. Just eat what's put before you. It's the first decent roast we've had since the war, and it's always been your favorite. We're having it especially."

"Tell us all about the war, Jamie," I say. "It must have been so exciting being right in the thick of it, firing guns and everything."

"Exciting?"

"You know. Kill or be killed."

Jamie doesn't answer right away. He stares at his plate as if he's trying to figure out what's on it. "Some of my friends were killed," he says.

"Now for dessert," Mother interrupts, "we have two kinds of pie."

Dad says very quickly, "My-oh-my, two kinds of pie."

I can't look at Jamie. Instead I stare down at my ragged fingernails and wish I'd never said a word. His *Dear Family* letters never mentioned friends getting killed.

"Jamie!" Mother taps the table beside him. "You've eaten almost nothing. There'll be no pie for you, young man, until I see a good portion of that plate cleared."

"Sorry, it's delicious. Too excited to eat, I guess."

Mother fetches the pies, apple and pumpkin, and places them in front of Dad to serve while I clear the table. Mary helps me, even though she's a guest, and is rewarded with a large slice of each of the pies to make up for the disappointing casserole. Jamie asks for a small piece of pumpkin and eats most of it.

I can tell Granny's getting agitated about something. She always sits very straight and wiggles her shoulders when she's about to make a pronouncement. Her probing eyes are on Jamie. "You've got too thin, my boy. Look at the neck on him, scrawny inside that shirt collar."

"Army-issue. They always go big on the shirts. Anybody mind if Mary and I go for a walk?"

Of course we mind, but before Mother can discourage

it, Dad says, "Go ahead, son. You two need a chance to catch up." Mother sighs audibly, but it's too late. They're already standing and pushing in their chairs.

"Can I come, too?" I know the answer will be a loud and blunt *no* and steel myself for it.

Jamie pokes his head back into the dining room. "Not this time, Rache," he says gently.

I think my mouth is hanging open like a character in a cartoon. He wasn't normally this kind before the war. My formerly vicious lips, now merely a pinkish smudge, turn up in an almost smile. War sure changes people.

"Thanks again for dinner, Mrs. McLaren," Mary calls. We hear the hangers jangle as she gets her coat from the hall closet.

When the door shuts behind them, I ask to be excused and go to the living room window. Our street, Wakefield, is like a stage subtly lit to resemble evening. I know a thing or two about stages because I'm in the school drama club. My dream is to act.

Jamie's arm is around Mary's shoulders. Hers should be around his waist, but it isn't. They spend a long time looking into each other's eyes before Mary looks away. I direct them to walk toward the streetlight, where they will be bathed in its golden glow, and they do.

"Snow," I whisper. As if on cue, snow feathers lightly from on high. This must be what it's like to write a play or direct one. *Stage direction: as they move closer to the streetlight, he bends down and she raises her face. They kiss.*

And they do. They kiss while snow falls on their heads and shoulders, and I let them until . . . until a little pang of longing says that's enough. *Move along*, I direct. And they do. The power of the director! What's wrong with the scene is the casting. Mary isn't the right girl.

It isn't until the next morning that I have a chance to get Jamie all to myself. I knock on his bedroom door, and he says, "Come in." He squints at my hair. "Quite a bird's nest you've got there, kiddo."

I have such thick, curly dark hair that it takes me about half an hour to get a brush through it. So, mostly I don't, until Mother shrieks at me, *I'm taking that head of yours, and I'm going to shave it bald if you don't . . . blah, blah, blah.*

I'm still in my pajamas, draping myself across the foot of Jamie's bed. I have lots of questions for him.

We can hear Mother rattling around downstairs, getting breakfast. Dad's bringing in the paper from the front veranda. We hear him call to our neighbor Mrs. Hall that Jamie's home, and Mrs. Hall burbles something back.

Jamie's chest is bare, and he draws his knees up, keeping the covers tight across his waist. He still looks like the boy who went away in spite of the dark hair sprouting on his chest. It wasn't there before, or if it was, I didn't notice.

I wonder if he wore his shorts to bed or if he's completely

naked. Mother put his ironed and folded pajamas on the bureau, and they're still there. If I tried that, Mother would know the instant my naked body slipped between the sheets, and she'd storm into my room with a lecture about personal decency. Every so often, I have the urge to be personally indecent. I'm developing a bosom now, and sometimes I take off all my clothes in front of my mirror just to admire it.

I sit up. "I'm thinking of writing a play."

"That's nice. About what?"

"The war. Kind of a romance."

"A romance about war?"

"It's going to be about a soldier who has to kill the enemy but at the last minute doesn't, and so he gets shot. But he doesn't die, and this nurse in a hospital looks after him, and, um . . ."

"Don't tell me, don't tell me, let me guess—they fall in love."

"Yes, actually." I look down and chew on my thumb nail. "It's pretty obvious, isn't it?" *Of course it is.* "It sounds stupid!"

"No, it sounds good. I hope it has a happy ending. After all the bombs and killing and destruction over there, I bet people want happy endings." That is the most grown-up, sensitive thing he's ever said to me.

"What was it like, Jamie? I don't know very much about war." I hug my knees and scrunch up his top blanket with my bare toes. "What was it like knowing there were boys and men out there who wanted to kill you?"

"You know, you've got eyes just like Granny's, the way they bore right into a person. If the two of you ever put your joint intensity together, you could tip the world right off its axis."

"Tell me," I say. "I don't know the first thing about war."

"What do you know about love?"

"I can imagine being in love. War is a different country. I can't imagine living there."

"Sooner or later, I'll tell you war stories. Right now, I want to shove the war right off the edge of the world."

"Jamie, come on . . ."

"In a war, it's like thinking about bullies. You could let yourself be bullied, or you could fight back."

"And what else?"

"I can't remember what else."

"But, how could you forget something like that so soon?"

He moves down under the covers, pulling them up to his chin. "If you squint your eyes half shut, you don't see as much. And you don't remember as much, either. It's as if everything is only half true." He draws his brows together. "I suppose you'll put that in your play."

"Maybe." I probably will, after I have more time to study my brother under my personal microscope of human behavior.

"Did many soldiers fall in love?"

"No one I knew. A lot of soldiers died."

"When people get shot, is it—not really, but sort of— like a balloon deflating?"

"No, of course not. I think you're trying to rewrite my memories."

"I'm not." I scowl at him.

"I had this friend, Herman Visser."

"Was he shot?"

"Yes. A scrawny guy. Unhappy. Kind of a deflated balloon while he was alive. His family was Dutch, but he had an unfortunate nickname—Herman-the-German."

"Did he have a girlfriend?"

"I don't think so. He had a mother."

CHAPTER

2

A week later, I turn fourteen, for all the good it does me. I'm still too tall, still too skinny, still scratching my arms raw, and still not allowed to wear lipstick to school.

The day after my birthday, I have an appointment with the doctor to have my arms examined. We're hoping that some new ointment has been discovered that will cure me.

Doctor Melvin's waiting room walls are plastered with large Dingbat calendars from the Charles E. Frosst drug company. Never mind leafing through boring, outdated *LIFE* magazines while you wait for the doctor. You can stay amused for hours looking at the cartoon scenes of curious buglike creatures, with antennae coming out of their heads. Some of the Dingbats are dressed as wartime Red Cross doctors and nurses; some carry injured soldier-bugs on stretchers; some wind endless rolls of bandage around the spindly arms and legs of the injured; some lie on cots and get blood transfusions from something that looks like a gas pump. There are also scenes of peacetime hospitals, where Dingbat nurses inject sick Dingbats with giant hypos or spoon medicine down their throats, and Dingbat doctors put casts on broken legs or hover over Dingbat patients on operating tables. And there are Dingbat pharmacists with their pills and medicines, and dentists with their lethal-looking drills. In Dingbat Land, all the little Dingbats get looked after, and I'm pretty sure they all get better.

There is no new miracle ointment (there would have been in Dingbat Land), so I have to use the same old smelly stuff that doesn't work very well.

"One of these days," Doctor Melvin says, "you'll outgrow this rash. You'll see."

Besides continuing to scratch my arms, I work a bit on the play I want to write, even though I don't know the first thing about writing one. I'm starting with the scene under the streetlight with the snow falling. But I bog down trying to write dialogue. And where should I set it? And how do I get the soldier into the war? Writing a play isn't as easy as it looks.

School is a series of low points. Drama club drags, mainly because I haven't been given a part in the play.

School sports get along better without me. Nothing is happening in my life.

It's first period, Thursday, English, Hamlet's soliloquy in act 3, scene 1. I've memorized it right down to the last comma. I want Mr. Mackiewitz to ask me to recite it because I want to prove I can act.

Besides being our homeroom teacher, Mr. Mackiewitz is director of the school play. If he sees me dripping with dramatic pathos, maybe I'll get a part next year.

But he doesn't even notice me beaming hopefully at him. He stands at his desk at the front of the classroom, his eyes wide with surprise, as if he can't believe he's forgotten the opening words *To be, or not to be.* . . . He falls into his chair and slumps over his *Hamlet.*

For seven seconds, our class of twenty-one students is in a state of total paralysis, until my friend Ruthie screams.

Hazel Carrington shouts, "I'll go get someone!"

She returns with the math teacher from next door, who checks Mr. Mackiewitz's pulse. "Somebody run to the office. Get them to call an ambulance!"

Hazel Carrington, the most responsible student in the class, runs to the principal's office. The math teacher tells us all to leave quickly and quietly and to wait in the lunchroom until our next class.

The lunchroom always smells like armpits mixed with either egg salad sandwiches or overripe bananas. Today it's egg. The air hums with the electricity generated by twenty-one nervous teenagers.

"Do you think he'll die?"

"I think he did. He's pretty old."

"Listen!" We hear the ambulance siren getting closer and then stop. We're quiet, imagining what's about to happen.

"I guess we'll be getting a supply teacher," someone says.

"I wonder if the school play will be canceled," Hazel Carrington says.

"The poor guy," someone thinks to say.

It was just after Christmas when Mr. Mackiewitz posted the cast list with no sign of my name on it.

"I know you're disappointed," he said to me.

"I thought my audition went pretty well."

"Sorry, I just couldn't picture you in any of the roles."

"But, I know I have great stage potential."

"Rachel, my dear," he said, "it pains me to have to say this, but you have a tendency to overact. Do you know what I mean?"

I nodded. Of course I knew what he meant. I just didn't believe him.

Later, I told Ruthie what he'd said, hoping she would scoff and say, *That's just stupid*, and make me feel better. Instead, she said, "Yeah, well, he's right."

"Ruthie! Why are you saying this?"

"I'm saying it for your own good because you never believe the things you don't want to be true."

"Like what?"

"Like somebody saying you tend to go way overboard."

"That's just stupid!"

Last time I ask her to stick up for me.

"Next year," Mr. Mackiewitz said back then, "I'll look very hard for a script that might work for you. If you believe you can act, then we'll give you all the encouragement in the world." I brightened a bit at that. "Right now, however, I need you to be the prompter. The job takes someone with a sharp ear and a quick mind, who can concentrate no matter what."

Grudgingly, I agreed to do it.

"And later," he said, "once we're into production, I'll need you to apply makeup."

I warmed up a little. Enhancing faces was something I felt I knew something about, the only bright star in the entire blank sky.

In assembly the next day, the principal announces, "Mr. Mackiewitz has had a severe heart attack. He is being well looked after in hospital, and we are all hoping for his early recovery. We are very lucky that he is still alive."

Everyone cheers.

"We are not expecting him to return to school for quite some time, if at all. Therefore, starting Monday, a supply teacher will take up his duties."

The following Monday, a Mr. Tompkins is writing on the blackboard as we straggle into the classroom. He doesn't turn around until everyone is seated, and *oh, my*! He is extremely handsome. And he's young—very young—hardly older than us, it seems.

Ruthie looks across at me and wiggles her eyebrows. *Woo-woo*, they say.

Below desk level, I move my hand back and forth. *So-so.* I feel a need to remain true to poor old Mackiewitz, a plump, balding man. No one would ever have wiggled so much as a big toe for him.

There is a general flutter among the girls, a few discreet chest-pattings to show throbbing hearts. The boys stare at us in wonder. One of them snickers.

"Turn to act 3, scene 1 in *Hamlet*, please," Mr. Tompkins says in a warm baritone.

When we finally move slowly to our next class, Ruthie says, "He's beyond handsome. He's an utter dreamboat."

Hazel Carrington screams, "He's way more than a dreamboat," and quickly plasters both hands over her mouth, afraid he might have heard.

I just keep walking. "Yeah, sure," I say. "I know his type. He puts on a dreamboat act when you meet him, but once you get to know him, he has as much charm as a cardboard box."

"Oh, pipe down," Ruthie says.

I shrug. To me, he's only a supply teacher, a supply play director who will never see in me the hugely talented actress I know I can be.

Ruthie says, "Those Clark Gable eyes. They really grab me."

Overhearing, another girl says, "More like Gregory Peck. It's that jaw."

"Come on, Rachel," Ruthie says. "Admit he reminds you of a movie star."

"He reminds me of a great big question mark."

"Huh?"

"Besides a cute face, what's he got?"

"Sex appeal," Ruthie says, and everyone hoots with laughter as we file into our next class.

"Girls, girls!" Miss Fiddler says. "Control the noise."

A week later in English, daydreaming, I catch myself gazing at Mr. Tompkins. He has very fine hands. You might even say artistic hands. And his shoulders are . . . I sit up straight and turn to act 4. Let the other girls go all soft and swoony. I have better things on my mind—my romantic play about war for one, which, for all the trouble I'm taking with it, refuses to fall into place.

Each day after school, Mr. Tompkins—or Tommy, as

everyone soon nicknames him—is surrounded by a gaggle of girls with questions about homework and tests. Not me, though. I observe from the doorway. A good-looking man like this is bound to be conceited, and I can't stand that in a person, especially in an adult, young as he may be. I do have a question, though, which I long to ask. By the end of the week, the queue for a private audience is considerably shorter, consisting primarily of Hazel Carrington, Ruthie Pritchard, and one or two other girls smitten with love. I join them.

I get right to the point. No woman-of-the-world smile, no eyelash-batting. "Are we still doing the school play?"

"Yes," he says, giving me the full benefit of his even white teeth and dark serious eyes. "We'll resume rehearsals at the end of next week, once I've had a chance to study it."

After school the next Friday, play practice, once again, is in full swing. To give him credit, Mr. Tompkins manages pretty well for someone coming to it cold. Sometimes, though, he seems lost in thought, especially when he watches Hazel Carrington, the lead, going through her paces.

Hazel must notice because she has to be prompted many more times than usual. This irks me. If I were lucky enough to be in the play, I'd have my lines memorized, as well as everyone else's, by the second rehearsal.

I give Hazel her line. "Try paying attention," I add, sounding a bit surly.

Mr. Tompkins turns to me with his Clark Gable eyes and says, "You're a hard-hearted woman."

"Huh?" I say, like the stunned bunny I am. No one has ever called me a woman. No one has ever said I was hard-hearted. "Sorry." Maybe I should have said it to Hazel.

"No, you're good. You should have been the director."

I'm all red and flustered. Hazel is madly searching for her line, but I haven't been paying attention, so someone else calls it out. Finally, the world starts up again.

Ruthie and I walk home together after rehearsal. This April weather is iffy—sun one minute, rain the next, turning my hair into something like a pot scrubber. The overhead clouds look threatening, but we poke along anyway, gabbing about the play practice.

"Hazel may be beautiful," I say, "but she can't act worth beans."

"If you're beautiful, you don't need to be able to act. She has class, she has high cheekbones, and she's blonde. That's all you need these days, besides great teeth. She's also tall and willowy." Ruthie goes to a lot of movies, so she knows what she's talking about.

"As far as acting goes," I say, "her finest attribute seems to be the strength of her voice. It probably carries from the auditorium stage all the way to the second storey of the school."

"*Ahem!* Are you jealous?"

"No. It's just that, with Mr. Mackiewitz in charge, the play was all about decibels, not emotion, not style. I'm just hoping Mr. Tompkins will be a bit more lavish in the passion department."

"He will be. You can tell just by looking at him, his second name is passion."

"If I were directing the play, I'd give the audience some grand sentiment to take home. I would have them gasp or shed tears or cower in their seats."

"Wouldn't that be more or less the playwright's job?"

"Initially, yes. But then the director has to go to work and wring every drop of emotion out of each word, comma, and period."

"Well, what about my role as the ding-dong maid? I don't know how you'd find any emotion in *Will that be all, Madam?* Not exactly high drama."

I would never mention this to anyone, but Ruthie has about as much acting talent as a dead guppy. "It could be *medium* high drama," I say. "Personally, I see your character as a vamp. Why don't you swing your hips a bit and say the lines with some passion in your voice? Maybe with a slight foreign accent."

"She's just a girl who answers the door and dusts the furniture."

"But she could be so much more!" I'm thinking hard. "She could have a little catch in her voice as she says *Madam.*"

"But, why?"

"Perhaps her lover was killed in the war."

"It takes place before the war."

"I'm sure there was a war on somewhere. Anyway, you're playing the maid too flat. It's highly possible that she has a dead lover. I think you should let her sound as if she's close to tears."

"I'll try it, but I'm afraid Tommy will think I'm ridiculous."

"Forget Tommy. Consider the audience. It needs to feel immediate sympathy. It needs to wipe a silent tear from its collective eye."

She doesn't look entirely convinced. "I'll do my best," she says.

She waves good-bye at the corner, and we scurry along our separate ways before the black clouds decide to dump on us.

CHAPTER

3

Granny's there when I get home. She comes in from the farm nearly every weekend to have dinner with us and sometimes to spend the night, more often now that Jamie's home. Her old dog, Bounder, prefers to stay with the hired man while she's in town.

During dinner she keeps staring at Jamie, lips pursed, as he stickhandles his food around his plate, without eating much of it. "That lad has picked up some foreign bug," she says. "He's eaten almost nothing. If I were you, Dora, I'd hike him off to a doctor right smart. Who knows what germs are roiling around inside him? Those foreign hospitals, where he had his leg looked after, are nothing but a breeding ground for all manner of diseases. It's a wonder anybody gets out alive. Look what happened after the last war. Everybody died of the flu."

"A few were spared," Dad announces from his end of the table.

Jamie puts his fork down. "Look, I've seen enough soldiers' spilled guts, along with quantities of their blood, to turn me off food for the rest of my life."

Mother puts her hands over her ears. "Oh, Jamie, stop! You're spoiling dinner for the rest of us."

He stares at a spot on the far wall and pushes a few forkfuls into his mouth. He chews and chews, and after every bite, he takes a couple of swallows of milk to wash it down. He's just trying to make a point. It's obvious that he's rebelling against Mother constantly telling him what to do.

"I'm every bit as alarmed as you are at his weight loss," Mother says. She has an edge to her voice, as if Granny's blaming her.

"It's merely excitement," Dad says. "Let's not over-mother the boy."

"I'm hardly a boy."

Mother brings in the coffee.

"There's absolutely nothing wrong with me," Jamie says. "It's just that I can't settle down yet. Everything's going so fast."

"What do you mean, fast?" Mother asks.

"I don't know. I don't mean anything. Just don't keep at me." He takes a cigarette package from his shirt pocket.

"You're smoking too much."

Jamie leaves the table and lights a cigarette, heading up to his room to smoke in peace. I don't blame him.

Letters not sent.

Everything is very hush-hush over here, but we all get the sense that we're about to give it to the Huns. Everybody's hoarding cigarettes.

I never thought I would feel the need to smoke, back when I was in high school. That sure changed the day I turned eighteen. It was a Friday. I went over to the armories after school and volunteered to have my life shot out from under me. Scariest thing I ever did.

Coop had already signed up for the air force. I chose the army, I guess because I thought I'd be safer on the ground than off it.

I was going to tell you all that day at dinner, Rachel, but I couldn't, not with Mother and Dad bustling around, making my birthday memorable. You gave me a swell magnifying glass, remember? You told me I could even start fires with it, if I got lost in the woods on a cold day. And then you added, "If the sun was shining and you happened to have it with you." You were sure pleased with yourself.

After supper, I went fishing with Coop. He
was still waiting to be sent to the airfield in
Dartmouth, Nova Scotia. He managed to get his
hands on a case of beer and also brought along
a pack of cigarettes. We lugged the beer out
to the river, along with our fishing rods, and
drank beer and smoked, but didn't do much fishing. It struck me funny that we were too young
to drink legally, but not too young to die for
king and country. Coop laughed at this. He said,
"You think too much, Mac." Remember how he always
called me Mac? He said, "Have another beer. And
here, have a smoke while you're at it." I'd tried
smoking once before but hadn't liked it that
much. I thought I'd better learn, though, before
I went overseas. It would prove I am a man.

Oh, boy, did I suffer next morning. My mouth
was dry and smelled like a sewer, and my head felt
like someone had hit it with a sandbag. But I had
something to say. Just to get it over with, I
confessed that I'd signed up. Remember how Mother
yelped? You'd think she'd been grazed by a bullet.
And she ran upstairs crying. You just stared at
me in this awful silence, and your eyes looked
like great overfilled soup plates. And Dad, all
he did was frown into his coffee cup. Finally, I
think he said, "Well, I guess you were bound to do

it sooner or later, son." And then he got up from the table and walked with a kind of stoop to his shoulders upstairs to calm Mother down.

A minute later, I ask to be excused from the dinner table. Upstairs, Jamie's bedroom door is half open.

"Can I come in?"

"Sure."

He's tipped back in his chair, his head floating in a fog of smoke. Stacked on the desk in front of him are the newspaper clippings about the war Dad saved, as well as a pile of papers with handwriting on them looped together with string.

"What's all that?"

"Nothing much."

He quickly bundles everything into the bottom drawer of his desk. I sit cautiously on the edge of his bed. Neither of us has much to say, it seems.

He doesn't look like he has anything wrong with him to me. Sure, he's pretty thin, but so am I, and nobody says there's anything wrong with me. Except for eczema. I sit there scratching the insides of my elbows.

He stumps out his cigarette in a saucer. "I don't know what I'm going to do with the rest of my life." He's not looking at me, but I catch the worry in his profile.

"I thought you were going to be a doctor. That's what you always used to say."

"Not now."

"Why not?"

"Ah, I don't know. Maybe I've seen enough smashed-up and broken people over there to completely turn me off that idea."

"You could be a pharmacist, like Dad."

"Yeah, I know. Go to university, take pharmacy, and end up selling pills and cough mixtures like a good little Dingbat, which would be all right, I guess, but then there's all that other stuff—hot-water bottles and women's stuff and all that junk—and, good God, no! I'm not doing that."

"They have hot-water bottles in Dingbat Land."

"Does Doctor Melvin still have those calendars on his walls?"

"Yup."

"Too bad this isn't Dingbat Land. I'd know what my role is."

"Listen, you just got back. What's the rush about a job? Why not take some time to be a regular guy? Wait until we get some nice warm weather before you decide what you want to do."

"Much depends on the weather, eh? Dad's philosophy of life. It *would* be good to put people back together instead of blowing them to smithereens, or at least try. But, right now, I don't have the courage to even consider becoming a doctor. I don't feel right. It's as if the war made something go wrong with my own insides. Maybe it's shell shock."

"What's shell shock?"

"I don't know."

"Rachel!" Mother calls from downstairs.

"Right. You see? The minute I get into an interesting discussion with my brother, it's time to go and help with the dishes. No one else can do dishes around here without good old Rachel pitching in."

Jamie grins, but shakes his head to sympathize.

I'm on my feet. "Look, why don't you visit the Coopers? Tomorrow's Saturday. I could go with you."

"Maybe next week."

"Why are you putting it off?"

"I'm not. I get sidetracked with other things."

"Just do it."

He stares into the dark beyond the window. "You know, I don't think I've ever felt as alone as I do now that I'm home. I miss my buddies. I miss Coop." He lights another cigarette.

"He'll turn up."

"Rachel!" Mother shrieks.

"Sorry, but I'm in a conference. Perhaps you would consider hiring a maid." I say this aloud but not loud enough for her to hear me.

I thump down the stairs hoping the noise adequately expresses my displeasure.

CHAPTER

4

In the morning, after the usual Saturday chores, I buttonhole Jamie. "Let's go to the Coopers'."

"I'll go by myself later. I have to get used to being a loner."

"You said I could go!"

I beam my fiercest gaze in his direction until he sighs and mutters, "Okay, okay."

Granny's in the kitchen rolling out pie crust. Quietly, we leave by the front door to avoid the where-are-you-going-and-why drill. "It's chilly out there," Granny calls before we can make our escape. "I hope you're warmly dressed."

"I'm wearing my pullover," I yell.

"Jamie?"

"I'm fine! At what point," Jamie whispers, "does your grandmother start to see you as an adult?"

"Maybe never."

As he closes the front door behind us, we fall immediately into Mother's clutches. Bundled up in a warm cardigan, she's on her knees carefully removing dead leaves from around the new sprouts in the flower beds.

"Going out?" she says.

We look at each other and bite our tongues. "Yup," we call, and walk quickly on.

"Cold wind," Jamie says, stuffing his hands in his pockets.

"The sun's warm."

"We're doing the weather thing again."

Someone's calling us. We look back and, sure enough, there's Granny coming after us with Jamie's jacket.

"I feel like running the other way, just for the hell of it," he says. But he turns back. "Gee, thanks, Granny. Didn't think I'd need it."

"If you weren't my own grandson, I'd say you were an idiot."

"Maybe I am."

"No maybe about it."

Mother plunges her hands back into the cold earth. "I could have gone in and grabbed his jacket," she says to Granny, "but I don't want to be one of those overbearing mothers."

"I'm only here to be helpful," Granny says.

We raise our eyebrows at each other and hurry down the street.

———

Mrs. Cooper's at home when we get there, also Coop's two sisters. Nancy, the younger one, opens the door and yells into the kitchen, "Jamie's here!"

I give Nancy a tiny wave with the tips of my fingers.

"And Rachel!" she screeches, and has a coughing fit.

"I'm in the kitchen, lad. Come on out, the two of you."

Mrs. Cooper seems to be trying to camouflage herself with flour. This doesn't prevent her from squashing first Jamie and then me into her, as they say, ample bosom, leaving us lightly dusted.

"Both girls have bad colds," she says.

If they lived under the same roof as Mother or Granny, they sure wouldn't be walking around spreading germs. They'd be tucked into bed, with mustard plasters on their chests, Vicks VapoRub under their noses, and glasses of ginger ale beside them.

"How are things?" Jamie asks, clenching and unclenching his fists. I'm sure he doesn't have a clue what to say. I lean against the fridge, ready to be helpful if needed.

Ellie washes dishes in a basin in the sink while young Nancy dries. Ellie keeps turning to look at Jamie. When he smiles at her, she nearly drops the slippery bowl she's putting in the drainer.

"Oh, you know," Mrs. Cooper sighs, "not so good sometimes, not so bad other times. Still no news."

Ellie and Nancy finish their task and hover closer to Jamie, not wanting to miss a word.

Mrs. Cooper says, "Back away, girls. Don't be spreading your germs. It's a bad time of year for colds. Will's gone out, but he'll be back soon." Will is Coop's younger brother. "How are you?"

"Fine," Jamie says. He coughs nervously. "Really, I'm fine."

"And you, Rachel, dear?"

"Fine, too." The yeasty smell of the bread dough is making me hungry.

"Jamie, you're looking thin. Have you lost weight?"

"A little bit, maybe."

Mrs. Cooper frowns as if she doesn't approve of people losing weight. She's a rotund little woman herself and has been as long as I've known her. She's still kneading the dough, roughing it up pretty badly.

"Mr. Cooper all right?" Jamie asks.

Mrs. Cooper looks up and shakes her head. "He's not over it. He's trying to find someone who will say they saw him alive, or . . . he needs to know for certain. He tried the Red Cross, but the best they could say was that his plane went down behind enemy lines during the bombing of Dresden. After that, who knows?"

"But he hasn't lost hope?"

"Who can say? He's up and down about it."

Jamie swallows hard and tries not to look at the girls. He's never been much of a talker.

Sounding half-strangled, I say, "It's good to keep hoping."

"It wears you down," Mrs. Cooper says. There's a long pause while she covers the dough with a tea towel and places it on the radiator to rise.

Jamie gives me a slight nod, indicating we should go. But we can't just *go*. He should be saying something comforting, not standing there in a self-induced coma.

"Go up and see his room," Mrs. Cooper says. "It's much as he left it. I made the bed up with fresh sheets so it's all ready for him, if . . . that boy never did learn the simple art of pulling the covers up and straightening them."

The Cooper girls follow us up the stairs, and Mrs. Cooper calls, "Let Jamie and his sister go on their own, girls. He doesn't want you shadowing his every move." We both see their eagerness change to disappointment.

"It's all right," Jamie says. "It's nice to have company."

Coop's bedroom door is open. Not much has changed since Jamie and Coop were kids. On his dresser is a framed snapshot of the two of them with their fishing rods, each holding up a smallmouth bass.

"I think we have a picture like that at home," I say.

On a long shelf are eight model airplanes. "There they are," Jamie says. "Wow, look at them. We put a lot of work into those. Well, it was mostly Coop. He had more staying power than I did. Nobody else was allowed to help, not even Will."

"They're pretty neat." I'm about to pick one up, but Ellie reaches out to stop me.

"We're not allowed to touch them."

"Why not?"

It's Nancy who answers. "Just because we're not. Our father says we're not to touch anything of our brother's till he comes home and says we can."

"Okay." I put my hands behind my back. I always thought Mr. Cooper was an ogre, and now I know.

Hands in his pockets, Jamie bends closer to admire the airplanes and to read the spines of Coop's books, most of them about pilots and planes and war.

Now, *I* want to leave. I feel out of place, as if I've stumbled into a museum by mistake and it turns out to be where somebody's buried. Not Coop, though. Coop's still alive; he has to be. It would be too sad for Jamie, otherwise, and I couldn't bear that.

I look out the window at trees blowing in the gusty wind. The silence in Coop's bedroom is oppressive. "That old Coop," I say, just to make some noise. "He's like a semi-brother at our place. He always messes up my hair and asks me if I've had it fumigated for rats."

"Sounds like him," Ellie says.

The next long silence is broken by Nancy's giggling. "Jamie, I remember how you used to say you were going to marry Ellie."

Ellie turns her back on us. "Don't be an idiot. He did not."

Red creeps up around her neck, and I feel a little sorry for her. Ellie's nearly Jamie's age.

"Sure, he did, and we had a big fight over him," Nancy says.

Jamie smiles. "I remember the fight." His face flushes, too, as he notices Ellie's embarrassment. "Of course, that was a long time ago."

Back downstairs, Will's home. "Hi," we say. He's two years ahead of me at school and only nods in my direction. But he can hardly take his eyes off Jamie, as if his presence brings his own brother closer to being found alive. Will's like his older brother in many ways—not as muscular, though, not as open-faced. Coop you can read like a book. Will takes some pondering.

Mr. Cooper is home for lunch, too, washing his hands at the kitchen sink. He doesn't turn around. I wish we could sneak away without saying anything to him. I think Jamie's just as afraid of him as I am.

At last, Mr. Cooper looks straight at Jamie. "You're back home, then, are you?" His face seems chiseled from hard rock, especially his hooded eyes.

"Yes, Sir," Jamie says.

Mr. Cooper turns away and grabs a hand towel from a hook near the sink.

"I'm sorry . . ." Jamie starts.

"What have you got to be sorry for?"

"He was, is, my oldest friend," he stammers.

"He was my oldest son. At least you can make new friends."

I can see Jamie struggling to say something, but no words come out.

"There's still hope," I say, my voice a high-pitched squeak.

Mr. Cooper's granite eyes are on me, now. "Do you know something I don't?"

Good Lord. Now would be a good moment to just make a run for it.

Jamie comes back to life. "No, of course not. She means, she can't, and I can't, believe he's . . . you know."

"Dead! Say it. The word is *dead*."

Mrs. Cooper takes Jamie by the arm and walks with him to the front door, with me practically treading on their heels. "Don't take what he says the wrong way, lad. He's worn-out with searching and grief. Every time he comes up against a brick wall, he has to grieve all over again. He doesn't know how to live with it without making everyone's life miserable, especially his own."

Outside, Jamie's eyes are about to overflow. The wind is sharp and makes my own eyes water. He breaks into a limping trot down the street in the opposite direction. I let him go. I have a pretty good idea where he's headed.

There's a swale on the edge of town. Near it is a sprawling hickory tree that just begs kids to climb it. Jamie and Coop used to play there. If Coop was busy, Jamie sometimes took me. He taught me how to climb. When Mother found out, she said, *Nice girls don't climb trees.*

High in the tree, I used to grin down at the world, glad I wasn't a nice girl.

I watch Jamie speed away as if he's trying to catch up to the past before it escapes his memory. Heading home, I recall how smooth the trunk of the climbing tree is, how vast and gray. Its branches start low, curving up like the trunk of an elephant. Life flits by too fast, I'm beginning to notice. It doesn't seem long ago that Jamie and Coop were gangly boys hanging upside down in the tree. But they've moved far beyond that. If he doesn't show up soon, though, Coop's going to turn into someone who exists only in a myth. The thought makes me shiver.

I wish I'd gone down to the tree with Jamie. He's probably standing near it, reaching out to stroke the smoothness of the bark. I can almost see the tufts of long grass and burdock that surround it, yellowish brown at this time of year, dry and brittle and lifeless. Beyond it, the swale is filled with the husks of bulrushes and the blackened skeletons of trees. Kids believe the swale is full of quicksand that will suck them down into the bowels of the earth if they fall in. Maybe it's true.

I look back to see if I can catch sight of Jamie returning from that ghostly swale and linger for a moment. No sign of him. The brisk April breeze carries the dank scent of marshy ooze.

I agree with Jamie, that he needs to move ahead with his life. But, what if he marries Mary Foley? He's too young. Once, though, I heard Mother say to him, *You're not going to marry a Catholic!* And Jamie said, *You sound a lot like Mary's mother. Only she says to Mary, you're not going to marry a Protestant!*

Stupidest thing I've ever heard. What possible difference could it make? It's the sort of thing that starts wars. If he does marry her, though, for sure he'll teach his kids to climb the tree.

Granny's placing her pies on the kitchen sideboard to cool by the time I get home. Mother's writing a shopping list, checking the fridge, the can cupboard, the bread box, getting in Granny's way, or else Granny's in her way.

"How was your walk?" Mother asks brightly.

"Fine."

"Did you go to the Coopers'?" Granny asks.

"Yup," I say and head up to my room.

A little later, Jamie comes home. I open my door and can hear Mother ask, "How are the Coopers doing?"

Jamie's on the stairs. "Not too good," he calls back, "but not too bad, either." He disappears into his room without saying anything to me.

Downstairs, Mother says, in a voice loud enough to carry, "What did I ever do to deserve such uncommunicative children?"

"You let them grow up past the age of five," Granny says.

Then comes the old familiar request, "Rachel, come and set the table!" I pretend not to hear. "Rachel!"

"All right, all right, I'm coming."

"Tell your brother to get washed and come down for lunch."

I pound on Jamie's bedroom door. "You have to get washed and come down for lunch."

"I heard. Tell her I'm not hungry."

I open his door. "You have to eat."

"I'm taking Mary out for coffee later. I'll have something then."

"Are you going to marry her?"

"Rachel! Why don't you just mind your own business?" He sits, brow furrowed, deep in thought. Finally he says, "If I get married, Coop has to be best man, so he'd better show up soon."

"He'll come back. Trust me." *Aha!* He does have marriage on his mind.

He opens the bottom drawer of his desk but doesn't take anything out. I think he's waiting for me to leave.

Letters not sent.

I'd like to return to this place after the war. If it weren't for all the damage, it would be beautiful. We are not far from an airfield. When the bombers go out, you feel like your whole

body is throbbing. Wouldn't it be odd if Coop
were here, too, and neither of us knew it?

I was thinking about Coop and me back when
Coop was making model airplanes. He used to
insist that the airplane was the best thing ever
invented by man. If someone else hadn't done it
first, he would have. All he could ever talk
about was flying. "Imagine what it must be like
to fly!" He probably said this a hundred times.

And I always said, "Yeah, it would be great."
Coop wanted more than that, though.

"No, but, Mac. Think about it, you'd be way up
there, so high no one could even see you. You'd
be above the clouds. You could fly among the
stars. You could just keep on going forever."

I said, "Sure, if you had enough fuel."

"Yeah, but think about it. Imagine the
universe."

"It's big."

"It's vast. Endless! And there you'd be."

I remember that entire conversation, especially the word "endless."

CHAPTER

5

Word is out that Mr. Mackiewitz is not coming back. Although his health is improving, he's decided it's time to retire. Our class has written letters, telling him how much he'll be missed.

On Monday, Mr. Tompkins stops me as I'm leaving English class. "You have such a good memory for lines in the play, it surprises me that you don't have a role."

This makes me all prickly, and I scratch my arms like mad. "Um . . . maybe next year," I say. "If we can find, I mean, if you can find a good play."

"I'm sure there are plenty of good plays out there, just waiting to be interpreted by you."

I catch my breath. What does he mean, and where's Ruthie when I need her most? At home with a cold, that's where, not on hand to decipher Tommy's utterances. Does he mean that he thinks I'd be a good actress if I just had a chance? No, of course not, he's only teasing. Laughing at me in that conceited adult way he has. He probably senses that I'm the type to overact, and he's waiting for a chance to prove it.

But, wait. His smile lights up the entire hallway, and I am charmed. *No-no-no!* "Charmed" barely covers it. I have a huge rush of adrenalin, as if I've taken a leap off the roof. I better get out of here before I come crashing down to earth.

"Yikes, I'm late," I bray and gallop off to my next class, like a lame-brained donkey. I spend the next half hour scratching my arms almost to the point of bloodshed.

That night, my arms covered in tarry-smelling ointment and wrapped round and round in strips of torn-up old bed sheets, I lie in bed seeing Tommy's dark hair falling a little bit over his forehead, his impish smile, his serious eyes. (He's not conceited.) I can even hear his alluring voice.

When I finally sleep, I dream I'm trying to swim across something like the swale only wider, wide as an ocean, and I keep getting sucked down into the quicksand. I wake up exhausted.

I drag myself off to school, only to find that rehearsal is canceled for the week because so many key people are at home, sick with colds and flu. It's hard to exist without drama after school and without Tommy's increasingly important presence to count on. I wait patiently, or as patiently as possible. If I could, I'd go to everyone's bed-side and pour ginger ale down their throats and smear them with Vicks VapoRub.

By the following Wednesday, most people are back in school, except Ruthie. I take some homework to her but don't stick around to catch whatever it is she has.

Ruthie croaks her thanks from the top of the stairs. "Oh, and by the way," she says, "I've been practicing my lines."

"That's good."

"Good! It's going to be amazing. I guarantee you will fall over in a dead faint. Everyone will."

"I can hardly wait. Hurry up and get better."

"I'm almost better now." Her voice breaks into a rous-ing, barking cough. "It used to be worse," she says when she catches her breath.

Hazel Carrington has taken to walking partway home with me after school. One day, she says, "My sister and I are having a party this Saturday. Can you come?"

I hardly know what to say. I like Hazel well enough, except for her loud voice, but I usually find parties boring and can't wait until they're over.

"My sister phoned your brother and invited him, too."

"My brother? You want me to go to a party with my brother?" He won't be too thrilled about that. He prob-ably won't want to go.

We're standing on the corner of her street. Hazel looks

down, sadly dragging a toe along a crack in the sidewalk. "I hope you'll come. If I don't have someone there my age, my sister will make me stay upstairs." When she looks up, her eyes are so wide with hope, it would be a criminal offense to disappoint her.

"Okay, I'll come. And I'll make Jamie come. He will if I tell him to."

"He will?"

"Of course. He always does what I want."

"We're inviting Mary Foley, too, so he'll like that, won't he?"

"Sure." I want to say, *No, he'll be happier just going with me*, but I don't. I'm starting to get excited about going to a party with the older crowd. I'll put my *Little Red Lies* lipstick to good use, but this time I'll prove my new maturity by not going overboard with it.

Hazel says, "I invited Ruthie Pritchard, but she's still sick."

At home, I throw my spring jacket at a hook in the back hall, where it almost stays, and yell into the kitchen, "We're invited to a party."

Jamie's at the table, poring over the newspaper.

Mother's scrubbing potatoes for dinner. "Whose party?" she asks.

"Oh, that Vera Carrington person. She's having a party," Jamie says. "She phoned me yesterday."

"It's Vera and her sister, Hazel, who are throwing the party, and we're both invited because I know Hazel."

"I don't feel like going," Jamie says.

"Don't be such a poor sport," I say.

"I hardly know the Carringtons."

"I think Vera's hoping to lure you away from Mary."

"Don't be ridiculous."

"It's true! Hazel told me."

"She actually told you her sister's making a play for me?"

I have to stop and think for a minute. Is this an outright lie or wishful thinking? Mary's nice in many ways, but she's not as madly in love with Jamie as I think she should be. Sometimes, she looks at him with an almost pained expression, as if he's, somehow, a disappointment.

I hesitate. "Hazel didn't come right out and say it, but you could tell by her face. It was a very broad hint."

"I hardly know Vera. I went overseas just after the Carringtons moved here."

Mother says, "They're such a quiet family, I'm surprised they're even having a party, the way they keep to themselves so much. Maybe some of your former classmates will be there, Jamie, and some of the boys who made it home from overseas. You really should go. Besides, Rachel will need a chaperone."

"Rachel's too young to go," he says.

"I am not. Don't be insulting."

Mother says, "If the younger sister invited her, it would be unkind of her not to go. She'll be all right with you there to keep an eye on her and to bring her home in good time. Besides, the girls' parents are lovely people, from what I hear—a bit standoffish but very refined. And they go to our church. I believe that Mrs. Carrington is a semi-invalid. I know it will be a quiet party."

"I'm not in a party frame of mind."

Mother sighs. "Oh, Jamie, it will be good for you to get out and socialize. Vera Carrington seems like such a nice girl. She spoke to me in the street the other day and asked if I thought you would like to go to choir practice with her sometime."

"I can't think of anything I would enjoy more, unless it would be having spikes driven up my nose."

Mother ignores him. "There are other girls in the world besides Mary Foley."

"Can't think of any nicer ones."

"People should marry within their faith."

"I thought we were discussing a party."

"You know what I'm talking about."

This is too good to politely ignore. "Mixed marriages never work. Stick to your faith or be a jerk."

"Rachel, this is not a joke. Go upstairs and wash your hands, and come down and set the table."

I flounce out of the kitchen but perch halfway up the back staircase, still within earshot.

"If a girl is brought up to believe that the communion bread and wine actually turn into the body and blood of Christ," Mother says, "then what's left to talk about? You'd never change her views if you discussed them all night."

"If I marry her, we might have other things to do at night than argue about the body and blood of Christ."

On the back stairs, I'm trying to smother a giggle without sounding like somebody strangling.

"Don't be vulgar, Jamie. I'm talking about marriage in general. Many a high school sweetheart has ended up a naive bride, thinking time and love is the balm to soothe all cares."

What the heck is she talking about? I can't resist. "Do you mean marriage is a time bomb?" I call out. "I don't get it."

"Rachel, I was speaking to your brother. Come and set the table for supper, as I asked you to do ten minutes ago. Wash your hands first."

I stomp up the stairs to the bathroom loudly singing, "Here comes the bride, fair, fat, and wide." I'll probably get my hair yanked later. Mary Foley is a little on the pleasingly plump side. "Here comes the groom, skinny as a broom."

CHAPTER

6

In a small town like Middleborough, neighborhoods are fairly close. People walked everywhere during the war and still do. Jamie and I drop by Mary's and then head to the Carringtons' stately brick home, shivering as we go. At least, I am. It's impossible to dress for the weather at this time of year, especially when you want your clothes to scream sophistication and charm.

"It's going to be pretty flat without Coop here," Jamie says as Mary rings the doorbell.

"A couple of other guys didn't make it home, either," Mary says. "Coop isn't the only one."

"I know." Jamie's voice holds a tinge of exasperation.

"I don't think you need to remind him," I say.

"I just feel kind of guilty about being here," Jamie says, "as sound as if I've never been over there."

"You've got a gimpy leg, for heaven's sake," I say. "What more do you want?"

The door is opened by Hazel, who bleats a welcome and bellows to her sister, "More guests!"

Loudness must be a family characteristic because Vera bellows back, "I'm coming, I'm coming. Anyway, it's your turn to take their coats upstairs."

"No, it isn't."

"We can take them up," I say, my voice a mere whisper by comparison.

"You can help me," Hazel hollers as she and Vera practically rip the coats off our backs. "I need a chance to talk to you, anyway."

Oh, oh. Why? Immediately, my arms start to itch with little pinpricks of nervous fear. Will this be about *Rachel, the hard-hearted woman*? Is Hazel just getting around to blasting me for sounding so mean to her when she bungled her lines?

We dump the coats on a bed covered in coats and sit down on top of them. I scratch; Hazel sighs.

"I need you to help me," she says.

"Me?"

"I wonder if you could come over sometimes after school and help me rehearse my lines? I can't seem to get them into my head."

"I'm sure it just takes practice," I say, trying to sound helpful. Privately I'm thinking she'd probably have trouble getting the words to "Mary Had a Little Lamb" into her head.

"I do try to practice on my own, but it's not working. I'm afraid everyone thinks I'm too stupid to play the lead."

She trains those huge hopeful eyes fully on my guilty ones, and I have to look down. Making people feel guilty, whether they are or not, is an art form. With me, it doesn't take much art. I sweat guilt.

"Nobody would think that," I say.

"Some would. Some think I got the part only because I have a loud voice."

I have to swallow once or twice while I come up with a reply. *Did Hazel overhear me talking to Ruthie? Did Ruthie rat?* I have an intense need to scratch the backs of my knees now. I know my face is deep pink.

"You have a voice that carries," I say helpfully. "A good thing for an actress to have."

Hazel gets off the coats and grabs me by the arm, grinning broadly. "Thank you for saying so." She pulls me after her, out of the room. "So, can we start on Monday after school?" she roars.

"Yes," I whisper. *What else can I say?*

Downstairs, Hazel leaves me to my own devices while she dashes off to shout at her sister to turn up the music. I don't think the party will be as quiet as my mother predicted. It turns out the Carrington parents are out of town for the weekend. The living room doorway is a good place to stand and mull things over. Maybe a sharp tongue is a bigger handicap than a loud voice.

Soon I catch sight of Jamie moving about the room, chatting with the people he knows, his limp more pronounced than usual. For a mere second, I wonder if he's exaggerating it slightly. But, no. That's something I might do—put on a little act to make sure people see me suffering—but not my brother. I join him and instantly hear his intake of breath. When I follow the direction of his eyes, I gasp, too. Across the room, his back to us, is Coop.

We both let out our breath. "It's *Will* Cooper," I say.

"Right."

I survey the dimly lit room. A small knot of boys laugh at someone's joke. A tight circle of girls, Mary among them, gasps over some piece of gossip. In a chair pulled back out of the way, in a blue fog of smoke, someone slouches and lifts a punch glass to his lips.

Jamie joins Will just as Roy Armstrong, a guy who's more in Jamie's age group than mine, smiles nonchalantly at me and takes my hand. "Let me get you some punch."

I'm flattered. It sounds like a line from a cocktail party scene in a movie. When no one's looking, I undo the top button of my blouse. No one notices. Not even Roy Armstrong, who hands me a glass of punch and immediately starts flirting with someone else.

I eventually make my way back to the living room. Will has moved on, and Jamie is talking to Vera Carrington now. Playfully, she shoves a plate of sandwiches under Jamie's nose, yelling, "Eat! You look half starved."

He takes the smallest sandwich on the plate, while she tries to get him to take two. "Is that Tom Klosky over there in the corner?" he asks, diverting her attention.

Vera nods. "He's in terrible shape." She manages to lower her voice a little. "I used to think he was a nice enough boy, but now . . . well, I just invited him out of pity, poor guy."

"I'd better say hello." Jamie crosses the room, while I snag a sandwich and follow him. "Tom, you old son of a gun, when did you get back?" Jamie offers his hand as Tom gets shakily to his feet. To steady him, Jamie reaches for his elbow but grabs only an empty shirtsleeve. "Sorry, pal," he says. "I had no idea. Where did . . . ?"

"Normandy. Listen, be a good chap and get me a drink. A real drink. None of the cat piss our gracious hostess is pouring."

"I wouldn't know where to look."

"Kitchen. Follow your nose, if it hasn't been blown off your face." Klosky sways. He notices me and grins stupidly. "And here's the little sister. All grown up, eh? You turned out pretty good. Who'da thought."

"Hi," I say. "I better go help Jamie."

Jamie's elbowing his way through a cluster of boys and young men in the kitchen by the time I catch up. I know many of them by sight. I think they were in lower school when Jamie left, and now they're swaggering upper school boys, not quite comfortable with cigarettes but working on it. Will's there, too.

I'm the only girl. I sidle in next to the fridge, where I won't be too obvious.

A guy named Eddy puts a bottle behind his back, but not quickly enough. "Give us a shot of rum for my friend Tom Klosky," Jamie says.

"For Tom? Oh, sure, poor sucker." He finds a used glass among the plates of cold cuts and pickles and bread and cheese that litter the kitchen table, flings the contents into the sink behind him, and almost fills it with rum, adding a splash of Coke. Nobody takes any notice of me, or else they don't care that I've invaded their inner sanctum.

"I had no idea he'd lost an arm," Jamie says.

"That's not all he lost," Eddy says.

"Oh?"

"Let's just say he'll never be a family man. Here," he says, scrounging up another glass, filling it with rum and Coke, and handing it to Jamie. "Cheers! Came out of the conflict pretty good yourself, eh?"

"I was one of the lucky ones."

"I'd have gone over if it had lasted longer."

"It lasted plenty long enough," Jamie says. He raises one of the glasses in salute and leaves.

I'm about to follow him, when Will Cooper notices me. "I'd be happy to walk you home, now, Rachel. I'm thinking of going."

"But, why? The party's not over."

"It could get a little rough. Just thought I'd ask." He sounds hurt, which makes me feel a bit, I don't know . . . hard-hearted?

"Um, I better wait for my brother. I promised I would."

"Sure."

When I catch up to Jamie, he's with Mary in front of Tom's now-empty chair. "Where's Tom Klosky?" I ask. "Has he left already?"

Mary says, "His brother took him home. All he does anymore is get stinking drunk and try to pick fights. Poor guy."

"Poor guy," Jamie echoes and downs Klosky's drink. It must have burned all the way down because it makes his eyes water, and he chokes a little. He starts working on his own. I've never seen him take a drink before.

"Come on," Mary says to him. "Stop moping around, and let's at least dance. Everyone says you're a wet blanket." She tries to soften the accusation by looking up through her lashes, her head tilted, a playful smile on her lips.

Dance music blares from a record player, and Mary drags the two of us toward it. Behind us, we hear the tail end of a crude joke. Jamie says, "Rachel shouldn't have come. I think we should head home."

Too late. Roy Armstrong grabs me by the waist and pulls me in among the dancers. He spins me around and moves me from one hand to the other, like a rag doll. I didn't even think I knew how to dance. A friend of Roy's grabs Mary, and soon she's dancing as wildly as I am.

When the music stops, Vera gets everyone's attention by shouting, "Game time!" She holds up two oranges and orders people to form two lines—boy, girl, boy, girl.

Amazingly, we follow her orders without an argument, and soon, while Jamie watches, we play a silly game that involves a guy tucking an orange under his chin and passing it to the girl behind him in line, who must receive it under her chin, no hands allowed. It looks like everyone's necking.

Before it's my turn, a girl screams, and the game abruptly stops. All eyes are on Jamie, blood spurting from his nose. He dashes from the room with his handkerchief to his face and bounds up the stairs. Mary and I follow, but he barricades himself in the bathroom. "Are you all right?" I call lamely, pounding on the door.

"Do you need an ice pack?" Mary asks. "Do you want more handkerchiefs? What do you need?"

"I don't need anything," is his muffled response. "Go away and leave me in peace." I wait for him near the bathroom door, but Mary goes back to join the necking game.

At last, he comes out. The bleeding has stopped, but he looks pale and wary, as if he's been attacked by a furtive enemy. I hurry to get our coats.

Downstairs again, I signal to Mary that we should go. Either she doesn't understand or doesn't notice, she's so busy pressing against Roy Armstrong, passing the orange.

Jamie says he doesn't like to leave without her. After all,

he brought her. "People are treating us like a couple now that she's left school and works full time in Woolworths."

Mary drops the orange and is out of the game. "It's okay," she calls to him. "Go ahead. I'll go home with Stella. She wants me to stay overnight at her place."

Jamie and I walk home from the party through the gently falling rain. "Getting pretty cold," he says. "This is a false spring. I shouldn't wonder if it turns to snow."

"Jamie, stop! You're turning into Dad." I pull my collar tight against the wind and glance at him sideways. "Are you all right?"

"Never better."

"You look awful."

"You're not too terribly stunning yourself."

"You know what I mean." I think I *do* look fairly stunning, with my *Little Red Lies* lipstick applied ever so discreetly.

I wish I had a scarf to cover my head so that my hair doesn't turn into the end of a mop. In my good shoes, I slip and clutch at Jamie's arm for support. He lets me hang on as we walk briskly along a side street.

When we near the corner, he says, "I feel like I'm dying."

"What?"

"You heard me."

"Because of a nosebleed?" I pull at him to stop. I need to look at his face under the streetlight. "Look, you're not dying. You got safely home from the war. The war is over."

He disengages me from his arm and walks on quickly. We're about to cross Main Street, alive with the usual Saturday night tribes of oglers and bored young people. I have to trot to keep up. On Wakefield Avenue, where we live, he starts to say something but seems to lose his nerve. I skip a little ahead of him in order to see his face.

"Okay," I say. "I guess we're all dying from the minute we're born. What a ghastly thought!"

"You don't understand." We turn into our own walk, heading for the side door. "Everything's slipping away from me," he says, "you, Mother and Dad, Granny, even Mary. Everyone's aging or changing somehow. I feel like there's a split growing between us all, as if there'd been an earthquake leaving me on one side of a huge fissure and everyone else on the other. Like a nightmare, only I'm awake."

I skid on my heel again, but he catches me by the elbow. "I don't get it."

"Neither do I. Anyway, skip it. I'm just talking through my hat. Too much rum at the party."

It's after midnight. Our parents are in bed but probably not asleep, not Mother at any rate.

"Has this earthquake thing got something to do with the war?" I ask.

"I don't know. I'm not talking about it anymore."

"Maybe you should write a book about the war."

"Nobody would read it if I did."

"Of course they would. Why wouldn't they?"

"Because everybody dies at the end. Like possibly Coop and a few of the other guys I knew."

"Oh, for crying out loud, Jamie, you're just being morbid."

"I didn't know you knew big words like that."

"Oh, shut up."

"Children?" From upstairs our mother's voice reaches us in the kitchen, where we stand bickering. "It's late. Go to bed and don't forget to lock up. And turn out the lights."

Jamie goes straight upstairs, leaving me alone to turn out the lights, a task I hate as much as he does. Neither of us likes to be left alone in the dark.

7

The true spring arrives at last. After the weekend's freezing rain, Monday opens onto a sunlit stage. It's almost a pleasure to walk to school. The sun has stopped being phony. It's beginning to warm things up.

There's no rehearsal this Monday, so I'm hoping to spend some time in the public library looking for a book of plays. Nearly every night, I make myself read five minutely printed pages of a Shakespearean play from the *Complete Works* before I go to sleep, the way some people read chapters of the Bible. I hope that some spark of playwriting talent will seep into my brain while I sleep. Night after night, this keeps not happening.

Shakespeare's all right as far as he goes, but, if you're trying to figure out how to write a play, when you get right down to it, there *are* other playwrights and other plots written in up-to-the-minute English. I need something more startling than "In sooth, I know not why I am so sad."

I try to dodge Hazel Carrington as much as possible, but, inevitably, she corners me after math, last class of the day. "Rachel!" she calls in a voice that carries down the corridor and into the cloakroom.

I was hoping to grab my sweater and leave the school as quickly and quietly as possible, not exactly sneaking out but moving with a certain amount of stealth.

Hazel dashes in and catches me by the arm. "You said you'd help me, remember?"

"Oh, sure. I guess it just slipped my mind." I keep up with Hazel's long-legged stride until we reach her house, only a few blocks away. Inside, Hazel asks me to wait for a moment while she tells her mother something.

Hanging my sweater on a hook near the back door, I hear voices coming from upstairs, one too soft to make out the words and the other, Hazel's, a loud whisper. "No!" I hear. "Stay upstairs! You don't need to come down!" It seems an odd way to talk to her mother. I wouldn't get away with that tone of voice for one minute. My mother is a great demander of respect.

Hazel returns, smiles cheerily, and leads me into the living room, shutting the door. Soon we're hard at work on the play, with me reading the lines that come just before Hazel's. *Will that be all, Madam?* I say, with a deep unknowable sadness that may or may not have occurred in the housemaid's obscure life. This is met with silence.

"Your line is, *Yes, thank you*," I say.

Hazel frowns.

"What's the matter? It's a pretty natural reply. I don't see why you find it difficult to remember."

"I know the line," Hazel says. "It's just that I don't understand why you're making the maid sound as if she's going to cry. I keep thinking I must have made a mistake and got her all upset, so I have to think back over my lines. It's very confusing."

Propping my elbow on my other arm, I press a knuckle into my teeth and wonder if I've made a grave error in judgment with Ruthie's role. "Um," I say while I think this through. Can it be that I am, in fact, taking liberties with someone else's work? The answer *yes* pops up.

"Let's try it again," I say. This time, I allow the maid to speak as if she has nothing more compelling on her mind than the location of her feather duster. Hazel sails along, belting out the rest of her lines almost perfectly, right to the end of act 1. We both breathe a sigh of relief.

"There, now. You see? You *do* know your lines. You don't need me to help you. You'll do fine at the next play practice."

"No. I won't. I'll get distracted. I always do. It's the stupidest thing, really. I get thinking about the way people talk or move in the play, and sometimes it just doesn't feel real."

"But it's not real. It's a play. That's the whole point."

"You don't understand. I see the people who are not in the play, the ones helping, and I think they're saying to themselves, *This is so phony.* The actors are just pretending to be real people. And when I think about it, I start feeling like some sort of windup toy, pointed in one direction and then another, and that's when I wind down and forget my lines. I'm afraid it will be just like that when we have an audience."

I stare at Hazel for a moment, wondering if she has just said something incredibly deep or something incredibly stupid. "But, plays are supposed to entertain, to be a break from reality, aren't they?"

"Then why write plays about real things?"

"Because it's entertaining for the audience to see what real life is like from inside someone else's head. You see, I'm writing a play myself," I confess (all right, lie), "so I've thought about these things." I've never really considered anything remotely like this. Not only that, my play, to date, consists only of a cast of characters; the heading act 1, scene 1; and a jumbled description of the set.

Hazel shrieks her delight. "A play! What's it about? What's it called?"

I don't really have a name for it, but I say the first thing that comes to mind. "*The Wounded Lover.* It's about this soldier who gets shot, and a nurse rescues him and tries to nurse him back to health."

"That is so romantic. Do they fall in love?"

"Of course."

"And do they get married?"

"No. The soldier dies."

"You can't let the hero die."

"He's not the hero, the nurse is."

Hazel has to think about this. "Yes, but who will the nurse marry? Stories have to end happily. Is there another lover?"

"I haven't got that far yet. I'll let you know how it ends when I figure it out."

Hazel frowns. "I don't like stories like that. I wish, just once, someone would write a story where nothing bad happens, where people have only tiny problems and get over them, and then everybody lives happily ever after." Her voice is unusually quiet.

"How boring! That wouldn't be a story; that would be the grade one reader."

Hazel has no comeback, in fact, she isn't even listening. Her eyes are on the closed living room door. We both listen for a minute and hear someone coming falteringly down the stairs, a woman, singing snatches of a song.

"Wait here," Hazel says loudly. She opens the door barely enough to slip through, then closes it tightly.

I can make out the muffled sounds of an argument, someone clumping up the stairs. Glass shatters. It's all I can do not to open the door to see what's going on.

Hazel comes back a few minutes later, face red, eyebrows fierce. Soon she relaxes. Her eyes show pain, or is it guilt? I'm not sure which. "I have stuff I have to do," she yells as politely as possible, "so I guess you'd better go."

"Will you be all right with your lines?"

"Maybe. If I can keep my mind on them." Hazel guides me toward the door.

"Forget about the audience. Forget anyone else exists," I say, hoping this is helpful.

"Easy for you to say." She's trying to keep her voice down. Her shoulders have the defeated droop of someone carrying an unbearable burden. Still, she's lucky enough to be the star of the play; she's beautiful; her family is rich. What more does she want?

I head for home, the spring breeze tousling my hair. Tousling? Ravaging would be the word. I must look like I've been electrocuted. My mind is still on Hazel and her strange family. The mother is obviously a madwoman they keep locked in the attic. She must have managed to get out somehow and found her way downstairs. But, what about the breaking glass? A vase. She threw it at Hazel in an attempt to kill her. Maybe I should be writing my play about that, about having a murderous lunatic for a mother. No wonder Hazel thinks stories shouldn't have bad things happen.

My mind strays back to my play, *The Wounded Lover*. Why kill off the soldier at all? To kill or not to kill, that is the question. Shakespeare had no qualms about killing off heroes. Look at *Romeo and Juliet*. Look at *Hamlet*—a complete bloodbath at the end.

I walk along with my head down, thinking hard about the best way to end my play, until at last I see that the only answer is to abandon it and write one instead about a madwoman who tries to murder her family. I'm so deep in thought, I don't notice that I've missed my corner and am now about to pass Woolworths. *Good.* A little bag of candies will get my brain working again.

Inside, I stand at the candy counter at the front of the store, pouring over the selection. Mary Foley's counter, where she sells cosmetics—including lipstick with enticing names—is near the back. I should go say hi to her, but I don't. I can see she's busy chatting with some of her girlfriends.

"May I help you?" the salesgirl at the candy counter asks.

Chewing my lower lip, I mull over the selection. I need to make the absolute best choice—peanut brittle or Liquorice Allsorts. "Liquorice," I say, and just as the girl is about to scoop some into a paper bag, I say, "Wait. I can't make up my mind."

She puts down her scoop. "Take your own sweet time, hon, I got nothin' better to do."

I stare hard at the peanut brittle, willing it to offer itself to be my choice, savoring in my mind the sweet-salty blend.

As I ponder the difficult decision, the girls who were talking with Mary come up to the candy counter. I don't actually know them personally, but I've seen them around. They're obviously continuing a conversation started a few minutes before. They don't recognize me. They don't even notice me.

One of them says, "He's so standoffish and above it all. I don't know why she doesn't drop him."

"Well, that wouldn't be very patriotic, would it?"

"No, but you know what I mean; he's let the war go to his head."

"Oh, for sure! And he wasn't even an officer or anything."

"You know Mary. Too nice for her own good."

I can guess who they're talking about. *Standoffish!* My brother is the farthest thing from it. At least he wasn't like that before he went away, I'm sure of that. Now that he's back, he's a tiny bit different, a little quieter. But, so what?

The girls buy a bag of chocolate kisses, each of them dipping into it, and leave without even glancing at me.

"Peanut brittle," I say confidently. The minute I pay, and the girl hands over the small bag, I wish I'd chosen a square of chocolate fudge.

CHAPTER

8

"They should give us a week off school every month," I say as I sprinkle more brown sugar on my cornflakes. It's the last week of April, and school's closed for the Easter break. "I love sleeping in."

"Eight-thirty isn't much of a sleep-in," Jamie says.

"It is if you normally have to roll out of bed at the ungodly hour of seven and force your eyelids to stay open for another scintillating day at school."

We're in the kitchen having breakfast. Mother has brought the ironing board down from the sewing room and propped it over the backs of two kitchen chairs. She flattens tea towels and handkerchiefs while she keeps up with the conversation. Through the window, we can see Mrs. Hall, next door, hanging out her laundry. Mother waves.

"I need to go away somewhere," Jamie growls into the newspaper he's browsing through.

"But you just got home," Mother says. "We've hardly had a chance to talk."

"Talk! About what?"

"About you, of course, about your war experiences."

"I didn't have experiences. The war was about fighting. I wasn't on a sightseeing tour. We were bombed. We were shot at. And we did the same back. Men died. And that was the war." He glares at the classified section.

Letters not sent.

It's quiet tonight. It won't last, not after yesterday's grim exercise. There were ten of us. We had to move quietly, in twos, crouching close to tumbled walls of bombed buildings, slipping into empty doorways. I was with Defazio, who grew up in downtown Toronto. He whispered something like, "This would be fun if I wasn't so scared I'm gonna crap my pants." I tightened up, too, because the same thought crossed my mind. Even so, it was a bit like the cops and robbers me and Coop used to play. Coop was always a robber.

We were in what was left of a small French village, where our job was to flush out a nest of enemy soldiers supposedly guarding a small munitions dump. It was one of those nights when the moon looked like a big silver dinner plate, just hanging up there. I was shaking like mad and couldn't stop. That's when I accidentally nudged an empty tin can, and it rolled down a grade and bumped against a stone wall.

Immediately, gunfire rattled and whizzed over our heads. It was coming from a bombed-out schoolhouse. I'd given away our position. My first thought was that I'd be court-martialed and imprisoned as a liability. My second thought was that prison would be a whole lot safer than this place. We kept low, slithering along, our faces nearly in the dirt. But at least we knew exactly where the enemy lurked.

We crept forward when we saw clouds tarnish the moon. We were half protected by an overturned vehicle and some household goods left behind by refugees making their escape. Just then, a dog jumped out of an abandoned car and barked at us. Our sergeant was lying low behind the tank, but he lured the dog to him, silently. I guessed he wanted to quiet him with a tidbit of something he pulled from his pocket, a moment of kindness in the face of battle. A second later, he grabbed the dog and slit its throat. Such is war.

Enemy fire rattled at and above our cover, but we moved stealthily forward. Everyone looked away from the bloody dog. Defazio silently threw up. The clouds drifted and we were close enough to see the Germans' faces.

"Jeez, they're just kids, some of them," the sergeant whispered. He passed me his binoculars.

Some of them looked younger than me. Could have been me and Coop and Tom Klosky back in about grade eleven. "They don't look dangerous enough to be Nazis," I whispered.

Somebody muttered, "Worst kind. Hitler Youth. Learn to kill in kindergarten."

On the order, we threw our grenades. I have to confess, I took the precaution of half-closing my eyes to avoid seeing the inevitable. We fell back to take cover behind a pile of rubble before whatever stores the Germans had were blown sky-high.

Can't finish this. We're on the move again. More later.

Mother rests the iron on its end and sighs. "Son, why are you *doing* this?"

"Doing what?" He sounds like a sulky kid.

"You're being sarcastic and sullen. You've changed. I want my old Jamie back."

He put the paper down. "What do you mean, I've changed?"

"You used to be a polite, loving son."

He snorts. "That's what war does to you, I guess. You're ordered to throw grenades into the midst of a bunch of schoolboys and blow them sky-high, and the next thing you know, you're being rude to your mother."

"Jamie, stop being so difficult!" I say.

He scowls into the newspaper. I scowl at my cornflakes. Mother, tight-lipped, is busy filling her clothes-sprinkling bottle at the sink. I feel like throwing my cereal bowl through the window to relieve the tension. If Jamie doesn't say something, I'm going to whack him on the head with my spoon.

"I miss my war buddies, I guess," he says. "I miss the camaraderie, even the taunting and teasing." The atmosphere improves. He nibbles on a piece of toast.

"You still have friends here," Mother says.

"It's not the same. I miss the sweaty smell of fear we all had, and the way we felt lucky and reckless at the same time when we came away from a battle, more or less whole. Once we found a small goat ambling along a road, and we slaughtered it on the spot. We put it on a makeshift spit and cooked it over a fire."

My mouth drops.

"How barbaric!" Mother says. She folds her tea towels, hem to hem, with mathematical precision, trying not to look at him as he talks.

"And then we devoured it, just pulled off gobs of meat with our filthy grease-soaked hands."

I'm making gagging sounds.

Mother says, "Obviously, there was nothing wrong with your appetite back then. You probably got food poisoning. That's what the problem is."

Jamie brushes toast crumbs from his mouth with the back of his hand and sips at his now-cold coffee. "My only problem is, I need a job. Also, I need to go away for a bit. There are a few people I should visit. My buddy Leeson's widow, for one. She lives in Toronto. And I'd like to go back to the Coopers', except that I don't have anything to talk about besides the war. That's the problem—I have only one thing on my mind. I need a job more than anything, that's what I need."

I take the paper from him and study the want ads. "'Farm laborer wanted,' it says here. Maybe you could work for Granny."

"Now, there's an idea!" He takes the paper back.

"I don't think you have any idea how hard farmwork is," Mother says. "Ask your father. Ask Granny. She worked that farm right along with your grandfather. She used to say she helped the Allies win the Great War by keeping them fed. 'Napoleon was right,' I've heard her say, 'an army marches on its stomach.'"

"So what if it's hard work? I'm just growing soft, hanging around here. I need to get back in shape."

Mother nods sadly.

"Sorry for being so difficult," he says.

She pulls the plug on the iron and leaves it on its end to cool. Coming over to stand near him, she pushes hair back from his forehead. I watch him clench his jaw as if it's all he can do to keep from jerking away.

"I guess it must be pretty hard to adjust to civilian life again," she says.

"I'm working on it."

Jamie doesn't object to me going along for the ride in Dad's car out to Granny's farm. He's going to see if she'll hire him for the spring and summer. We roll down our windows to feel the breeze on our faces. At full volume, we sing, "'How' ya gonna keep 'em down on the farm, after they've seen Paree?'" We have to hum the rest because we don't know all the words. But who cares?

"I'll have to get a car of my own, if my plans work out."

"Can you afford one?"

"Sure, a little secondhand coupe, if I can find one. I have my army pay. I wasn't a big spender overseas."

"Granny will pay you," I say.

"I don't want her to pay me. I'll work for room and board."

"You mean, you would actually move out there?"

"Of course."

"No! You're not allowed. We need you at home."

He laughs. "Not half as much as I need to get away."

That takes a little of the joy out of my day, and I sulk

as we drive up the lane, rutted from a spring rain, and park beside Granny's truck. Bounder, the old farm dog, lies in the sun, soaking up the warmth. He barely raises his head but wags his tail enthusiastically when I give him a good tummy rub. Jamie bends over to pat him and staggers a little when he stands up, as if the effort makes him dizzy.

"What's wrong?"

"Nothing. Why does everybody keep assuming there's something wrong with me?"

He knocks on the kitchen door and opens it. "Hi, Granny," he shouts. A muffled shout answers from below the floor. He opens the cellar door to see Granny on her way up the ladder-like steps, with a bowl of last fall's apples.

"Well, this is a nice surprise," she says. "To what do I owe the pleasure?"

"I'm looking for work."

Granny raises her eyebrows at me. "Have those parents of yours put you out to work, too?"

"Why would they do that when they can use me for slave labor at home?"

"True enough," Granny says. "And what about you, young buster, what kind of work do you have in mind? Not farmwork, surely."

"Why not?"

She eyes him with her shrewd seeing-through-disguises look. "I'd have pegged you as more of a city boy."

"A man can change." He stresses *man*.

She purses her lips "Touché. However," she adds, "I've already hired a man to help me this spring. He's just back from overseas, too. By midsummer, though, I'll need more help, if you can afford to wait a few months." Jamie's shoulders slump. "But since you're here, and since I've had a great hankering for pickerel lately, and since I hear they're running, how about taking a couple of Grandpa's rods and trying your luck?"

Jamie shrugs, I grin, and soon we're trudging through the pasture, with rods and tackle box, to where the river separates the farm from the forest.

"I'm feeling lucky," I say.

"Bully for you." He shifts the tackle box to his other hand.

"This is just what you need, a good day's fishing. Back to nature and all that."

"No, what I need is a job."

We squelch through the ruts in the pasture. Not far away, cattle bend their necks over the new hay. Some raise their heads to scowl at us.

"To think I used to be afraid of those stinkers when I was a kid," Jamie says.

"I wasn't. Only thing I was afraid of was stepping in a fresh cow pie. Yikes! I just did." I scrape my heel through the grass trying to get rid of the mess. "What a staunch!"

"I gather you mean stench."

"Remember coming down here when the whole herd would come right for us?" I say.

"Not really."

"You used to stop dead. You couldn't move."

"I don't remember."

Looking up now, the cattle take it into their heads to investigate at closer range and plod toward us. Jamie sticks out his chest, waves his fishing rod, and says, "Out of my way, cows, I'm coming through!" They back right up, and he grins.

"They're steers," I say.

Our favorite place on the riverbank is an outcropping of rock, a shelf of limestone slabs overlooking the widest part of the river. From the hunk of unsliced bacon Granny gave us for bait, Jamie cuts us each a couple of pieces with the fish-skinning knife. We bait our hooks and cast our lines.

"Give your wrist more of a flick when you cast," he says, showing me how.

Reeling in, I think I feel a nibble, but I'm mistaken. It's a perfect morning—sun for warmth, clouds for shade, swallows flitting and diving. A breeze blows off the river, keeping the blackflies at bay.

"This is like old times," I say.

"This is like heaven," Jamie says. "Maybe I could get a job selling fresh fish to people in town."

"First, you have to catch some."

I sit on the rock, dangling my feet above the water, reeling in slowly, thinking about the way the river has about six shades of color in it.

Jamie's the first to get a bite. He pulls in a small fellow, not quite big enough to keep. Then I do the same. Probably the same fish. About fifteen minutes later, Jamie's line bends almost double.

"Maybe you're caught on a log," I say.

"No, there's something there, all right. It feels like a whale."

Once it surfaces, we see that he has a good-sized pickerel on his line—a keeper for sure—and it's putting up a pretty good fight. I get ready to scoop it up in the net as soon as Jamie reels it in close enough. In it comes, tail flipping, body writhing in a last battle against the inevitable.

"Granny's going to love this," Jamie says. He gets the hook out, bonks the fish on the head with the small club Grandpa used to use, and cuts off its head and tail.

"Maybe she'll invite us to stay."

Jamie's busy gutting the fish and doesn't answer, but then he yelps. He's cut himself on the fish knife and is bleeding more than the fish. I whip a handkerchief from my pocket and offer to bandage the gash.

He pulls away as blood runs up his wrist and arm. "Is it clean?"

"Of course it's clean." Quickly, I wrap up his hand as

best I can. Once the makeshift bandage is in place, I add, "At least it was clean last week. It may have been used once or twice since."

Granny just shakes her head when she catches sight of Jamie dripping blood through the handkerchief onto her freshly scrubbed kitchen floor. "Well, I never in all my born days," she says.

"At least we caught a fish," I say, plunking the scaly thing down on the table.

With enough pressure, she gets the bleeding to stop, cleans the cut, and bandages it properly.

"It's not that deep a slice," she says. "I wouldn't think it was worth that amount of blood. How do you feel?"

"Fine." Jamie doesn't look fine.

"Well, your face is as white as that fish's belly. Maybe you should lie down."

Surprisingly, he does what he's told and goes into the parlor to lie on the settee.

Granny puts the fish on a cutting board and wipes blood off the table.

"What do you think is wrong with him?" I whisper. "Do you think he got blood poisoning from my hankie?"

Granny shakes her head, her lips tight with concern.

Eventually Jamie gets up and dutifully drinks some sweet hot tea at the kitchen table. Bounder is inside now, in his usual spot under the table, hoping for crumbs to fall. Jamie looks a little better. He nibbles on a bite of the fish that Granny has just cooked and served, along with homemade bread slathered in butter.

"I guess I'm more of a liability than a help around here," he says.

"You'll be fine once you get your steam back," Granny says. "If I were your mother, I'd have you at the doctor's so fast, you wouldn't know what hit you. Now, I'm telling you straight out, son. You're old enough to look after yourself. You make an appointment with old Doctor Melvin, and he'll prescribe a tonic for you, or pills, or *something*. It's no good ignoring your health, lad. Look what happened to your grandfather. Caught cold, took pneumonia, and died. Just like that."

Hesitantly, Jamie says, "I think I'd just be wasting Doctor Melvin's time."

"It's not a waste of time to find out if there's something wrong, lad."

"But maybe it's only that I need to settle down and get married. I don't need a doctor to tell me that."

"Oh, Lord!" Granny says, slapping her hand to her head. "And support a wife how?"

Jamie flushes. He stands up, arms folded, glowering at the green fields he can see through the window and the sky with its darkening clouds.

"Sit," Granny orders him, and Bounder, his head in her lap, looks up to see if she means *him*.

Jamie continues to stand. He leans against the kitchen

sink, looking like the god of war. He's left a few bites on his plate, and I fork them down before Granny can bawl him out for not eating.

"Does your hand still hurt?" she asks him.

"No."

The way he's cradling it, I know it does.

After several moments of listening to the clock tick, Granny breaks the silence. "Much as I'd love to have you around on a permanent basis," she says, "I really wonder if farmwork is right for you. I don't know if you have the heart for it, love. I'm not talking about cutting yourself, now. I mean, generally. The land either captivates you or it doesn't. And then it kills you, the way it did your grandfather.

"He wouldn't quit, even when Death was staring him in the face. It was as though he'd said, 'I'm going, but not before I'm good and ready.' He got the hay in, sold off most of the livestock, all the while hacking up his lungs. It was what he did that was important to him. His job was to provide food for others, and that's what needed to be done before his illness got the better of him. When he finally did lie down, he kept looking at the bedside clock, waiting, it seemed, for the train to heaven and it was late. I could almost hear Death say, 'Ha! Now you have to wait for me.'"

Thunder rumbles in the distance. I hope it will rain, storm, keep us here for hours so the talk can continue. I wish I'd brought a notebook to scribble down the conversations.

"I never thought Gramps liked me very much," Jamie says.

"He did, though he had trouble showing it. He was a hard man to please, hard on your poor father, too. At the end," Granny says, "he reached out and squeezed my hand with the little bit of strength he had left. That was always his way of saying *thank you*. His final gesture. That's when I knew the safety net was in place."

"What do you mean?"

"Safe for him to go. Safe for me to stay, I guess."

"Are you afraid of death, Granny?" I ask. She's the only old person in the world you could say this to without fear of being told not to be so rude.

"It's not death I'm afraid of, love, it's redundancy. The day I discover everybody can get along better without me and would prefer to is the day I'll cheerfully croak." She grins at us. "I don't want to be relegated to the rocking chair while the work of the day goes on around me."

"No chance that will happen!" I say.

"As I see it, you young people are at a disadvantage. You see just the suddenness of death. You can't accommodate yourselves to the shock. Whereas, at my age, you see life getting a little frayed around the edges. The cracks in your ability to do the things you used to do start to show. You slow down, you stiffen up. You have time to accept that you can no longer walk a tightrope carrying all your baggage and still keep your balance. The idea of death creeps through the cracks little by little, and you see it as not such a terror, really, just more of the same. The ultimate slowing and stiffening, you might say. And then you fall off."

"Is there really a safety net?" Jamie asks.

"Of course. And it's exactly what your needs or beliefs want it to be."

Jamie goes over to look out the window again. Black clouds roll by, but there's still no rain. "How about giving me some good advice? You always say you know me better than I know myself. What do I want to do with my life?"

"Not waste it."

"Too easy."

She waits a moment before she speaks. "You have to be part of the world, not just an innocent bystander, love. When—notice I'm not saying if—the Martians land, you need to be able to answer this one question, because you can rest assured they're going to ask it. 'What's it like,' they'll ask, 'what's it like to be a human?' And you'll have to tell them what it's like to suffer and what it's like to rejoice."

"Jeez, Granny! That's too hard."

"You asked. I told you. And that's just the basics. Now go and get a head start. I have work to do. I want to nail down some shingles on the shed roof before it starts to rain."

At home, I follow Jamie into his room and he doesn't even kick me out. His window overlooks the back garden, where the apple tree is coming into bloom. The clouds are still heavy with rain. He opens the window, and we both breathe in the sweet, familiar smell of spring, of new grass yearning for a drink.

"I think I must be homesick," Jamie says.

"How can you be homesick when you're at home?"

"I don't know."

"I think you just need a job. Dad will put you to work in the drugstore."

"No, thanks. I would hate being forced to smile and be polite to all the old ladies who come in for their pills, or have to take wisecracks from the high-school crowd who come in for Cokes and laugh with them and pretend I have a good sense of humor."

"But, you do have a good sense of humor."

"Sure, for about one hour every three days."

"What about university?"

"The thought of studying makes my bones ache." He fills his nostrils with one last breathful of grass and new leaves and pending rain and shuts the window. "Maybe I'm just homesick for my youth."

"Rachel!" we hear. "Stop bothering your brother and come down and help me fold the sheets as I take them off the clothesline. It's starting to rain."

I manage a theatrical sigh. "I am nothing but a slave in this house. A slave to her every whim."

The rain doesn't last long. I'm on my way back upstairs

when I meet Jamie on his way out. "Where are you going?"
I ask.

"Out," he says and leaves without further discussion.

Half an hour later, he's back. I peek into his room, and
there he is lying with his arm over his eyes as if he has a
headache.

"Where did you go?" I ask.

"Nowhere."

"I'm just being friendly. Tell me."

"You're just being nosy."

I keep it up and keep it up, so just to shut me up, I
think, his voice flat with disappointment, he tells me the
bare bones of the rest of his afternoon.

Here's what I think happened. I'm adding descriptive
detail and dialogue because that's the way my imagina
tion works.

He walked down to Woolworths, pushed through the
swing door, marched straight to Mary's counter, and stood
there until she finished selling a jar of cold cream to a customer. When the woman left, he spread both hands on the
counter and told her he had a question.

"Hang on," she said. "Madam!" she called to the depart-
ing customer. "You've left your parcel."

The woman had to reach in front of Jamie to get her
cold cream, and it took him a second to understand he
was in the way. When he moved aside, another customer
stepped in front of him. And then Mary had to go to the

stockroom, and after that there was a department meeting.

"Sorry," she said, "I can't get out of it."

And then he came home.

"What did you want to ask her?" I kind of knew already.

"Nothing of any importance to you."

CHAPTER

9

School resumes. Daffodils begin to appear in flower beds. The buds on the trees burst into leafy lace. And the sun, toasty by midday, tells us to put away our winter woollies.

Ruthie's back at school. Her voice is still a little raspy, but she's not coughing as much.

After the final bell, we go to play practice, an extra one to make up for lost time. As prompter, I take up my position in the wings. Mr. Tompkins stops the action once or twice to offer suggestions, but on the whole the first act of the play rolls along smoothly. Remarkably, Hazel keeps all her lines straight, until Ruthie's line comes up: *Will that be all, Madam?* But Ruthie doesn't stop there. While Hazel's character waits to shout her next line, Ruthie's character grasps her hand dramatically and says, *I do hope so, Madam, as I must go to look after my poor fiancé, who was badly injured in a terrible war, and I'm so afraid he might die.* She emits a loud sob and places the back of her other hand on her brow.

The actors stand openmouthed, and Hazel pulls back as if from a burning coal. Mr. Tompkins climbs the steps to the stage, sputtering and shaking his script.

I shield my eyes with my forearm from the pain of seeing the entire rehearsal shattered, knowing that the fault is largely mine.

To give her credit, Ruthie explains her decision to change the lines without mentioning my coaching. Deep in the wings, I find a chair and sit hunched over my knees, feeling like Doctor Frankenstein.

After the actors return to their places and resume their roles, and after Hazel gets back into the swing of belting out her lines with the help of my prompts, and after it's over and everyone leaves for home, Ruthie and I walk along the street to her corner.

"I didn't think it would matter all that much," she says in her own defense. "There's always so much going on, I didn't think anyone would even notice. It's mostly your fault, though."

"I didn't tell you to add more lines. You don't go in and make changes that the writer wouldn't approve."

"Mr. Mackiewitz changed a couple of words that Hazel had trouble pronouncing," Ruthie says.

"That's different."

Ruthie snorts. "So it's all right if I act as if I'm sad, even though nothing in the script tells me to, but it's not all right to say I *am* sad and why."

After a moment, I say, "No, it isn't. I was wrong to suggest a change at all."

Ruthie grins at me. She loves it when I'm wrong. She says, "It's too bad, really, because I kind of enjoyed beefing up my role. It felt right. I felt like a true actress."

We part then, Ruthie hurrying along to her house. I poke along to mine, but, as I amble in, I hear Jamie almost shouting, "I'm *not* getting lazy!"

"Well, you need a tonic, then."

"All right, all right! Stop badgering me. I'll go to the doctor!"

I half-expect Mother to tell him to go to his room, but it's Mother who leaves.

"Maybe I should take your advice and start writing a book about the war," he says to me.

I hang my spring jacket on a kitchen chair, knowing Mother will come back and tell me to move it. "Of course you should."

"Mother thinks I'm a lazy bum."

"No, she doesn't."

"Oh, but she does. She said as much. Now, if I were to say I was writing down my war experiences, I could stay in my room with the door shut and no one would see me doing nothing. That's what upsets her. She can't stand to see a member of this family being idle. You can read a book, but not for too long and not in the morning because that's when chores *have* to be done. Useless to imagine you can put them off until the afternoon. You can listen to records or the radio, but not for more than an hour and not every day. And you definitely cannot lie around sleeping in the daytime, especially when the sun's out, without someone telling you to go to the doctor."

"I think you need to have a plan. She would stop pestering you if you had a plan of action."

"I have a plan. I'm going to start winding my watch on a regular basis and just go on from there."

"Ruthie said you told her sister you were going to become a commercial artist. I didn't know you were good at drawing."

"Good at drawing! *Ha!* I can barely draw a breath." He laughs so hard at his own joke he chokes, and Mother returns to pound him on the back and hand him a glass of water. "I'm just a little out of shape," he gasps.

"We'll go to the doctor first thing in the morning," Mother says.

"Not we, I."

"I think you need me to go with you."

"Mother, I'm a grown man. Why would I . . . ? Can you not just leave it up to me?" He leans on the table with his head in his hands.

"I go with your father," she points out. "It's better if there are two heads to take everything in; that way I can remind your father to take his pills, or do whatever it is he's supposed to do."

"God!"

"Don't swear."

"Does he go with you when you have a medical problem?"

"Well, no, of course not. He doesn't want to be involved with women's things. Why would he?"

"Good God," I hear him mutter as he goes upstairs.

I head up shortly afterwards and, through his half-open door, I can see him at his desk reading from a sheaf of papers tied together with string.

Letters not sent.

A week has passed since I last wrote about the night we attacked a bombed-out schoolhouse full of German soldiers. I still can't get over how young they all looked. I can't move on till I finish this because I can't get it out of my head.

Nothing happened after our grenades went off. The silence was worse than the expected explosion. When the dust settled, weapons at the ready, we went in to search the ruins for ammunition but didn't find any. Instead, among desks

and benches, we found bodies and body parts of
the young soldiers. In the now-bright moonlight,
we moved carefully around the debris. As I've
said before, I don't have the heart for this job
of killing people. The enemy, the ones still with
faces, in death looked like children pretending
to be asleep.

Part of the floor above us remained intact,
and so did a staircase against one wall. The
sergeant ordered me to go up and check out the
space above. I climbed thinking each step would
be my last, shrinking as much as I could against
the wall. When I was high enough to look around,
I moved my rifle in a slow sweep. I heard a sharp
intake of breath. At first, I thought it was my
own, but in the moonlight I saw a young guy, a
kid really, sitting, aiming a revolver at me.
His eyes were glistening with hatred or tears.
I don't know which.

Writing about it now, well after the event,
I'm sure I gave the kid a chance to surrender.
I'm pretty sure. I also remember the immediate
(almost immediate?) blast from my gun. But I have
this disturbing sense that my trigger finger was
part of the gun's mechanism and that the gun
went off without a conscious effort on my part.
I was actually shocked when the kid slumped to

one side. Rachel, he was like one of the cast-off
dolls in your bedroom closet.

Outside his door, I call, "Have fun at the doctor's tomorrow." Before going into my room to do my homework, I add, "You'll be able to check out the new Dingbat calendars. They're even funnier than the old ones."

"You're the Dingbat," he says.

"No, you are."

"So, what's the verdict?" I ask him the next day, when I get home from school.

"Doctor Melvin says my blood's low, whatever that means. That's why I have no energy and no appetite. I have to take pills and a tonic." He's stretched out on his bed.

"Your blood is low?"

"I think I'm registering only about half a tank."

I'm picturing the Dingbats getting blood transfusions from something that looks like gas pumps.

"The doctor explained it, but I wasn't listening," he says.

As spring warms into a promise of summer, Jamie religiously takes his tonic and pills and seems a lot better, as far as I can tell. Not only that, he's been accepted into Arts & Science at the University of Toronto, admitted under the Veterans Charter, so no tuition costs. Now, unfortunately, he has time for his love life.

He invites Mary over to listen to records in the living room, one evening near the end of May. Our family tactfully goes to bed early, although I have to make several trips downstairs—once to find the book I'm reading, once to make myself a brown sugar sandwich, and then to find my fountain pen. I'm sure I left it in the dining room. It isn't my fault that they don't notice me searching under the table for it.

I can't help overhearing Jamie say sweetly, "Mary, why don't you move to Toronto when I do? You could probably get a better job than the one you have here."

"I'm not sure I want to live in a big city. And my mother wouldn't let me."

"But this is your life, not your mother's."

"Try telling her that."

"Listen, you're old enough to stand up for yourself. I feel as if your mother is beside us every time I try to hold your hand or kiss you."

"Well, I can't help that."

"Tomorrow is Saturday. Let's just go somewhere. I'll borrow Dad's car; he won't mind. We'll drive up to, I don't know, somewhere beyond Claymore. We'll lose ourselves in the woods. There's a lake about half a mile from the road. We can go swimming."

"I threw out my last year's bathing suit."

"We'll swim in our underwear."

"Our underwear!"

Beneath the table, I clap my hand over my mouth to stifle a gasp. If this idea doesn't make Jamie's heart pump more blood into his system, I didn't know what will. Mine is certainly going a mile a minute.

"Yes."

"It's still only May. The water will be too cold."

"We'll just wade."

"I have to baby-sit."

"Sunday, then."

"After church."

"Of course."

If his voice is anything to go by, I think his blood level's dropped to an all-time low.

Mary says, "I don't know if I could do that after church. I mean, I'd be thinking about it all the while I was in church, and I wouldn't be accepting the Blessed Mother into my heart with a pure spirit. I mean, we'll be next to naked. And then what? That's what I'm worried about."

Jamie lets out a long trying-to-be-patient-but-failing sigh. "We'll keep our clothes on."

"But, what will we do? It sounds kind of boring."

"I'll bring a deck of cards." His voice is hollow with disappointment.

"I'm not allowed to play cards on Sunday. The Blessed Mother—"

"Blessed Mother! Blessed Mother! There are just too many mothers in our lives."

It rains on Sunday, buckets, and it keeps on all day, with occasional thunder and lightning. Not to mention wind. People coming out of church have their umbrellas blown inside out. Anyway, as it ends up, Mary has to baby-sit, again.

My pen, I discover, is on the desk in my room, so that's a relief.

At school on Monday, I catch up to Ruthie in the corridor before our first class. "I'm afraid Jamie's going to pop the question to Mary any day now," I blurt.

"What do you mean 'afraid'? I think that's exciting."

"She'll take him away from us."

"Doubt it. She'd never leave Middleborough. I wish my sisters would get married and move a hundred miles away. Then they wouldn't be able to boss me around."

"But, she'll take him away from *me*," I say.

Ruthie looks at me as if I have snakes in my hair.

"Do you have any spare cash?" Jamie asks me a week later, before I set off for school. My impulse is to say no. I have a sock stuffed with small change and small bills in my underwear drawer. I'm saving up for a typewriter.

"I might have a little. But you have to pay me back. What do you need it for?"

"I don't think that's any of your business."

"It is if I'm the banker."

He scowls. "I'm taking Mary out to lunch at Wong's

Grill, if you must know. I want to make sure I have enough and some left over for a tip. You'll get it back, don't worry."

"Hmm. Wong's Grill, eh? I suppose you're going to pop the question."

"What?" He's blushing.

"You're buttering her up so she'll agree to marry you."

"Look, if you don't want to lend it to me, just say so. I can easily go to the bank, but I was there just yesterday."

"So where did your money go?"

"Shoes. Clothes. Didn't know they were so expensive after three years away and in uniform."

Against my better judgement, I produce my sock and invite him to take what he needs. It isn't Mary I'm against, necessarily. Mary's all right. It's the idea of losing my brother that bothers me. Once he gets married, he'll never again take me along to Granny's just for the ride, never fish with me, never confide in me and me alone.

Wong's Grill, I muse as I pack up my homework to take to school. Ruthie's sister Joan usually takes her lunch break there with her work pals. A plot is beginning to form.

Nearly all the booths are taken, and the noise level is high, when Ruthie and I slip into Wong's Grill on our lunch break from school. His back to the door, Jamie doesn't notice us sneak in. I keep my hand half over my face. I should have a trench coat, but the turned-up collar of my blouse is all the disguise I can manage.

"There they are!" Ruthie says, pointing to a booth where Joan and her friends from the Bell, where she works, are forking down French fries.

I frown and put a quick finger to my lips, but Ruthie ignores me. "We're joining you," she announces loudly as she squeezes in beside her sister, pulling me after her. The older girls protest but shift to make room.

Jamie and Mary sit opposite each other at one of the tables in the center of the room. I notice Mary glance, with what looks like embarrassment, at *her* friends from Woolworths, in a booth on the other side of the room, the ones she usually has lunch with. Maybe she wishes she were with them, instead of Jamie. Or, maybe she has an inkling about what Jamie's going to ask her.

Mr. Wong brings their orders—hamburgers, fries, and Cokes as well as separate bills. I watch Jamie snatch up Mary's bill with his own. He probably wants to make sure she knows it's his treat. She doesn't seem to notice.

"Are you skipping school?" Joan asks us.

"No, we're going back. It's lunch hour," Ruthie says. "Rachel wants to ask you something."

"I do?"

Ruthie encourages me with a tight smile.

"Oh, yes, I want to ask you something."

Joan leans towards me, puzzled. "This better be good, kiddo."

I haven't had time to think this through. "Um, Joan,

I was wondering if you have, um . . ." I pause to glance around the restaurant. "Oh," I say, "my brother's here. What a surprise!"

He isn't taking his eyes off Mary as he nibbles a long French fry on the end of his fork. Mary tucks into her hamburger as if she's been fasting for days. I keep ducking in behind Ruthie so Mary won't see me. Jamie still, more or less, has his back to us.

"Oh, yes." I turn back to Joan. "I was wondering if you have, um, um, if I could borrow . . ."

Jamie seems to be asking Mary a difficult question. She stares at him, her eyes round and startled as if he's confessed to strangling cats.

Joan says, "I'm all ears. What do you want to borrow?"

Mary turns bright red, but she keeps on chewing.

Still looking at her, waiting for her response, Jamie finishes off the fry and slowly, deliberately, forks another. I wish I could lip-read.

"What?" Joan prompts, poking my arm. "Spit it out."

I pull my eyes back into my head. "Books," I say. "Do you have any good books I can borrow?"

Joan stares at me suspiciously, as if this is a trick question.

I take another peek at Jamie, who looks brokenhearted. His shoulders droop. He's staring hard at his plate.

Mary drinks her Coke and chokes. When she recovers, she looks at her watch. "Oh, dear!" I *see* more than *hear* her say. She jumps up, making some sort of excuse to Jamie.

She gives a quick wave to her friends across the restaurant, and the bell over the door jingles as she leaves.

Jamie keeps his eyes on his plate, still heaped with food.

Mary's friends, mouths agape, crane their necks to glimpse Jamie, who's staring hard at his hamburger. It looks to me like he's willing it to disappear. He even cuts it in half with his knife and fork. He swallows some Coke. He picks up a fry with his fingers, eats it, and wipes his hands on his thighs.

I bend in across the table to Joan. "Books?" Joan says turning up her nose. "I have a lot of movie magazines you can borrow."

I have to look again at Jamie. He takes a paper napkin from the dispenser on the table, wraps half his untouched hamburger in it, and jams it into his pocket.

I practically lie across the table to avoid notice because now he's going to the cash register, which is close enough to us that I can overhear him talking to Mr. Wong.

Mr. Wong looks back at what's left on his plate, half a burger and most of his fries. He says, "You no like my food?"

"Oh, yes. I do. For sure. But, you know (he looks at his watch to make the point), my fianc . . . my friend had to get back to work. She forgot she'd promised to cover for someone else. But it was very good. Delicious."

Mr. Wong is about a hundred years old. Jamie wouldn't want to upset him.

"You have nice snack in pocket for later. Okay. Bye-bye."

Jamie says, "Bye-bye," and leaves, his hand covering his bulging pocket.

Joan and her friends titter behind their hands. When they catch sight of me, they look a little embarrassed. I wish I'd never come.

"Movie magazines! Oh, sure, I'd love them." I hate movie magazines. Sort of.

As soon as Jamie's safely out of sight, Ruthie and I run outside and back to school. We're ten minutes late and both get detentions.

Before serving them, we go to the auditorium to explain that we won't be at rehearsal. Just as we open the heavy door, we meet Mr. Tompkins coming out.

"I was just going to send someone to look for you," he says.

"We have detentions," Ruthie says.

"Whatever for?" Mr. Tompkins has a way of looking at girls as if they're breaking his heart.

"We were late after lunch," I say.

"Ooh, no! You girls are so-o-o bad!" He puts his hands on both our shoulders and gives us a little shake. I feel his hand slide up my neck under my thick hair to tweak my ear.

Releasing us, he shakes a finger and says, "Don't miss tomorrow's practice. Final fitting for costumes. First performance this Friday!"

Back he goes into the auditorium, leaving us both breathless. The warmth of his hand on my neck, the pinch of his fingers on my earlobe, linger, making me dizzy with excitement.

Ruthie's mouth hangs open. "Confess," she says. "You are secret lovers."

"Don't be an idiot," I whisper hoarsely. I put my hand on my neck where his had been and relive the sensation.

All through our detention, Ruthie teases. "You're in love. Confess."

"He's a teacher, for Pete's sake."

"He's in love with you."

"He just likes to tease." My heart is thumping loud enough to be heard.

"Every girl in this school will be so jealous."

I put my fingers in my ears to block out Ruthie's taunts. But it has no effect on my imagination. I see myself running towards something huge, like a volcano, something dangerous.

CHAPTER

10

I decide not to talk about my detention at home. It would just raise embarrassing questions. As I walk in, I hear a commotion upstairs. Mother's voice is one notch below hysteria, and Jamie's is gruff, protesting.

Upstairs, I park myself in his open doorway. Jamie's in bed, pajamas and all, with a cold compress on his forehead and a glass of water and pills on his bedside table. Mother bustles about, clears his chair of clothes, and pushes it nearer to the bed.

"What's wrong?" I ask

"Jamie fainted on his way home, after having lunch in a restaurant. Food poisoning, again, no doubt. The doctor should be here any minute."

"People from all over town came to watch me fall down on Main Street," Jamie mutters. "They figured I was drunk."

"You're feverish," Mother says.

"Maybe I have that kind of flu everybody died from after the last war."

"Don't talk nonsense."

The doorbell rings, and Mother rushes down to let the doctor in. Jamie looks scared, like a kid afraid of a needle.

Doctor Melvin hunches through Jamie's doorway as if he's had to stoop all his life to avoid knocking his head on low ceilings and doorjambs. But he's only a little taller than I am. His stoop makes him look about ninety. I know he isn't. Dad once said he's in his sixties, but he's practiced looking mature and responsible for so long that it's prematurely aged him.

"Move out of the way, Rachel," Mother says.

The doctor has Jamie unbutton his pajama top before he pushes and prods his belly. At one point, Jamie winces with pain. In his exploration, the doctor comes back again and again to that upper left side of his abdomen, pressing, but not as hard. "Hurts, does it?" he says.

"It's his appendix, isn't it?" Mother says. "I just knew it. That, or food poisoning."

"No, it's not his appendix. If you have something to do downstairs, I suggest you and Rachel go down and keep busy, Mrs. McLaren." Usually he calls her Dora. "We'll be all right here. Jamie's a big boy, now."

Jamie tightens his lips. "I fought in the bloody war," he mutters. "I'm not a big boy; I'm a grown man. When is anyone going to recognize this fact?"

The doctor harrumphs and says, "Quite right, quite right!"

I follow Mother downstairs while she sighs and mutters. "I try to be a good mother, heaven knows." At the bottom, she turns back and shakes a finger at me. "Just wait till you're a mother, then you'll know the heartache."

"I don't plan on being a mother." I scratch my arms as if I would erase them.

"Stop scratching," she says. "You'll make your eczema worse."

"It's already worse."

In the kitchen, she says, "I knew there was something wrong with him almost from the day we met him at the train station. But, I held my tongue, and now, of course, the blame falls on my shoulders."

"No one is *blaming* you."

She rinses out the dishcloth and begins scrubbing the stove top, then the table. Both were already in immaculate condition. "I noticed how thin he was, but it was your grandmother who drew everyone's attention to it, as if she were the only mother at the table."

"Don't worry about it. He'll be okay."

"He's been a worry from the day he was born. Colicky until he was six months, whooping cough when he was three." She's wiping down the front of the fridge, now. "Doctor Melvin said at the time that it wasn't whooping cough, it was croup. But, as a mother, I did know a thing or two back then. It was whooping cough."

This is old news from the days when Doctor Melvin presumably didn't look a day over eighty-nine. I get out soda crackers and peanut butter for a snack. I have a feeling dinner will be a long time coming.

"Does Dad know Jamie fainted?"

"I phoned him. He said that the drugstore was extremely busy for some reason. I said, 'You have two assistants. They don't need the druggist there when there's an emergency at home.' Now, if it were me, I'd drop everything and race home to find out what the problem is. I don't think men have the same capacity for caring that women do when it comes to their children."

She lifts the hair off the back of her perspiring neck and looks around for something else that needs to be done. Filling the kettle with water, she places it on the back burner and says, "I really don't know why I'm doing this."

"For tea, maybe?"

"No, something else. It's what my mother used to do in times of stress—fill time with a known habit. I remember when news came that my older brother was missing in action during the last war, my mother boiled water and cleaned every available surface, plunging her hands into the pail until they were as red as cooked lobsters. I was about your age."

"Maybe you should go for a run around the block."

"Why run? I'm not in a hurry. I'm upset. In my day people worked off their emotions; they didn't try to run from them." She's now on her knees, scrubbing the table legs.

I head for the stairs.

"Where are you going?"

"To my room."

"Well, don't bother the doctor."

"I'm not going to!"

I leave my bedroom door open but, at first, can hear only muffled sounds from Jamie's room. As I listen hard, I hear Jamie say, "That's a lot of blood you're siphoning off. I'll be running on empty soon."

"You might be a wee bit sicker than we thought."

I move closer to my doorway.

"Will I need an operation?"

"No, I don't think so. I want you to get as much bed rest as you can. I'll tell your mother."

I hear Dad come in so I go downstairs. When the doctor comes down, the two men shake hands. "Something about his blood cells, is it?" Dad asks, but Doctor Melvin won't commit himself, even to Howard McLaren, pharmacist, father of the patient.

"Could be," he says. "We'll know better once we get the lab report." He leaves a prescription for pain relief with Dad and says he'll be in touch.

When he's gone, Mother says, "What do you think it is?"

Dad frowns. "No idea." Although he tries to hide it from Mother and me, the expression on his face shows that he might have an inkling.

We all go upstairs to worry over the patient.

"What did he tell you it is?" Mother asks.

"He didn't say."

"Oh, that annoying man! Why we continue to go to him, I don't know." When she puts a hand on Jamie's fore-head, he shifts out from under it.

"I think it's reasonable to wait for the lab results," Dad says. "No use fretting until we have scientific proof there's something wrong."

Mother means to sigh, I think, but it comes out as a snort. "Surely he told you something," she says to Jamie.

"He doesn't think I need an operation."

She brightens. "Well, I guess that's something."

I catch sight of bruising on his arm. "What happened to your arm?"

Mother's eyes widen. She pushes up his sleeve. "How did this happen?"

"When he siphoned off my blood."

"Good heavens! The man's a butcher! You shouldn't have all that bruising. I mean, I do know something, and this is definitely not right. A little bruise, perhaps, but this . . . this is scandalous." She turns to Dad. "We're get-ting another doctor, Howard. This is deplorable. There's that new chap. I've met his wife, and she seems very nice. Could you just phone him? Please, Howard."

"Hmm," he says, frowning over Jamie's bruise. "I'm sure everything will be fine."

Downstairs again, Mother bangs pots and pans on

and off the stove while Dad picks up the evening paper. The paper rustles; his hands are shaking.

I set the table without being asked. I'm thinking of offering to help with dinner, but when Mother tries to take a baked ham out of the oven without oven mitts and screeches like a tormented animal, I think it safer to go back upstairs. When I peek into Jamie's room, he's lying very still with his eyes closed.

Letters not sent.

Half my mind says, don't write about it, and the other half says, get it out of your system. So all right, here goes. It's taken me almost a week to be able to write about this. It's about trust. It's about wondering if we can put our trust in anything.

The heat that day was suffocating. My eyes stung from sweat, although not exactly the worst thing I had to put up with.

We could hear the drone of bombers and knew they were ours, Halifaxes. Coop could be flying up there, for all I knew. Lucky son of a gun. Not down here with us, creeping like ants on the baked earth with the stench of battle in our nostrils. But as I looked up, my envy turned to horror.

"Good God!" someone yelled. The bomb doors were opening right above our heads. The Allies were bombing us.

Some of our transport vehicles roared ahead. Others stopped abruptly, and men tumbled out to dive under them. Some of us took to a nearby wooded area. The last things I saw before I started to run were parts of machinery and parts of men flung into the burning air. I dove behind a clump of trees, and there was Leeson, trying to dig a foxhole with his bare hands. I'd known him only a few months, yet, it felt like a lifetime. I joined him, two dogs after the same bone, no time even to unhinge our spades. We huddled together, half-protected by a shelf of moss-covered rock, praying the bombs would miss us and drop a quarter mile ahead, forward troops be damned.

Leeson was a married man. Once, he showed me a picture of his wife, a plain girl with a sweet smile and slightly protruding teeth, but big eyes that saved her from being funny-looking. "She looks nice," I told him. He put the picture back in an inside pocket, nodding, satisfied. Leeson was one of the few in our platoon who didn't go looking for women whenever the opportunity arose. I tended to stay behind with him and one or two others.

Again bombers pulverized the air overhead. Someone threw a Union Jack out onto the field just beyond our half-dug trench, but it lay furled in on itself as if trying to avoid the onslaught. "Get your head down," our captain yelled at me.

I thought we should spread out that flag to show the bombers they were blasting their own side. The utter stupidity of Allied bombs dropping on Canadian soldiers turned whatever fear I had into anger. "Coop, you stupid bastard!" I yelled and crawled over the rock to give the flag a flick, to make it at least recognizable.

Leeson yanked me back by the legs, and I slid again into our homemade dugout seconds before more bombs could do their worst. The attack was punishing beyond anything I'd ever imagined, the more so because of its irony. We burrowed in like moles while clots of earth, rocks, metal-debris of all kinds-pummeled our backs.

At some point, I passed out. I came to face-down on top of my rifle in a mud puddle, held there by an impossibly heavy weight. When I got my face out of the oozing earth, I discovered that the deadweight was Leeson's body and the puddle, Leeson's blood. I managed to squirm out from under until, by kneeling on him, I could

hoist myself over what was left of the makeshift
trench and roll out. I wiped his blood off my
face with my sleeve. My leg was ripped open below
the back of my knee and bleeding, but I managed
to stand with the help of my rifle.

Carnage everywhere. Bodies of men looked like
hunks of meat. Bloody, mangled, strewn. I kept
vomiting until all that came up was sick-tasting
slime.

Then it hit me that I had actually knelt on
Leeson, with his helmet knocked off and his
brains spattered everywhere. I owed him my life,
and yet I practically stood on him. On a recruit-
ment poster, I once read "Let the army make a man
of you." It should have said "Let the war make a
mound of earth of you."

Leeson took his wife's picture everywhere.
I thought it was likely still in his pocket,
drenched in blood, maybe. I made a quick survey
of the sun and the land to get my bearings and
hobbled a short distance away. I was still thinking about the picture and wondering if his wife
would want it. But, why? I wouldn't care about
having a picture of myself.

I was in a real daze at this point. I decided
to walk in the direction of Falaise, hoping to
find some live, whole human beings. Blood from

my wound was dripping into my boot, and my leg stung like billyo.

That's when I dragged myself back to Leeson, because what if his wife would love to have the picture back and to know that her husband carried it with him everywhere? I managed to move Leeson enough to reach into his pocket and draw out the picture without smearing it with blood and put it in my pack. I had a roll of bandage in my kit and wound it around my bloody leg. By the time I struggled to my feet again, the bandage was soaked through. The pain was a killer, but—

Hang on. An announcement. Big move. Orders from on high. I'll finish this later, maybe a lot later.

As I stare at Jamie, he barely seems to breathe. Beside him lies a sheaf of papers, tied at the corners with string.

I go in. "I know you're not asleep," I say loudly. "And I know you're not dead, you big faker!" I watch his chest to make sure it's still moving up and down. His eyes remain shut. "Jamie!" Nothing. "I want to know what's wrong. Why are you sick?" I grab his arm to look at the spreading bruise.

Suddenly, his eyes pop open and he bares his teeth like a mad dog. I jump back startled. Quickly, he covers the papers with a blanket.

"Don't manhandle the war wounds."

"You gave me such a scare. Why is your arm like that?"

"The doctor went a little overboard trying to bleed me dry."

"What's that bunch of papers all about?"

"It's about how to make your sister mind her own business."

"Liar."

Doctor Melvin makes another house call the next day. Just as I get home from school, he comes into the kitchen and says to Mother, "I want Jamie to see a specialist in Toronto."

"What kind of specialist?" She puts down the potato she's peeling and turns to face him, one hand gripping the sink for support.

"He specializes in diseases of the blood."

"What's wrong with Jamie's blood?" My voice is squeaky, panicky.

Mother frowns. "Don't interfere, Rachel."

"Well, it's a long story, I'm afraid." He hunches his shoulders more than usual, as if the weight of what he has to say is too heavy. "To be brief, Dora, we think your son's blood is low on normal white cells. This means he can pick up germs more easily, so we have to be careful about keeping him well and making sure he gets plenty of rest." He takes a notebook from the pocket of his suit coat and squints at it. "I've gone ahead and made an appointment for him to see a chap in Toronto this coming Monday afternoon." He tears the page out and gives it to Mother. "If the day doesn't suit you and Howard, just phone and they'll change it." Putting his hat on, he nods consolingly at us and leaves.

Mother and I look at each other as if we've never met.

"I'd better get dinner ready," she says and goes back to peeling potatoes.

I brighten suddenly. "You know what? He's going to be fine."

"Oh?" Mother's still frowning.

"Yup, I just know it. He got home from the war all right, didn't he?"

CHAPTER

11

It's early June. Jamie's trip to Toronto will take place the day after closing night of the play. In these final few days, excitement runs high for both the actors and the backstage crew. Mr. Tompkins draws me aside to say, "I don't want you to feel underemployed. How would you like to be props mistress?" So, besides prompting and doing makeup, I am in charge of making sure the bowl of apples is on the table in act 1 and that two apple cores are beside it in act 2, things like that. I now seem to be responsible for all the bits and pieces required for the smooth running of the plot. I don't mind the extra job; it's not acting, but it's important. That's what I tell myself.

I try to avoid making eye contact with Tommy, as much as possible. I need to focus on my backstage jobs. The play is to run for two nights, Friday and Saturday. My family has tickets for the final night.

On my way home after the dress rehearsal, I run into Mary Foley coming from work. We stop to greet each other. She seems a little shy and in a hurry to go.

Quickly, I say, "Jamie's sick in bed with something horrible."

Startled, she says, "What's he got?" Her face is chalk white.

This is a good omen. If Mary and her friends know he has a mysterious health problem, they might show him a little respect or at least take him a little more seriously.

"We don't know for sure, but he fainted after he had lunch with you."

I think this will make her gasp, but all she says is, "Is he getting shots for it?"

"I'm not sure. Why?"

"They give the boys shots for that disease they pick up overseas."

"What disease?"

Mary shrugs. "Just something I heard my older brothers whispering about. They had to get shots for something they called the clap. I don't know what it is." (She's blushing, which makes me think she does know.)

"You could phone him," I say.

"Sure, I'll do that."

And she does, that very evening.

I answer the phone downstairs in the front hall, where we keep it on a little table. I call up the stairs to Jamie to pick up the extension in our parents' bedroom. Intending to hang up, I keep the phone to my ear to hear when Jamie comes on the line. I hear him say hello, and Mary say, "Hi, Jamie," and Jamie say hi back.

"I'm sick," he says.

"So I hear." There's a long pause. "Um, I was wondering if you're getting shots for it."

"No."

"Well, you should." For some reason, she sounds angry.

"Why? Shots for what?"

"For, you know, that disease you get from being with, you know, strange women."

"What strange women?"

"Um, bad women."

The silence that follows makes me think the phone has gone dead for a moment.

"The clap?" he sounds horrified. Suddenly he yells angrily, "Rachel, get off the phone!"

I hang up quickly.

Mother calls from the living room, "Who was on the phone?"

"Mary."

By the time I head upstairs, Jamie's back in bed, but I go into his room anyway. "Sorry for not hanging up right away."

"You shouldn't eavesdrop."

"I didn't mean to. I didn't even get it. What was she going on about?"

"Never mind. It's just some stupid idea Mary's got into her head. That girl has some growing up to do."

I feel a little bit forgiven, but I'm still in the dark.

The next day, Jamie's up and dressed and nearly collides with me on my way downstairs.

"I thought you were supposed to stay in bed," I say.

"It's impossible with the sun pouring through the window. I can't explain this, but now that I have permission to be lazy, I feel anything but."

"Guess what? Jamie's all better," I announce as the two of us go into the kitchen for breakfast. I glance back at him, hoping he'll look better, but he's still pale in his white shirt and so narrow his trousers hang low on his hips. He needs to punch another hole in his belt.

Mother studies him with her hands on her hips. "Jamie, you go right back up to bed. I'll take something up to you in a minute. Honestly. You're a grown man. You would think you'd at least be able to follow the doctor's advice."

Jamie and I glance at each other with raised eyebrows.

"I've suddenly been promoted," he says under his breath.

"I beg your pardon?" Mother says.

"Ever since Doctor Melvin took all that blood, I've felt fine. I think it was just holding me back, too much blood in my system." His bruises are still a rainbow of colors. He sits down and eats toast and honey for his breakfast.

As I'm leaving for school, he says, "I'll be fit as a fiddle for Saturday night's play."

"The auditorium will be alive with germs. You're not going," Mother says.

"I'll be fine, and I'll be there," he says with conviction.

I grin all the way to school.

Friday night's performance is about to get under way. Mr. Tompkins gives a little pep talk to the actors backstage, just before the curtain goes up. "Resist the temptation to look for your parents in the audience. You won't be able to see them over the glare of the lights, anyway. Now break a leg, all of you."

From my position on a tall stool in the wings, ready to furnish anyone's forgotten lines, I can glimpse the audience, at least the first row or two.

Hazel Carrington comes up behind me and whispers, "My father's coming. He promised to sit near the back." She looks really excited and proud of herself, and she has big red spots on each cheek radiating through the makeup. If I were in her shoes, I'd be just the same.

"What about your mother and sister?"

"My mother has a headache, and Vera's coming tomorrow night."

Mr. Tompkins looks at us pointedly, his finger to his lips. I don't think Hazel is aware of how loud even her whisper is. The houselights go down; the footlights come on; the hush in the audience is immediate. Beside me in the wings, Hazel peeks at the first few rows and, with a hand over her mouth, smothers a high-pitched squeak.

"What's wrong?" I whisper.

"My father *and* my mother. In the front row. I can't go on."

"You have to."

Hazel looks shattered.

I stand up. I am the same height and stare ferociously into her eyes. "Do it, or I will write a play about the day you spoiled everything for everybody."

"Psst!" the male lead whispers and pushes Hazel toward the stage. She glances back at me.

Quickly, I go through the motions of writing on the palm of my hand. It's all she needs. From that moment on, Hazel begins to act as if her very life depends on it. She gets through the entire play without needing to be prompted once.

Ruthie does well, too. Her scenes are brisk and smooth, and she plies that feather duster like a pro. One thing, though: she adds a petulant tone to her voice. Did I recommend that? It certainly isn't in the script, but it works pretty well for the thankless role of the maid.

From time to time, I keep an eye on the front row. After the intermission, with the play in the homestretch, Mrs. Carrington nods off to sleep against her husband's shoulder while Hazel booms out her lines onstage. Hazel doesn't seem to notice, thanks to the glare of the footlights, otherwise she would need my prompting service with every second line. The play ends, and Mrs. Carrington comes to with a start. The audience claps loudly and someone even yells bravo.

For Saturday night's performance, I arrive at school early to get the stage ready. It strikes me that I'm a bit tired of the play. If I were one of the actors, it would be a different story, but being behind the scenes is wearing thin. Once the stage is set, I go into the classroom we're using for makeup to open the jars of cold cream and grease paint and to prop up the mirror.

Hazel hasn't arrived yet, but we all go about our business. She's often a little late but always bustles in, eventually, ready to shout out her lines. Mr. Tompkins is looking at his watch when the school janitor knocks on the door to say that he's wanted on the phone. He returns five minutes later with a long face.

"Hazel has broken her leg!" he moans.

Everyone gasps.

"How could she?" Ruthie says. "Is this a joke?"

"She really did break her leg," Mr. Tompkins says.

"Isn't that just something you say to actors to mean the opposite?"

No one hears me. They're crowding around Mr. Tompkins asking questions.

"Now what are we supposed to do?" someone asks.

"My parents waited until tonight to come," Ruthie says.

"Do we have to refund the audience their money?" I ask. The proceeds from the two nights' performances were to go towards expanding our costumes and props department.

Mr. Tompkins—chin on his chest, hands on his ears, eyes closed—is trying to think. A moment later, he opens his eyes and looks directly at me.

"You have to play Alexis Ravelthorpe. I know you know the lines. I've watched you prompt without even looking at the script. It has to be you. We have thirty minutes to make sure Hazel's costumes fit you. Dressing room. On the double." I stand there like a brainless statue. "Ruth, you go with her. Quick!"

I feel hot and cold at the same time. "I can't do this," I say to Ruthie as I put on the first-act costume, a ruffled blouse and a fancy emerald green suit. I can see in the mirror that the costume fits and even looks kind of snazzy on me. My cheeks are so red, I'll hardly need makeup.

"Of course you can do it. You could say all Hazel's lines backwards, standing on your head, if you had to."

"But, I don't know how to act."

"Yes, you do. You taught me everything I know. You can see when a person's acting is too flat, and you know how to fix it. If you can do that, you can act."

Ruthie hands me the high-heeled shoes, a little tight but wearable. I wobble when I take my first few steps but soon get my balance.

"Mmm. Maybe you're right."

I'm absorbed by my reflection in the mirror. I have just been transformed into a sophisticated rich lady in an elegant green suit. And suddenly, that's who I am. All I need is a few dabs of pancake makeup, a slash of my *Little Red Lies* lipstick, and the role is mine. "Okay, I'm ready to become Alexis Ravelthorpe."

Mr. Tompkins will prompt in my place. He goes onstage before the play starts and announces the change in cast. "Miss Hazel Carrington, playing the role of Alexis, will not be with us tonight due to an injury. The role of Alexis Ravelthorpe will be played by Miss Rachel McLaren."

I hear a buzz of surprise in the audience. I cannot even imagine how astonished my parents, my grandmother, and my brother must be. If their hearts are racing half as fast as my own, they'll be having heart attacks. I feel like a starlet in one of Ruthie's sister's movie magazines, getting my big break, my chance to show the world my magnificent talent.

Standing in the wings, I can't think of my first line. My leg bones are rubbery. If I scratch my arms one more time, they'll bleed all over the green suit. In the second before I am to make my stage debut, with the houselights down and the audience silently awaiting the action, I experience a moment of truth. I'm not a good actor; I'm a good critic. I have no idea how to act.

I walk quickly onto the stage, dressed in Hazel's costume. Ruthie, as maid, is busily dusting the fake pictures on the fake walls. I say my lines mechanically and not very loudly. I sit on a fake chair, knowing this is what I'm supposed to do, rise when my elderly fake mother enters stage left, and speak my lines rapidly because I can't wait to get them out of the way. At the end of my scene, I walk briskly through a fake door into another room of the nonexistent house.

Backstage, Mr. Tompkins nods encouragement. He shakes his shoulders around. "Loosen up," he whispers.

I want to go home at intermission, only I can't find my clothes. I think Ruthie hid them somewhere.

I do not loosen up. My acting does not improve. When the curtain comes down and the audience applauds politely, I do not go out for my curtain call. I run back to the dressing room and tear off Hazel's costume. I scrub at my makeup with a handful of absorbent cotton, not even bothering with cold cream. I'm out of the room and out of the school moments before the audience surges out through the front door. I'm in bed before the rest of my family returns, and when they do, I refuse to talk to them through my locked door. Tonight I blindly leapt from the steepest cliff I will ever encounter, never to rise again. I lie beneath it, splattered and shattered.

———

Sunday morning, my eyes are red and puffy. I didn't mean to cry half the night. But, every time I remembered the disastrous play, I heard my own voice rattling out the lines like popcorn popping as I rushed to get through them.

I go down to breakfast knowing I am a disgrace.

"Don't say anything," I'm at the kitchen doorway. "I know it was a disaster."

"It wasn't that bad," Jamie says over his coffee cup.

"It wasn't bad at all," Mother says. "You spoke a little quickly, that's all."

"I thought you were great to step in and save the day," Dad says. "Magnificent, in fact."

"Liars," I say.

I hurry back upstairs because my eyes are filling again. Passing my parents' room, I see their open suitcase on the bed. Beside it is Mother's best blouse, and on the floor, Dad's polished shoes. They intend to drive Jamie to Toronto this afternoon to see the specialist tomorrow. I wasn't planning to go, but now I think I will. I can't face school. I throw what I'll need into a small suitcase and put *Little Red Lies* into my skirt pocket, I don't know why. It didn't help me pass myself off as an actress. I feel like a fraud.

But, I wash my face, soak my eyes, and go back down. "I'm going with you." I say it loudly and firmly. I will not be talked out of it.

"But you have school tomorrow," Mother says.

"I'm never going back."

"Oh, now, now," Dad says. "Never is a long time."

"Give her a break," Jamie says. "She's had a traumatic experience."

"Oh, I don't think it was as bad as all that," Mother says. "There's no need to be quite so dramatic, Rachel."

"I'm not going!" I glare, not at them, but through the window, my arms folded majestically, my brow a firm line. Mrs. Hall, sweeping her steps next door, sees me and waves. I turn my back.

Dad says, "Dora, she'll miss only a day or two."

So he thinks, I say to myself.

"It's silly to give in!" She takes another look at me. "Oh, well—but bring your books. You'll have to study."

I run upstairs to get my bag. I pull my hair closer around my face and, at the bathroom mirror, add a smear of *Little Red Lies* to hide my puffy lips. With a little imagination, I look fine. The lipstick's back in my pocket.

Downstairs, Mother takes one look at my lips and says, "Hand it over."

"What?"

"You know very well what." She's staring at my mouth. "It makes you . . . look like someone you're not. Give it to me."

"But I bought it with my own money," I say as I put it in her outstretched hand.

She places it in a corner of the nearest kitchen cupboard. "There it will sit until you're twenty years old. By then, maybe you'll be old be enough to see that less is actually more. Now go and wipe your face."

Sullenly, scratching my arms to shreds, I sit next to Jamie as we drive to Toronto. We're spending the night with Dad's second cousin Betty, an elderly woman who lives alone in a big house.

She welcomes us by bustling in and out of rooms, showing us where we'll be sleeping, asking if we'd like a cup of tea, and giving Jamie and me the critical once-over.

"Rachel," she says, "Is something wrong? You look as if you're moping."

I bare my teeth, which she can take as a smile . . . or not. If I had an ax handy, I'd wedge it in her head.

To Jamie, she says, "Dear boy, what have you been doing to yourself? You're awfully frail, my dear. Do they not feed you?"

He draws himself up tall, as if he can make up in height what he lacks in width. This will not be a pleasant visit.

Promptly at nine, next morning, I mope along behind the others to the specialist. Jamie goes into the doctor's office while the rest of us stay in the waiting room. After about twenty minutes, Doctor Latham calls us all into his office.

"I'd like to admit Jamie to hospital here for further testing," he says.

Jamie's arms are folded defiantly. "Actually, I feel fine now and have for the past week. I think it was just some bug I picked up."

Dad says, "Jamie, have the tests. We'll come back for you as soon as they're over."

Mother says, "I'll stay."

"No need," Jamie mutters. "Go with Dad. This is a waste of time."

"I'll take Rachel back," Dad says. "She should be in school."

"I'm not going back to school. I'll take correspondence courses."

Doctor Latham clears his throat.

"This is something we'll discuss later," Dad says.

CHAPTER

12

I get my wish. They let me stay with Mother. I try my best to be nice to Cousin Betty, and she rewards me by letting me look at all her books, of which she has hundreds. "Choose whatever one you like," she says, "as long as it's appropriate."

I start looking for something racy and come up with *The Anatomy of the Human Body*, a textbook for medical students with her brother's name on the flyleaf. Flipping through it convinces me I'll know more than I ever wanted to about people's private parts.

Each day, we visit Jamie in hospital. Visiting hours are two to four, so we always get there sharp at two to make the most of them. He shares a room with a man who spends most of the day snoring, but Jamie is lucky enough to have the window side.

"I don't mind the snoring," he says, "I just wish he'd talk

a bit." He has to rely on books and magazines for company.

Thursday afternoon, we get there at two as usual, and Mother pulls the curtain between Jamie and the snoring man. We have been there just five minutes, me leaning against the windowsill, Mother tidying Jamie's bedside table, when Doctor Latham comes in. He stands at the foot of Jamie's bed, brow furrowed, pulling on his lower lip as if he would pull it right off.

"The diagnosis is confirmed," he says, "or as confirmed as it can be, at this point. We believe you have leukemia."

"Leukemia," Jamie says. "What's that?"

"It's a condition that prevents your bone marrow from producing enough normal white cells."

I watch Jamie frown and nod like a fellow scientist.

"You have a proliferation of abnormal white cells crowding out the normal ones along with the red cells and platelets in your blood."

"I see," Jamie says.

I don't see. All I know is, none of this sounds good. I am scratching my arms before they're even itchy.

"It means your blood has a hard time clotting. To be blunt, it's . . . cancer of the bone marrow."

At the word cancer, Mother says, "Oh!" and collapses into the bedside chair. Jamie's pale face looks whiter than ever. As for me, my heart is jumping around my chest in panic. Mother presses her hands into her cheeks. I watch Jamie swallow a couple of times before he can speak.

"Is there . . ." he clears his throat ". . . a treatment for it?"

"Yes, indeed," Doctor Latham answers heartily. "We can give you transfusions of normal blood, and there are drugs we are trying with some success."

Jamie has dots of perspiration on his forehead, and two red spots appear on his cheeks. Looking through the window at the patch of blue cloudless sky, he asks, "Am I going to die?"

Doctor Latham follows his gaze and says, "We have to look at this positively. We have treatment; we have hope. Let's leave it at that."

"But," Jamie insists, "am I? I need to know."

"You were a soldier. You knew you had to fight for your life over there in France. No one told you whether you would live through it or die. Well, here, on the home front, it's much the same. Chin up, Private McLaren. There's a war on. We'll keep you here for another week or two to start treatment." He pats Mother on the shoulder and leaves.

I can barely bring myself to look at Jamie, can't stand to watch him clenching and unclenching his jaw, flaring his nostrils, blinking hard.

Mother grasps his hand and, for once, he lets her. In that instant, he loses all his fight—soldier or not.

I turn to the window, feeling empty, weightless. I have a vague idea that if I don't hang on to something, I might drift right through it to become the first cloud in a perfectly clear sky.

"There's a war on," Jamie mutters. "Right. It never ends, does it?"

When I turn back, Jamie pulls his hand from Mother's grasp. "So, I'm sick," he says. "Cancer. I could die. Ironic, isn't it? I spent most of the war afraid I'd be killed. Now that I'm home safe and more or less sound, damned if there isn't a sharpened meat cleaver still dangling over my head." He flings his arm across his forehead, shielding his eyes from view.

Mother tries to mop up the tears running down her cheeks with her hankie, but she can't keep up to them. "I'm going to find a phone so I can talk to your father. Will you be all right, Jamie? Rachel's here."

The room feels hollow after she leaves, taking her lilac scent with her. The man in the next bed snores on. I don't know what to do, what to say. I want to throw my arms around Jamie, but I know how he hates mushy stuff.

"Maybe I'll find Coop," he says, "if he really is dead, if there really is a nice place to go after death."

"Don't," I say.

"Ah, what's the use of sentimentality? When you die, you're dead. There, now. That's the way I see it. There won't be any Coop drinking beer beside some heavenly river teeming with holy fish." He rubs at his eyes.

"When the doctor said there was a war on, he meant you have to fight for your life. So, start fighting."

"Any minute, now."

"How can they be one hundred percent sure of what you have?" I get right up close to him, my hands on my hips. "Listen, they'll give you transfusions, and just like in Dingbat Land, you'll get up and walk away from this. You will. Believe me."

We hear Mother's heels coming along the corridor. He blows his nose, and we both blink hard, trying to look normal.

She sits in the chair near his bed and reaches out to hold his hand, but he pulls away and clasps his hands behind his head. "How's Dad?" he asks.

"Terribly upset. He'll come tomorrow." Her voice is so high-pitched, she sounds like a little girl.

"I expect once they get going on the treatment," he says, "that'll do the trick."

"Oh, Jamie!" she says. "What will we ever do? How can we stand this?"

I watch Jamie's facial muscles tighten. "Stop!" he says. "I'm the one going up the scaffold, not you."

"Sorry," Mother says, searching for another hankie.

A nurse comes in, all starchy and bright, bringing Jamie some fruit juice to sip. She stands between him and Mother, sticks a thermometer in his mouth, and holds his wrist to take his pulse. Mother manages to pull herself together as the nurse makes perky comments about the noisy pigeons and the blue sky and what the temperature is outside.

Patting Mother's shoulder, she says, "It won't take your son long to start feeling better. You'll see." She leaves, taking her optimism with her.

The heaviness in the room feels like a thunderstorm brewing, in spite of the brilliant sky. Jamie's pretending to be interested in a magazine about cars. Mother is in his tiny bathroom bathing her swollen eyes.

I stand at the window, grinding my teeth. *So this is what the end of the world is like.* Jamie has a possibly fatal illness, and I am the school outcast. I would cheerfully trade places with him, right about now. At least people would feel sorry for me, instead of hating me.

Realistically, though, he isn't going to die. Young people just don't. In a month or two, the doctor will be telling us that he doesn't actually have leukemia, just something like it, something that won't kill him. I, on the other hand, will live in infamy forever. No one will ever forget what a fool I made of myself and how I wrecked the play for the whole cast, not to mention the audience.

Ruthie must despise me. What a windbag, what a faker she must think I am, pretending to know all about acting. My life might as well be over. I could jump out this window as quick as take a breath, and that would be the end of it. I try to raise it higher, but it's blocked. I could probably slip through feetfirst, I'm skinny enough. Except for my head. I'd be left dangling by my neck.

"Put the window down a bit, Rachel," Mother says. "You don't want to give your brother pneumonia on top of everything else."

I slam it shut and walk out of the room. The world revolves around my brother, who probably doesn't even have leukemia. I wish I had my lipstick to smear on about two inches thick. If I did, maybe people would notice my down-turned mouth and feel sorry for me, for once in my life. No one has time to spend worrying about me and whether or not I harbor dark thoughts. If I found a sixth-storey window that opened wide enough and jumped out, would they take their mind off Jamie's rotten blood and say, *How sad?* No. They would look at my smashed-up body and say, *What a mess! Pity old Rachel can't clean it up for us.*

I'm sure Doctor Latham must have doubts about his diagnosis. *As confirmed as it can be*, he said. By now I've reached the end of the corridor. But, what if something really *is* desperately wrong with Jamie? My heart is thumping wildly. *No!* I block any further thoughts in that direction and train a spotlight squarely on myself. Everyone and everything else fades into the blackness.

Retracing my steps, I pass the open doors of other patients' rooms. There are bottles with tubes attached to people, one of them a pale bony girl no older than me. I hear a man groan with pain. Along the corridor coming toward me, a nurse pushes a little boy with a big head

and bulging eyes in a wheelchair. His spindly legs dangle
uselessly.

"Hi," he says.

"Hi," I say, not very loudly.

"You bad guy," he says.

"Scotty," the nurse says. "That's not very nice."

He stares at me with his bulging eyes and says it again.
"You bad guy!"

I give him a vampire-sneer, with my fangs hanging out,
and notice my spotlight fading as the houselights come
up. There is no applause.

I go back to Jamie's room. He doesn't look very sick
at all.

Two days later, we gather in Jamie's room to say good-bye.
Dad has laid down the law. Glaring at him, Mother says,
"I'm leaving against my wishes, but we'll come back for
you, Jamie, when you're well enough to be released."

"No, I'll take the train."

"You most certainly will not. Think of the germs. Trains
are traveling cauldrons of toxic bacteria, especially in this
weather."

"I'm going to take the train There's something I have
to do while I'm here."

"Jamie!"

"I'll come home by train after I deliver something to
the widow of a friend."

I'm proud of him for standing up to Mother. He's James to the nurses and doctors, and it suits him. He's outgrowing Jamie.

He's been lying on top of his hospital bed in pajamas and bathrobe. Standing now, he towers over Mother, forcing her to look up. He staggers slightly, a little dizzy from getting up so quickly. "Would you let me look after myself now, Mother?"

She looks into his unwavering eyes, mesmerized, and says, "Whatever you think is right, dear." She pulls his head down for a kiss on the cheek and leaves the room.

I lag behind, wanting to hug him or just shake his hand. Anything.

"Go," he says. He reaches out and gives my hair a yank. "I'll be home before you know it."

I grab his wrist to make him let go of my hair and squeeze it until he winces.

"You're lethal," he says.

"Get better."

"Okay."

13

School is out of the question. I refuse to go back. I argue, stomp up the stairs, slam my door, but my father is right behind me, pounding on it.

"I will call in the truant officer. I will tie you up and drag you, if necessary," he says. "I will get the chief of police to handcuff you. You *will* return to school."

Sitting in my room, I try to imagine a life without school. Home all day.

With my mother.

Sometimes you have to admit defeat. I set off at the usual time, but take the long route to avoid meeting up with Ruthie or anyone else I know. Dragging my feet and expecting to be stoned or spit-balled or even worse, shunned, I get to school seconds before the bell and slink into my homeroom seat.

No one gives me a dirty look. No one laughs or points or whispers. Their lives have moved on. Hazel's broken leg is more newsworthy. How it happened, no one knows for sure, but everyone has a story. Her mother, who has a screw loose, pushed her down the stairs was the favorite. My disastrous stage debut is entirely forgotten. Even this makes me sad. I must be a complete nothing to everyone to be so quickly forgotten. With final exams only two weeks away, teachers give me extra homework to get me caught up.

On the way home, Ruthie says, "How's Jamie?"

"He's getting better. He'll be home soon, good as new."

"You don't look very happy about it."

"It's not that. It's the play. I'm so sorry I wrecked it."

"You didn't wreck it. You just had a case of stage fright. It could happen to anyone. Even the finest Hollywood actresses freeze sometimes."

"How do you know?"

"I read about it in a movie magazine. Olivia de Havilland slashed her wrists when it happened to her."

"But she lived."

"Deanna Durbin drank turpentine."

"Go on, I don't believe it."

"It's true. Would *Silver Screen* make it up?"

Had I really imagined hanging by my neck from a sixth-storey hospital window because my head was too large to go through? How unpleasant. This is not something I want to discuss.

"Let's change the subject," I say. "Did Hazel really break her leg, or was she just too discouraged to go back onstage after her mother slept through almost her entire performance?"

"Yup. She fell down the cellar stairs at home and landed hard on the concrete floor. Her leg is still in a cast. I take schoolwork to her nearly every day. That family is very, very weird. She wishes you would go and see her. She wants to thank you for taking her role."

"I can't. She must know how I botched it."

"Oh, who cares? It was just a play."

"A play is never just a play," I say. "It's a work of art."

We part at our usual corner, but I don't feel like going home, where Mother keeps cleaning and tidying the house. The minute I walk in the door, she'll ask me to help. Instead, I turn up the street leading to Hazel's house.

Hazel's sister, Vera, opens the door and ushers me into the living room, cool after the heat of the day, where Hazel sits beside the radio with her leg propped up on a hassock. A plaster cast covers her lower leg and foot. Only her toes peek out. Crutches lean against her chair within easy reach. She roars a welcome. It actually cheers me up a little to be roared at so happily. She turns off the radio.

"How's your leg? Does it hurt a lot?"

"Not as much as it did. It's my ankle, really."

"How did you break it?"

"I fell down the cellar stairs. Just an accident. Could have happened to anyone." A flush rises up her neck and into her cheeks. "Thanks for saving the play."

I snort. "I guess you heard about the terrible mess I made of it." I sit down, gingerly, on a frail, velvety antique sofa. The last time I was here, I didn't notice how big the room is or how many pieces of uncomfortable-looking ancient furniture it contains. It makes me think I should sit like a princess, back straight, ankles crossed. I slump down, legs sprawled in front.

"Can you imagine anybody else able to step in and know all my lines off by heart? I don't think so. I heard you were amazing."

"Huh?"

"Sure. You saved the day for everybody. All the other actors. Everybody worked hard on that play and they all had a chance to shine, even though I broke my stupid ankle and nearly spoiled it all. It could have been such a disaster."

"Oh."

I hadn't really thought in terms of the other actors. My long-awaited chance to act was foremost in my mind. It was my personal failure that made me so embarrassed.

Before I can say anything else, the door creaks slowly open. Hazel's mother, in an elegant royal blue dressing gown, face heavily lined, golden curls cascading down her back, drifts into the room.

Hazel's face freezes. I sit up straight, cross my ankles,

and watch her mother open a drawer in a cabinet and paw through it. She finds whatever she's looking for and hides it in her sleeve before slamming the drawer shut. She doesn't look once in our direction, but wordlessly wafts out again. What is she concealing? A murder weapon, very likely. A jewel-handled dagger. Even a long, sharply pointed ice pick would not surprise me.

"Sorry," Hazel says. "My mother is not very well." Embarrassed, she looks at the floor, at her cast, wiggles her toes. "So, anyway, thanks for taking over. No one else could have."

Just then, her father, all hearty and booming, brings in a plate of brownies. "Made them myself," he says. "I'm becoming quite a good cook and not a bad baker. When Life kicks you in the teeth, take my advice. Make brownies." He passes them to each of us, takes two himself, and leaves with a wink, closing the door behind him.

While we're busy devouring the delicious brownies, I can't help wondering if the closed door is to protect us from getting murdered by Mrs. Carrington. Hazel and her sister probably speak loudly as a kind of warning to be on the alert, and the decibels are now second nature to them.

My madwoman play is still in my head. Nothing yet has been committed to paper, but these things take time. I'm hoping I can write, because I've proven I sure can't act. I'm beginning to wonder if it's even worth my while to be in the drama club.

"I can't wait to get back to school," Hazel says, "even if it's only to write exams."

"I know the feeling. Home can get on your nerves." I glance around and think *especially this place*.

"Where have you been?" my mother asks as soon as I get home. "I've made hair appointments for both of us. We have less than ten minutes to get there."

"What?"

"Smartly, now! Yours is first. Just a trim."

"But—"

"No buts."

We have to walk quickly, even though it's broiling hot. Sweat runs down my back in torrents.

Just before the hairdresser's, we notice a sign on a telephone pole: ARE YOU SUFFERING? *Yes*, I think as I rub an arm across my damp forehead. On the next pole: THERE IS HOPE. *Yay!* On the next pole: COME AND BE HEALED BY FAITH!

Mother says, "It must be summer. The snake oil salesmen are back."

"What do you mean?"

"The faith healers. They apparently shake the very devil out of you, and you're supposedly cured of anything from leprosy to ingrown toenails. And if the cure isn't immediate, they sell you some sort of holy oil to hurry it along."

"You mean the revival meetings they have in that tent in the park? Maybe they could cure my eczema."

"Don't you dare go near them! They're charlatans, most of them. I would be mortified if my daughter was seen going to a faith healer."

At the Crowning Glory Beauty Salon, the door is open to allow what little breeze there is to penetrate the stifling shop, with its mixed bouquet of sulfurous permanent-wave solution and perfumed shampoos and setting lotions. I skulk near the door, waiting to be called, while Mother sits down beside a vaguely familiar woman, a Mrs. Harmon. Mother says a polite hello. Mrs. Harmon doesn't return the greeting. Instead, she gets up and moves across the room to look out the window. A bit deaf, I guess. There are two other women waiting and three more having things done to their hair who avoid looking at my mother.

Creeps, I think. *Has Mother got bad breath or something?* I nab a magazine and become engrossed in an article about teenage girls and whether or not they should kiss on a first date. Not a problem for me—I've never had a date.

Another woman, Mrs. Glidden, pays for her hairdo and, before leaving the shop, stops in front of Mother.

"Hello, there, Dora. Have you been away?"

Mother looks up. "Why, yes," she says. "I've been in Toronto. My son's in hospital there."

Mrs. Glidden looks shocked in a phony kind of way, as if she knows a secret. She glances at the other ladies: one being shampooed, one being snapped into metal curlers, and one under a dryer. My mother looks puzzled when everyone stares.

Mrs. Glidden bends close. "He must have an awful bad dose of it, then," she whispers as loudly as she can. Simultaneously, the dryer reaches the end of its cycle and is turned off; the rinsing of hair under the tap finishes; all chatter ceases. The Crowning Glory is all ears.

"I'm not sure what you're talking about," Mother says, frowning. She glances at me and shrugs. Just then, I'm called to a sink to have my hair washed.

When I emerge from under the tap, I hear someone say to Mother, "It's awful what these boys bring home with them from overseas. Even the nice ones." I'm led to a chair to have my hair combed out and the ends trimmed.

Mother's voice is even. "Jamie's disease has nothing to do with the war. He has something called leukemia."

I think I hear someone mutter, "Is that what they're calling it these days?"

"I'm ready for you, Mrs. McLaren," Bonnie, the stylist, says.

In the mirror, I watch Mother sit with her back to the sink while Bonnie swirls a cape about her, fastening it tightly at the neck. She looks a little sick, as if there's something nasty about the topic Mrs. Glidden has raised.

With her face turning red, she pulls at the neck of the cape until Bonnie says, "Is it too tight? Here, let me fix it." Something unfair is going on. Mother looks wounded, as if she has just figured out what it is.

The girl finally gets her comb through my thick hair and begins to cut it.

After Mother's shampoo, Bonnie ushers her to the styling chair beside mine and begins to trim away little feathers of her wet hair. "They say it's going to cool right down tonight," Bonnie says.

"It can't happen too soon for me," Mother says. "Toronto was like an oven." She continues to talk a little louder than she normally would.

Mrs. Glidden, on her way out, stops to chat quietly with Mrs. Harmon.

"Bonnie," Mother says, "I hope you will never know what it's like to have a desperately sick child."

"I heard something about your boy. What's he got?"

"I'm afraid it's leukemia."

"What's *that*?" Her nose wrinkles. "Is it serious?"

Beside me in the mirror, I can see Mother swallow hard. "Yes, I'm afraid it is." Taps are off, again; dryers off for readjustment. "It's a type of cancer—cancer of the bone marrow, the specialist told us."

A quiet hum of sympathy goes through the place. "Oh, dear! I'm so sorry to hear that," Bonnie says. "Is there anything they can do for it?"

"Blood transfusions, mainly, I guess. We have our hopes pinned to that. He wants to start university in the fall, but we'll just have to wait and see."

A few heads are shaking at the magnitude of what they've just heard. *Imagine! What would you do if it was one of yours?* They aren't vicious, I guess, not really. Mrs. Glidden goes over and pats Mother on the shoulder before she leaves the shop.

I'm finished first and go home. I don't know what all the innuendos were about, but, I wonder if they had anything to do with something Mary said to me the day I told her that Jamie fainted.

"What," Mother asks, "is the basis of this horror story going around?"

Dad and Granny and I are all in the kitchen before dinner. Mother is mashing the very devil out of the potatoes.

"Shall I do that, dear?" Granny asks. "I fear for the bottom of the pot."

"No, thank you."

Dad's reading the paper at the table. "What horror story?"

I gather up salt and pepper and a plate of butter to set the table in the dining room but stop to listen.

Granny pauses in her self-appointed task of removing the cutlery from its drawer and wiping out the various sections, muttering, "Hasn't been done in months—dust, crumbs, who knows what all."

"What story?" I say.

"That Jamie picked up some hideous disease when he was overseas."

I think for a minute. "The clap?" I ask, without a clue.

Dad looks up abruptly from the paper, his face almost purple. Mother looks as if she's just filled her mouth with piping hot potatoes. Granny lets a handful of forks clatter to the floor.

It eventually becomes clear, with my help, in a round-about way, that it has to do with something Mary Foley said on the phone to Jamie before he went to Toronto, something I asked my friends about, something my friends must have asked their mothers about—friends who are on much more intimate terms with their mothers than I am with mine. I didn't know it was something disgusting. How would I? No one ever tells me anything. I still don't know exactly what it is, but I'm thinking it has something to do with head lice. I've been scratching my own head ever since.

All I know is, it has nothing to do with Jamie or his condition. We talk to him long-distance every second day. He's getting better, he says, just as I knew he would.

CHAPTER

14

Jamie is home looking ghostly, but, little by little, color is coming into his cheeks. He seems to spend a lot of time in his room. Once when I peeked in, he was writing at his desk, with that pile of papers near him, tied at one corner with string. I wish I had X-ray vision; I'd love to know what he's doing. But I left him in peace. Sometimes you have to.

Letters not sent.

I guess it's a bit of a cheat, writing this now that the war is over, but it's sort of about the war. Anyway, it seems right to include it, so here goes.

I had some time before I had to catch the train home, after I was discharged from hospital. I

found the street where Leeson's widow lived, with
the help of a street map, and spotted the house, a
small bungalow hunched in between two other almost
identical bungalows. But, then I got cold feet.
I really ought to have phoned first, in case she
needed a chance to comb her hair or something.

I walked to the end of the block and studied
the picture of Dulcie Leeson. She wasn't really
all that funny-looking. There was something
rather charming about her teeth. The way they
protruded slightly, made her look naive, in need
of a strong man to protect her. No wonder Leeson
had married her before going off to war. In some
ways, I wished she was my girlfriend. On the
back, she'd written "Love and kisses, Dulcie."

I felt a few drops of rain and drew in a big
breath. It was now or never. I needed to just walk
back and knock on the door before I lost my nerve.

It was definitely Dulcie who answered the
door, with a smile on her face that quickly
changed to curiosity. She looked terrific. It was
obvious that she didn't need any time to run a
comb through her hair. It was shining and lovely
and pulled back with barrettes.

A little kid in overalls ran up behind her yelling, "Daddy, Daddy." Embarrassed by his mistake,
he pulled back, hiding behind his mother's skirt.

This brought me pretty close to tears. The poor little guy was still waiting for his dad to come home from the war. Hadn't his mother explained? I'm not very smart about little kids. I figured it was a boy, but with all that curly hair, it could have been a girl. No idea how old—three, maybe.

I introduced myself. "A friend of your husband's during the war," I said. Her jaw dropped a little in surprise. "I'm returning your picture. He had it . . . with him when . . ."

She went kind of pale, which made me wonder if I'd done the right thing in taking the picture from Leeson's pocket. Maybe, given a chance, he would have said, "Bury it with me." How can you know people's minds when it comes to death? What if giving her back the picture was the most heartless thing in the world?

Perhaps this was why I'd waited so long. Or maybe it wasn't. I think the truth is, I didn't want to get embroiled in somebody's sadness and have to stand there and try to think of the right thing to say. I'm no good at that.

"Oh, my goodness!" she said. "Come in, come on in." She hung my damp coat on a hook near the door and led me into a cozy living room.

The little kid, probably a boy, stared at me, then buried his head on his mother's knee.

She picked him up. Sitting across from her in
Leeson's living room, the child peacefully suck-
ing his thumb, I was clearly aware of what Leeson
was missing. And then I saw him frantically dig-
ging a hole in the ground for protection, saw
him mashed and bloody, lying in the hole that
became his grave. And I thought, What's the
point? What's the point of anything? And that's
when I became aware once again of the trembling
earthquake that I was afraid was splitting me off
from the rest of the world. Crazy, eh, Rachel?

I handed her the picture. She studied it,
smiled sadly, and put it on a small table out of
the child's reach. "Thank you," she said. "You're
very kind."

"Sorry it took so long for me to get it to you."

"That's all right. These things can be, well,
pretty awkward."

I said, "Leeson, I mean your husband, never
said anything about a baby." Cripes, I couldn't
even remember Leeson's first name.

She said, "The letter never reached him. The
army returned it to me, along with several others
that hadn't caught up to him." She brushed the
kid's hair back from his face and said, "Freddie
looks just like his dad did." And I could see
it. Fred Leeson. Of course.

The front door opened, and a tall heavyset man came in. He leaned into the living room, puzzled, and said, "Hi, there. I'm Jeff Emerson."

Dulcie said, "This is James. He was a friend of Fred's in France. Here, Jeff, take Freddie." She wanted to go to the kitchen to get us some coffee.

The little boy squirmed willingly down from her lap and ran to Jeff saying, "Daddy." Jeff picked him up, kissed him, and sat him on his knee.

"Dulcie and I are married," he said. "Did she tell you?"

I wondered if I looked as shocked as I felt.

"No," I said.

"Six months ago."

"Oh."

Jeff looked at me as if he expected me to say something else. So I said, "That's nice." I felt like saying, "Could she not wait a bit?" Jeez, Leeson was hardly dead a year. Well, close to two years, I guess. Still, he'd been so proud of her and loved her so much, no question about that. This would not have made him happy, having this big lug take his place and the baby calling him Daddy. Cripes, where was her heart? I wanted to get up and leave.

Dulcie came back in with cups of coffee on a tray.

Jeff said, "I told him about us getting married."

Dulcie smiled at me. "It's what Fred would have wanted," she said.

How would she know? It would have broken his heart, that's what. Maybe I should have said congratulations. Bit late. I drank my coffee. Dulcie passed me a plate of cookies. Store-bought.

I swallowed my coffee too quickly and burnt the roof of my mouth. Trying hard to put on a bright face, I said, "I should be going." Dulcie walked me to the door.

While I was putting on my coat, she said quietly, "I mourned him. I cried myself to sleep most nights, knowing that he would never see his beautiful boy." And then she said, "One day I woke up and realized that the sun was shining right in my eyes. I think it dazzled me into saying to myself, 'My life continues.'"

She was looking at me. I knew I looked anything but happy, anything but understanding.

I said, "It's hard to comprehend that other people's lives go on." I opened the door and stepped out. The rain was only a light drizzle.

"Thank you for coming and for bringing the picture," Dulcie said. Suddenly, she called after me, "I'm sorry you're still grieving."

I nodded, waved, not trusting my voice. What
an ass I was! What a phony! It wasn't exactly
Leeson I was grieving for. I almost felt like
running back and telling her about myself.
Instead, I continued plodding along, trying
to avoid the puddles, until the street ended
in a turmoil of drivers and streetcar-riders
and pedestrians, each of them owning their
own small portion of the world while mine was
slowly crumbling.

Exams are over. I didn't ace anything, but I passed. Summer
stretches before me like the open sea. Wish I had a boat
or even a raft, because we're sure not going anywhere or
doing anything that sounds like fun around here. At least
I've stopped fantasizing about Tommy. I dream about him
occasionally and wake up feeling as if I've been running a
race and losing.

By the end of July, I notice that Jamie has color in his
cheeks, a smile on his face, and energy to burn. Maybe not
to burn, but he's more like his old self. His classes at U of
T will start in six weeks.

"Why not stay home and take correspondence courses?"
Mother suggests, hopefully. She's at the stove, boiling up
the last of the strawberries for jam. I lean over the pot,
taking in the aroma, almost drooling. "If you go away,
who will keep an eye on you? Who, in the entire city of

Toronto, let alone the university, will worry about you?"

"No one," Jamie says, grinning. I stand beside him at the open window, taking deep, carefree breaths of summer—sun on grass, on snowberry bushes under the window, on the peeling paint of the back veranda. "Right now, I feel wonderful. If all it takes is a bunch of blood transfusions and some drugs, then I can live with that. If I start to wind down a bit, I'll just check into hospital and get my engine battery recharged. I feel like I've moved to Dingbat Land."

"Toronto isn't Dingbat Land," I say. "Where are you going to live?" I don't want him to go. I can't imagine him living anywhere but here.

"I've been looking. Found something in the *Toronto Telegram* yesterday. Not too far from the university, a bed-sitter with kitchenette and bathroom. I've got an appointment to look at it tomorrow."

"I'll go with you," Mother says.

"No, thanks. I'll go on my own."

"I think you need me to make sure it isn't infested with bedbugs or cockroaches."

"I have eyes, Mother."

And that was the end of it.

"What does 'remission' actually mean?" I ask a week or so later. I don't try to hide the fact that I read the letter on Mother's desk from Doctor Latham. We are still at the table finishing dessert. It's Saturday and Granny is with us.

"It means my disease has been sent back to hell, where it belongs," Jamie says.

"Jamie!" Mother's reproachful voice.

"For good?"

"Rachel! Don't quiz your brother." Mother has sudden tears in her eyes, an event that happens often these days.

Dad scrapes up the last of the chocolate pudding in his dish and clunks his spoon down. "Let's be open and honest about Jamie's condition. I think it's time we all had a chance to discuss this, dear."

"Discuss what?" Mother's voice is edgy.

Granny makes an issue of clearing her throat, usually a warning sound.

Dad doesn't back off. "I think we all need to clear the air a bit and be perfectly honest with each other. About the nature of Jamie's disease and about remissions."

Mother puts her napkin on the table and takes her own and Granny's dessert plates. "Come along, Rachel, I need some help in the kitchen."

"Wait. I want to know what Dad means."

"Your father is trying to open a great big hole, and we're all going to fall into it and never be able to pull ourselves out."

"I don't get it."

"Dora, just sit down a minute," Dad says.

I notice Granny beam her powerful eyes at Jamie. Mother does not sit down.

Jamie says, "Look, um, I don't know what to say. I feel fine right now, and I don't want to spoil that. I'd like to be excused from this discussion." He pushes his chair out. Mother hurries to the kitchen.

"You're going to get sick again, aren't you?" I blurt.

There is silence. The bomb has dropped. We wait for the explosion.

We can hear Mother in the kitchen, crying in big drowning gulps. I get up from my chair beside Granny and go around the table to my brother. I try to cradle his head against me, but he bucks me away. He stands up, letting his chair fall backwards with a clatter. In the kitchen, Mother drops, or maybe throws, something that smashes.

Jamie leaves the room. Dad remains at the table, his head in his hands. It's Granny who begins to pick up the pieces. "Get yourself out there to that wife of yours," she says. "She needs you, badly."

"Why? She thinks I'm useless."

"Well, you're a useless stump in here. Go!"

With great effort, he pushes his chair back and leaves. Granny sits, slumped like an old crone, and I go weeping up to my room. I don't know which is worse—my brother's disease or my mother throwing a fit as well as a dish hard enough to break it. If I did that, she'd be flaming mad at me for the rest of my life.

I actually know what remission means. I looked it up when I saw the letter from Doctor Latham lying open for anyone's eyes on Mother's writing desk. I just want to know what it means when applied to Jamie. A remission is like a holiday. If he can stay on holidays for the rest of his life, that'll be just fine. That's what I want to hear someone say.

I hear footsteps on the stairs, Mother's. I bury my head in my arms in case she comes in. I don't want to talk. The footsteps go past my door and into her room. And then I hear Dad. He, too, passes my door and quietly but firmly closes their bedroom door. I sit up and get a hankie out of my pocket. I can hear my parents talking in low voices, but I can't make out what they're saying.

It's Jamie who finally looks in. "May I come in?"

"Yes," I mutter into my arms, facedown on my bed, again.

"So, what's up?" he says.

I groan into my bedspread. "What's up? Our family is coming apart at the seams, and you wonder what's up?" Rolling over, I sit up. "What's happening to us?"

"Nothing," he says. "Everything's fine."

In one minute, I will have to leap at him and slap the sides of his face to wake him up, to make him give me a straight answer. But the minute passes. He leans his elbows on my dresser with his back to me, examining pictures stuck in the mirror.

"How come you have this picture of Coop and me? It's an antique." They're posing with their fishing rods and the day's catch, almost a match for the one in Coop's bedroom.

"Just for the fun of it. You can borrow it if you like." I watch him tense, clench his jaw, his fists, keeping his emotions from escaping.

"Why would I want to borrow it?"

"Who knows?" My voice is flat. "It's only a picture of you and your best friend, who's missing in action." Leaning against my headboard, knees drawn up, I can see in the mirror over my dresser how red my nose and eyes are. He sits on the side of my bed and lets himself fall back.

"What's going to happen, Jamie? I'm so scared."

He sits up again, his eyes straining against tears. "Nothing," he says. "Ha-ha! Get it? Something, then nothing. Someone, then no one."

"Jamie, stop."

"No sense letting fear get the better of you." He stands up. "I think I'll go over to Mary's," he says and leaves.

I guess that's how he plans to keep out of the clutches of fear. He has his big crush on Mary to hide behind. I can hear my parents getting into bed, early as it is. At least they have each other's comfort. I hug my knees until I think they'll crack. And who do I have? Me, myself, and nobody. Except Granny. What I really need, though, is someone my own age.

Ruthie's away at her aunt's cottage. Even so, I couldn't go over. This fear of losing someone you love isn't a topic you can share with a girl like Ruthie. Yes, she's my best friend, but it doesn't mean our minds are on the same wavelength. It's like pain. You can describe it, but you can't make anyone else feel it.

Wait a sec. What did it say on that sign? I'm remembering something I saw a few weeks ago. Maybe there *is* something I can do to fight this monster.

I scramble off my bed, thump my knuckles against my teeth as I plan my next move, and grab a couple of books from my bedside table. I shoot down the stairs.

It isn't even dark yet. "I'm going to lend Hazel Carrington some books," I call to Granny in the kitchen, where she's finishing drying and putting away the dinner dishes. I wave my books in the air.

"Don't be late."

I set off in the direction of the Carringtons', but change course as soon as I see the first sign on a telephone pole: ARE YOU SUFFERING?

It takes me twenty minutes to walk there. A huge tent is pitched in a clearing in Kavanagh Park, beside the community center. Crowds mill about the tent entrance, waiting for the action to start—mostly women, but a few men and a scattering of noisy children. I stay back under a tree, ready to change my mind, shivering in spite of the heat, my heart thumping because what if this works? What if I find a way for Jamie to be cured?

Just then, a man comes out and ties back the tent flaps.

People push through, plowing their way toward the seats in the front. When nearly everyone is inside, I sidle in and stand at the back so I can see but also escape if this thing turns out to be as stupid as my mother says it is. Just inside the entrance, two young girls about my age hold baskets, in which people drop coins and sometimes bills. I have no money, but they say it's all right.

The tent is stifling. Sweating bodies are crowded so close, they overflow onto each other's chairs, welded to each other like a string of cutouts by their upper arms and thighs. I breathe into the books I'm carrying to block out the smell of body odor.

The preacher, Reverend Lennie Lasco, glows, maybe from sweat, but it may just be his personality. His eyes beam huge behind glasses that make them seem even larger, as if he can see more than the average person. His teeth are almost luminescent. He flashes them around the tent like searchlights. He wears a shiny dark blue suit and highly polished brown shoes.

"Repent and ye shall be saved!" he shouts, making me jump. "Have faith and ye shall be whole!" The tent almost balloons with the force of his resonating voice. There's a lot more babble about how he's a messenger of God, how he has been singled out to heal body and mind. "An angel of the Lord has spoken to me, Ladies and Gentlemen. In the audience tonight, there is a young person sorely in need of help. This I know!"

Tingles go up and down my spine, and I feel myself turning red. *Can he mean me?*

"There is a young woman here tonight who can be helped. Yes, there are many, tonight, who will be helped and made happy and whole, I say, by the Lord's power burning through me."

This is followed by Mrs. Lennie Lasco striking some chords on a piano. The same girls who collected the money sing a duet in two-part harmony. Their faces gleaming, eyes focused on a vision near the top of the tent, they sing about light and darkness and beating on your drum to make the devil run.

Again Reverend Lasco takes the microphone. His voice gentler now, he almost whispers into the mike, his flashing eyes taking in the entire audience as if he were looking at each member personally. "All ye who are troubled and who are heavy-laden, come forward. All ye who would seek a cure, step up to the fold. There is healing in the air. The Lord is with us. All rise and accept the presence of the Lord."

As everyone stands, a hush descends. Lightbulbs, hanging from the ceiling, go out. The only light emanates from two tall candelabra near the altar, where the preacher stands.

A line of people forms near the altar. With everyone standing in front of me, it's difficult to see clearly what's happening. "Praise the Lord," the audience murmurs from time to time. I worm my way over to the side of the tent for a better view.

As a person in line reaches Reverend Lasco, the two singing girls move in behind him. The preacher takes the sufferer by the shoulders and seems to press down. He stares hard into his eyes while he whispers to him, gives him a shake, and releases him. The girls steady him, and an usher accompanies the healed man back to his seat.

I recognize three of the people. One is the old bum who hangs around the beer parlor at the Empire Hotel, looking for handouts; one is Mrs. Russell, a woman who sits a few rows ahead of us in church, who had her entire arm and shoulder removed because of cancer. And one is Mrs. Popkey and her little boy, Danny, in a wheelchair, who live in the apartment over Dad's drugstore. From what I can see, they return to their places unchanged.

The line is becoming shorter. A red-haired young man with a face full of freckles appears next on crutches, dragging one useless leg. After his shake-up, he falls a bit sideways, but the girls catch him and he straightens up. Suddenly he stares at the ceiling of the tent, his eyes aglow. With both hands, he grabs the top of his head as if it's in danger of blowing off. Then his crutches fall away from under his arms, clattering to the ground. His smile is radiant as he walks, shakily at first, arms out for balance, but almost without a limp by the time he gets back to his seat.

A sigh goes through the audience, as well as whispers. *Did you see that? Who was that? This preacher's darn good.*

Jamie should be here. Not me. I edge past people to leave and hurry home in the deepening dusk.

Granny is waiting for me. "Well," she says. "I was about to send out a search party. Did the Carringtons have to kick you out?"

"Yup," I say and go straight upstairs, clutching my books close so she won't see that I'm bringing them back home. I have too much to think about to continue with my book-lending lie.

According to the posters downtown, the healing tent is open for business Tuesday and Thursday afternoons as well as weekday evenings. I decide to go back in a few days. I know I'll never get Jamie to go, but I have a plan that might just work.

Tuesday it pours rain, so I don't go. Ruthie is still away, so on Thursday after lunch, I say I'm going back to visit Hazel Carrington. Who needs lipstick called *Little Red Lies*? Not me. I walk swiftly to the park, hoping to get a chance to talk to the preacher before he starts healing people. The tent entrance is closed. I walk all the way around it, looking for another way in. The flap at the back is also closed, but behind the tent, I discover a trailer attached to the back of a truck.

From inside I hear voices getting louder and louder. Before I can knock on the door, it bursts open, and one of the singing girls storms out, almost stumbling on the three steps to the ground. She calls back into the trailer, "I'm a singer, not an actress!" Behind her, the door slams. She notices me then and says, "I wouldn't go in there if I were you. He's liable to bite your head off."

I take her advice and wait for the show to start. It's much the same as the last one—not as crowded, but just as smelly. This time I find a seat closer to the front. Both girls are in place, ready to warble their song accompanied by Mrs. Lasco at the piano. When the line forms, they take their places behind the sufferer. I don't recognize anyone in the line. There's one gray-haired woman with glasses who is terribly hunched over, her chin almost on her chest. After her shake-up, she stands nearly straight and returns to her seat, glowing with surprise and relief and looking years younger.

I'm determined to talk to Reverend Lasco. I make my way with difficulty against the throng pushing their way out of the tent. By the time I reach the front, Reverend Lasco is nowhere to be seen. Mrs. Lasco is at the piano, gathering up her sheet music and putting it into a carry-all. I quickly squeeze past the last of the audience and manage to catch her. I know how hot and sweaty and red-faced I look, but she's mopping her face, too. She's a fleshy woman with a cinched-in waist that makes her look as if she's wearing a corset a couple of sizes too small. Coils and waves of blonde hair are intricately pinned up on top of her head, but a few wisps have escaped.

"I need to talk to Reverend Lasco," I blurt.

"He's resting," she says. "He's always done in after these sessions. It's hard work, you know." She edges away slightly.

"But I just need to ask him something."

"And what do you want to ask? Perhaps I can help."

"Well, um . . ." I need to get right to the point. "Can a person, a sick person, my brother, actually, be cured by long distance?"

"Why? Is he too sick to come here?" She screws up her face as if it this is the stupidest question she's ever heard.

"Not—not so far, but—"

"He has to attend. It's the laying on of hands. It's the faith. Tell him."

"But, I'm afraid he won't come."

She has everything packed away and edges toward the back door of the tent. "God helps those who help themselves. Tell him. We'll only be here for two more weeks, and then we set up in Durhampton. Tell him."

All right, I will tell him. But, I need to be convincing.

Mulling over arguments he'll likely give me, I head toward the other end of the park, not ready to go home until I've thought this through. I can't get the red-haired young man who let his crutches drop out of my mind. I'd like to describe the whole scene for Jamie. On the other hand, he'll stop listening if he thinks I'm exaggerating. And the thing is, I probably will exaggerate. It's hard to know the best approach.

This end of the park straggles into a wooded area that I don't like to go into. The train tracks go through it, and hoboes often camp in a gully there. You can sometimes see and smell smoke from their campfires. My father says it's a dangerous place and girls should steer clear of it. Some don't. Ruthie says if you go down there on your own, you'll end up pregnant or dead. Take your pick. Some choice.

There's a footpath on the other side of the tracks that goes deep into the woods, behind a factory that makes farm equipment, and then back into town. It comes out near the swale, not far from Coop's house. It would be a shortcut for me, and I'm tempted to take it on this boiling hot afternoon, but, actually, I don't have the courage. Ruthie could be right.

Just as I turn to go back up through the park, I hear kids giggling and look behind me to see two girls come running up from the tracks out into the clearing. They throw themselves down on the grass, out of breath, laughing fit to bust.

"But, he was so cute!" one of them gasps. She couldn't be any more than eleven years old.

The other one looks a little older, but not much. She gets up and pulls the younger one to her feet. "Let's get out of here before he finds us."

"But he was so dreamy!"

"Come on. I'm going." She starts to run, and finally the younger one catches up to her.

I'm about to carry on toward home when I catch a glimpse of a man coming out of the woods. Something about the way he walks looks familiar. I keep going but glance back over my shoulder. *Wait. How ridiculous!* He waves at me.

"Rachel!" Mr. Tompkins calls. "Hang on a sec."

I haven't seen him since the last day of school. He looks younger than ever, with his shirt slung over one shoulder, his undershirt showing off his muscles. He stops for a moment to put his shirt on. "What are you doing down here on a hot day like this?" he asks.

"Nothing much. Just walking." I feel as if I'm not in my real life, as if this is someone's made-up version of it. I can't think of anything to say to him.

"It's way too hot," he says, buttoning his shirt now and tucking it in.

"Were you with those, um, girls?" I ask him.

"What girls?"

"Two girls came out of here. I just wondered."

"I didn't see any girls. I was just taking a shortcut. You're not going into those woods, now, are you? *Woo!* It's a pretty dangerous place for a girl like you. I would have to go along to protect you." He smiles down into my eyes, and I feel as if my legs are made of melting chocolate. He looks away just as I hear the girls laughing, again. They're coming back.

Mr. Tompkins takes a peek at his watch. "Good heavens," he says. "I'd better get going, or I'll be late. Sorry."

Before the girls get very close, he hightails it out of the park, crosses a busy road, dodging cars, and I don't even see which way he goes. He's gone. The girls sit on the grass.

I move on, but I can still hear them.

"He said he wanted to take me to the movies," one of them says.

"As if," the other one says.

"He did. Honestly."

They must be talking about someone else. Mr. Tompkins would never have said that.

"Just listen to me! Don't say no before you even hear what I want you to do."

"I'm not going to some quasi-religious sideshow to parade in front of a lot of quacks and Bible Belters! I'd probably just lie right down in front of them and croak, anyway. Spoil their show."

"Oh, shut up, Jamie. I'm only asking you to go and observe. We can go late, stand at the back, leave early. This guy really can cure people."

I'm in the doorway of his room, but he edges out past me. "See you later," he says. "I have more important things to do than waste time on pipe dreams." He clatters down the stairs, leaving me standing there, defeated. It isn't a pipe dream. If he would just observe what goes on, see something like what happened to that red-haired guy, he'd be convinced. I was, and I certainly had my doubts before I saw it happen.

Jamie has decided to help Dad in the drugstore for a few weeks, until it's time for him to leave for university. That's where he's off to in such a rush. I'm in the workforce, too. Two days a week, I go in to tidy shelves, dust off containers and boxes in the back room, and sweep the floor. I even get paid a pittance for doing it.

That's where I am a few days after our conversation, when Mrs. Popkey, the lady who lives over the drugstore, comes in with Danny. She leaves his wheelchair outside and carries him in. His head flops against her neck, and his arms hang uselessly at his sides. He looks about three, but he's actually six.

"Well, how's little Danny today?" asks Margaret, the cashier.

Danny's head bobs around in Margaret's direction, and he manages a lopsided smile.

"He's doing not too badly," his mother says. "We've been going to see Reverend Lasco, down at the tent, every week, and I really think I notice a difference. He's stronger, I think—a little bit, anyway. He's over his cold, and he's eating better, so I think the preacher is doing him a world of good."

"You need a lot of faith for that, don't you?" Margaret says.

"Yes, you do. But, I have enough for both of us. I don't go to church every Sunday, but I go to the tent three times a week."

I peek at Jamie behind the counter and I know he's listening, even though he's not part of the conversation. He's counting out pills and putting them into a small pink prescription box. He has to stop and start over again.

"I didn't know you had to go so often," I say.

"You probably don't," the mother says. "But it can't hurt. I feel wonderful just watching the people who are healed. It keeps your hopes up. Why, even Mrs. Russell, that poor woman with only one arm, says she feels a hundred percent better. The cancer is completely gone. She says it's something she just senses. But, they'll be packing up their tent and moving on soon. I believe this is the last week. They'll be back next summer, I expect. For Danny and me, it's a question of trust."

I glance at Jamie again, but he's busy writing something in a ledger. When he raises his head, he looks as if he's off in a world of his own.

After supper, a few nights later, Jamie says he's going for a walk. I have to help with the dishes, of course, but all the time I'm drying knives and forks and shoving them into the drawer, I'm thinking about where Jamie might be heading. When the last plate, glass, and pot are put away, I say, "Ruthie's home. I think I'll go see her."

"Don't be late," Mother says.

I change direction once I'm far enough away from the house. It's a muggy evening, the air sultry with unshed raindrops. I run most of the way and get to the tent in Kavanagh Park in a lather of sweat. The tent flaps are still open, but Reverend Lasco has already started to speak. I slip inside, keeping well back, and start looking for Jamie. Sure enough, there he is in the second to last row, almost directly ahead of me.

People are standing, now that the healing ritual has started. I watch Jamie crane his neck for a better look. Luckily, I find a wooden box to stand on, next to the wall of the tent. There is the usual line of people—some who look healthy; some leaning on canes. Two soldiers come along on crutches and, behind them, another one in a wheelchair.

I see Mrs. Popkey at the front of the line with little Danny. Reverend Lasco doesn't put as much pressure on Danny's shoulders and doesn't even look very deeply into his eyes. I wonder if he resents having repeat customers, who never seem to get healed.

A soldier, still in uniform, with a bandage around his head that covers his eyes, shuffles along near the end of the line. He's being led by a pretty young woman, her black hair tied up with a big floppy bow. The soldier, tall and heavyset, moves forward with his hands stretched out in front of him. As he gets close to the preacher, he stumbles and nearly falls into the candelabra, but he's kept upright by the two singing girls and the woman with him.

Reverend Lasco unwinds the man's bandages and hands them to the black-haired girl. The soldier gropes blindly until the preacher grasps his shoulders, staring hard into his eyes. He whispers to him, then gives him a violent shake. Immediately, the man staggers, catches his balance, and puts his hands up to his eyes, looking stunned. When he takes them away, he turns to the audience. "I can see!" he shouts, "I can see!" He throws his arms around the woman he's with and kisses her passionately on the lips. She must be really self-conscious, because she pushes at him to get free.

The audience goes wild. They're clapping and yelling, "Praise the Lord!" The soldier himself is yelling something, but no one can hear him. The ushers try to get him to move away, but he keeps embracing the girl. Finally, Reverend Lasco puts his hands on the man's shoulders and turns him toward an usher, who takes him firmly by the arm and leads him back to his seat. The audience is still clapping and praising the Lord. Before the soldier sits down, he faces the audience and raises his fists like a successful prizefighter.

I'd give anything to be able to see Jamie's reaction. I see him look toward the door of the tent, as if he might be thinking about leaving, and decide to make my own getaway first. I don't want him to know I've been spying on him. It's nearly over, anyway.

Two days later, I barge into Jamie's room, where he's lying on his bed reading. I feel he needs another push. "Why don't you go to the tent in the park tomorrow? Just this once." I have to pretend I don't know where he was the other night. "What have you got to lose?"

"I don't want to discuss this."

"Reverend Lasco is moving on to Durhampton next week. This is your last chance."

He puts his book down on his stomach with a long pained sigh. "It's not my last chance. I'll go to Durhampton. That way, I won't run into anyone I know. And I won't care about making a fool of myself."

"You mean you'll go? How are you going to get there? It's fifty miles away."

"Borrow Dad's car. I'll think of some excuse."

"I want to go, too."

He has his nose in his book again.

"I really want to go."

"I'll think about it."

A week later, we're on our way to Durhampton in Dad's car. As far as our parents know, we're off to buy some of Jamie's textbooks from an ex-student who's selling them at half price. I'm just going along for the ride.

"So what made you decide to do this?" I ask in the car.

"I went to have a look at this Reverend Lasco for myself, last week, and saw a soldier get cured of his blindness. On the way out, I got talking to the guy, and it turns out he was in the same bombing raid I was when we were fired on by the Allies. He said that's where he lost his sight. He was pretty excited about being able to see. He might even have been a little drunk. He invited me to join him for a drink, but I didn't really feel like it. I gave him some sort of excuse. He made a big impression on me, though. I saw a few other guys after that bombing raid who were blinded and deafened, among their other injuries. If I get my nerve up, I'll give it a whirl."

In Durhampton, we have to ask for directions but soon find the tent. The same two girls are collecting money at the doorway. I think one recognizes me, the one who yelled through the door of Reverend Lasco's trailer that she was a singer, not an actress. Inside, the setup is much the same as it was in Middleborough—lit candles; no electric lights; Mrs. Lasco at the piano. Soon the proceedings are under way.

When it's time to line up, I watch Jamie fidgeting.

"I don't think I'll do this," he says.

"You just have a case of cold feet. If you don't go, you'll regret it. Go ahead. Do it."

"It's not going to work. It's not like I'm blind, or anything."

"Stop making excuses. All you need is faith that it'll work." I stare hard into his eyes, imitating the preacher.

Finally, he blows air out between his lips and stands up. He edges slowly past the people in our row and is last in line.

Each time I watch the ritual, I'm fascinated. I'm transported somewhere beyond the intense heat and the odor of people packed so closely together. The magical gloom inside the tent and the flickering candles high on the candelabra put me into a kind of dream state, where I'm aware only of the preacher's powerful voice. It sends a thrill up and down my spine.

Near the end of the line, just a few people ahead of Jamie, a gray-haired man with a beard makes his way on crutches, dragging one leg. When he gets his shake-up, he nearly loses his balance but is kept upright by the two girls. He stands bolt upright, stares at the ceiling, puts his hands on top of his head, and the crutches fall out from under his arms and topple to the ground.

I stand bolt upright myself. I've seen this before. My mystical mood shatters as I recognize the red-haired guy with freckles. Suddenly, I know The guy pretending to be cured is in disguise, an actor. While everyone's clapping and yelling praises to the Lord, I try to get to Jamie to tell him it's a waste of time. But the crowd is so excited that no one pays any attention to me—I'm blocked on all sides.

The line moves forward, and finally it's Jamie's turn. He has his shoulders pressed and shaken and his eyes stared into, and soon the crowd opens enough to let him return to his seat. He won't look at me, at first, but when he does, he seems dazed. His eyes have a wide hollow look, as if he's just waking from a dream.

"I think it worked," he says. "I feel funny. Different."

I take a big breath, open my mouth to tell him it's all a sham, and suddenly close it again.

"I don't know what it is, but there's something to all this," he says. "I feel as if I'm cured."

On the way home in the car, I fight to keep tears from running down my cheeks.

"You're quiet," he says.

"I'm just trying to take it all in."

"I know what you mean. It's pretty astounding." After a while, he says, "Let's not tell Mother and Dad until later, just to be on the safe side."

"Good idea," I say.

When Jamie has his last medical checkup before he leaves for Toronto, Doctor Melvin says he didn't expect him to be in such great shape.

"I didn't tell him about the preacher," Jamie says. "I was afraid he'd lose his faith in modern medicine."

I don't know what to think. Maybe it's possible that Jamie and Mrs. Russell and a few others actually are cured. Maybe the preacher hires actors just to make it a bigger show. That's possible. Because, it's certainly as much a show as any play put on in a theater. There's suspense and drama and special lighting effects. There's a dynamic leading man, background music, an eager audience. While I argue with myself about whether or not to tell Jamie about the actor, or actors (the blind soldier might have been an actor, too, as far as I know), I can hear him in his room, whistling as he opens and closes drawers, packing his clothes for Toronto. He's happy and relaxed, and I probably have no right to take that away from him.

On the other hand, is it right to let him go on believing a lie? Could it mean that he won't look after himself and skip future doctor's appointments? Jamie goes off a new man, looking forward to attending university.

As for me, school starts again. To mark the occasion, I take my lipstick from the back of the kitchen cupboard, just to dab on a bit before I leave for school. I put it back and scoot out the door before Mother even notices.

I need to talk to someone about the faith healer. Granny always has good advice, but she has problems of her own at the moment. She's worried about her sister, who has to have an operation. Her main worry is leaving the farm long enough to go and stay with her after the surgery. I consider Ruthie, but trudging along on the first day of school, listening to her chatter about how she hates school and how the only good thing about it is Mr. Tompkins, I know she won't concentrate on me and my problems. Besides, I can hardly get a word in. I'm almost ready to interrupt and tell her about Tommy coming out of the woods with his shirt off that hot day, but I don't. Something about those giggling girls bothers me. I'm not thinking about it anymore.

"Oh, Tommy," I say at last. "Isn't he old news?"

"After he put his hand on your neck, that time? Hardly."

"Oh, that! I've forgotten all about it." Talk about little red lies! I get goose bumps thinking about it.

Tommy's not our homeroom teacher, this year. Ruthie and Hazel and I glance into his classroom from time to time, only to find it aswarm with the usual flirty girls, mostly grade-niners. We have a legitimate question for him. By the end of September, the crowd is somewhat diminished, and we wait our turn to ask him what play the drama club will be doing this year.

"I haven't really thought about it," he says, when at last we have his ear. "I have a list of possibilities. Let's look it over together and decide." He retrieves the list from a desk drawer. As we pour over it, he says, "Perhaps Rachel should be assistant director."

"Me!" I say. "I don't know anything about directing."

"I could teach you everything you need to know," he says. "You look like a young woman of many talents."

Ruthie and Hazel give each other a quick raised-eyebrow glance.

Hazel says, "She really is. She's writing a play, you know."

"No, I'm not," I say. "I've given it up."

"Why? It sounded great," Hazel says.

"I have too much on my mind to be able to think about it."

"Girls don't have anything on their minds, do they?" Mr. Tompkins says. "Besides boys?"

Ruthie and Hazel laugh politely at his feeble joke. I feel slighted. How would he know what problems are weighing on my mind? Maybe I should tell him.

On the way home, Ruthie says, "I hope you're not going to get all stuck-up and everything, just because he said you have talent."

"*Look* like I have talent," I say. "There's a difference."

"What kind of difference?"

I say, as modestly as possible, "I think he means I'm interesting-looking. Sort of."

"Whatever that's supposed to mean."

"No, it's simple. I'm certainly not as beautiful as Hazel, but I *am* interesting-looking."

"Most people think horny toads are interesting-looking."

"Ruthie, you have no soul."

"You've got a bad case of it, I think."

"What are you talking about?"

"Admit it! You are dangerously in love."

"When I fall in love, believe me, you'll be the first to know."

"You are in love with an older man—a married man, at that."

"How do you know he's married?"

"Everybody knows, and his wife is going to have a baby."

My face feels hot. I admit, I once had a daydream, a sort of love story involving Tommy and me, but it was about doomed love because of the teacher-pupil thing; it was about eternal but innocent yearning. Something you could turn into a successful movie starring Gregory Peck and a wonderful new, young, talented actress. A movie where everyone in the audience leaves the theater mopping their eyes, unable even to speak to each other. Later, though, they phone their friends and say, *You simply must see this new movie starring Gregory Peck and a wonderful, new, young, interesting-looking actress.* I sure didn't bargain on a wife, in my daydream movie, and certainly not a baby.

We part at the corner, and I drag my feet the rest of the way home.

So, the Tommy-dreams are over. If he has a wife, he's definitely off-limits. Officially out of my life and out of my thoughts.

At school on Tuesdays and Thursdays, I watch Ruthie play basketball, and I cheer in the right places. I watch the football game with Ruthie after school on Friday. Will Cooper scores a touchdown. I cheer. Our school loses, anyway. I say, "How sad," at the sock hop after the game, but I couldn't care less. Will Cooper asks me to dance. I didn't think he even knew I existed. He's quite good-looking and, while we dance, I see Tommy watching us from the sidelines. He looks a little jealous, I think, but maybe I'm only imagining it. He and Miss Felden, the phys ed teacher, are chaperones. Of course, I stumble all over the place and can hardly follow Will. But I refuse to think about Tommy.

Not for one moment am I thinking about Tommy. At home, I become aware of my parents penetrating the fog of thoughts clouding my brain, which hasn't happened for many weeks.

There's something funny going on with them. It's hard to put my finger on it. My mother seems tired and worn out. My father goes around in a daze. Except when Granny comes for dinner, we're like three ghosts occupying different parts of the house. Dad says I can no longer work at the drugstore.

"How come?"

"Because Mother needs your help more than ever. She's . . . she's not herself these days. Someday you'll understand."

No, I won't. I'll never understand why they're trying to turn me into the family slave. I go up to my room and slam the door.

"Rachel!" I hear. "If you've finished your homework, I could use your help in the kitchen."

"I haven't finished," I yell through my closed door.

I'm trying out a new hairstyle, with it all piled on top of my head and secured with five hundred bobby pins. But the effect is more metal than hair, so I give up.

Downstairs I hear a crash and my mother wailing, "Oh, no! I spilled it!"

I hear my father hurry out to the kitchen. "Now, now," he says. "You go and lie down. I'll look after it. Rachel!" he calls. "I need your help!"

What can I do? I claw the pins out of my hair, shake it to resemble a lion's mane, and listen to my slave chains, as they clank all the way down the stairs.

As the weeks go by, anger and resentment become my best friends. I'm angry with Jamie for getting sick, because, obviously, it's worry over him that's turning my mother into someone I've never met before. I'm angry that he won't tell her about being faith healed, to put her mind at rest. And I resent the fact that he made me promise not to tell. On top of this, I know, or at least feel sure, that the whole thing is a fraud. So, how is it possible that he's cured?

I don't know what to do. Should I tell Jamie the whole thing is a sham, or should I tell Mother that he's been miraculously cured? If I ask Ruthie, she'll tell me that movie stars are always being miraculously cured and not to worry. As for Hazel, well, I don't really know her well enough to ask. Anyway, she always seems wrapped up in problems of her own. What I need is mature advice. Granny's out of the question for the time being. She's gone to Kingston to look after her sister.

At school, I am barely aware of what's going on. In

English, we're supposed to read *The Barretts of Wimpole Street*. I haven't even started it. One day in class, Mr. Tompkins discusses Elizabeth Barrett's mysterious illness, and Robert Browning's growing tenderness toward her, with such compassion that I actually pay attention. Everyone says he's the most sympathetic teacher in the school. Maybe he is.

After the bell, I wait while some grade thirteen girl bends his ear over nothing. I'm surprised by my own impatience. I scratch the insides of my arms and try to think about peeling potatoes and carrots, which I will be doing in about one half hour, oh joy, oh rapture.

At last, it's my turn. I start by saying, "I need some advice."

"All right," Mr. Tompkins says. "I'll try my best."

"It's about my brother. He has leukemia."

He looks startled, shuffling papers on his desk into a pile. "Oh, dear," he says. "That's terrible. I'm sorry to hear it. Is there anything anyone can do?"

"The thing is, he believes he's been cured by a fraudulent faith healer."

"How do you mean?"

I tell him about the red-haired guy on crutches, who turns up with a beard and gray hair in Durhampton and is healed all over again.

He frowns. "What a cheat! He should be reported to the authorities."

"Well, yes, I agree. But right now, I need advice on what to do about my brother."

"That's a toughie," he says. "There's a right way and a wrong way to tackle this, but I'll try my best." He pulls an extra chair up close to his desk and asks me to sit down. "This is much too hard for you to deal with alone. I'm glad you told me."

I'm so relieved to find him being sympathetic and helpful that I nearly burst into tears. Swallowing hard, I say, "What do you think? Should I tell him it was all an act?"

"That's a hard one," he says. "Don't do it yet. Don't be in a rush." He takes my hand in his for a moment and then releases it. "Let me think about this for a day or two. I know someone who might have some good advice. I'll get back to you. Would that be all right?" He's already gathering up his papers, putting them into his briefcase and preparing to leave.

"Sure," I say.

He walks with me to the classroom door. "Don't be discouraged. I'm sure there is a right way to handle this. It will just take a little time." He gives me a pat on the shoulder, leaving his hand there for the merest moment. It burns through my blouse, making me shiver inside in spite of my worries.

I stand gazing up at him, and he down at me, with my schoolbooks clasped nervously to my chest. I'm aware of another student walking past, but I can't move my eyes away

from Tommy's. Football practice is over, I guess. It must be
getting late. Mr. Tompkins says, "See you tomorrow."

Will Cooper catches up with me as I'm leaving the
school. "I saw you with Tompkins," he says.

"So what? He *is* my English teacher, you know." Is that
guilt in my voice? I don't need to explain anything. Anyway,
what business is it of Will's? He's two grades ahead, but that
doesn't give him the right to check up on me. And, while I
think about it, Will isn't really all *that* good-looking.

"He's a terrible flirt," Will says.

"He's not interested in me. Why would he be? He's
married."

"No, he's not. A friend of mine asked him, and he said
he isn't."

"There's no law against talking to a single man, especially if he's your teacher."

"They say he was fired from his last job."

"Who says?"

"That's the scuttlebutt."

"That's stupid. I expect he was overseas, like all the
other young men."

"Apparently not. A guy in my class asked him. He was
turned down because of flat feet."

"Well, he wasn't fired. If it were true, he'd hardly be
hired here."

"The school needed someone in a hurry. Remember?
Mr. Mackiewitz left suddenly."

"I think someone's spreading nasty stories," I say.

We walk in silence to the next corner, where we pause before going in different directions.

"Well, he's sure got the girls eating out of his hand," Will says.

I picture soft-eyed does, coming tamely from the forest toward his outstretched hand, and imagine I hear the crack of a rifle.

"He's just giving me some advice," I say, a trifle haughtily. I don't want to, and don't need to, go into details, and so I leave it there.

"Well, take care," he says and lopes off down the street.

Scuttlebutt's a good word. Imagine old Will Cooper using a word like scuttlebutt. The world is full of surprises.

I walk on, and in spite of everything reasonable, I find myself back inside a daydream, Tommy's hand singeing my shoulder, his gaze burning my face. My worries are tucked away in some dark cold cave at the back of my mind.

CHAPTER

16

Golden autumn gives way to winter almost overnight, it seems. Leaves sweep and swirl ahead of me, each day, as I trudge to school. We have a few light snowfalls, but nothing permanent, yet. I wear earmuffs to school, spurning a hat, and continue to sport bobby socks and saddle shoes, ignoring my mother's warnings that my legs and feet will get frostbitten and my toes fall off. I wait, as patiently as possible, for Mr. Tompkins to come up with the promised advice, but he always seems busy, always rushes off to do something else.

One day after English class, he says, "The friend I want to talk to about your brother is away until after Christmas. I hope you can wait that long for me to advise you."

"I guess so," I say. I'm disappointed, but I fake a smile.

"This person is an expert, so it's going to be worth the wait, I'm sure."

"Okay." I try not to look glum, but I think I fail. He puts his hands on either side of my face and stretches my lips into a smile. And then, I do smile.

Every week or so, I write to Jamie in Toronto, and amazingly, he writes back. "Do me a favor," he writes, "and ask Mary to send me a letter." He's written two letters to her, he tells me, and needs to hear back.

So, I go into Woolworths. "Oh, for sure," Mary says, "I keep meaning to write. It's just that I'm really busy these days." She turns pink and ducks her head under the counter, looking for a tin of talcum powder that she knocked to the floor. "Maybe you should give me his address again. I think I lost it." I write it on a scrap of paper torn from my notebook.

I try to wait patiently for Mr. Tompkins to advise me, but it's really hard. What makes it even harder is listening to Ruthie tease me about him, calling me a home-wrecker. She doesn't believe me when I tell her that Will Cooper said he isn't married.

There's something about Hazel that bothers me, too. In English class, with our heads bent over a poem we're dissecting, I sometimes look up, and with a shock, notice Mr. Tompkins' gaze falling directly on Hazel and staying there. It makes me sad and, at the same time, nervous, although I don't know why. Sometimes I see Hazel glance up at him with an expression I have trouble translating. Is it adoration, or is it something like panic?

In my letters to Jamie, I try to describe what's happening at home:

> Your parents (*I like to pretend they have no connection to me*) have gone completely off their nuts. Your mother doesn't get out of bed until after I leave for school. Remember how she used to rout us out of bed if we dared to sleep in until nine o'clock, on a Saturday, no less? She's really slipping. And your father goes around looking haunted.
>
> Granny is back from Kingston and is the only one who remains normal. The sad news is, poor old Bounder died. She says she's going to get a puppy in the spring.
>
> Your mother said, "Don't you think you're a bit too old to be taking on a puppy?"
>
> Granny gave her a nasty look and said, "If you ask me, that's a lot like the pot calling the kettle black."
>
> Your father got up and left the table.
>
> I said, "Couldn't we all just practice being normal, so that when Jamie gets home for Christmas, he won't feel like he's in a lunatic asylum?"

Jamie writes back:

> We've always known the parents are mildly psy-
> chotic, so why be surprised? I've been feeling great,
> by the way. No need to go back into hospital for
> refueling. Doctor Latham is quite satisfied with me.
> See you soon.

Three days before Christmas, we're slouching on the living
room sofa, supposedly admiring the tree.

"Too short," I say. "A tree for gnomes."

"Not enough decorations," Jamie says. "Looks like it's
been through the Depression."

It doesn't take Jamie long to see what I meant in my
letter about our parents. "What's the matter with them?" he
whispers. "They seem so vague, as if they're only half here."

"This is only a theory," I say, "but I'm afraid some alien
being has taken our parents and exchanged them for two
Martians who look just like them."

"Although not quite," Jamie says. "The mother they
gave us is fatter."

"And moodier," I say. "If she's not humming to herself
and grinning, she has tears running down her cheeks, as if
the world has come to an end."

Next day, I convince Jamie to go Christmas shopping
with me.

"How can I buy you a present if you're standing beside me?" he says.

"I'll turn my back."

We put on our coats and hear Mother on the phone, saying she's awfully sorry about something. "I hate to miss it, but I've nothing to wear." She lowers her voice. "Nothing fits, now."

"She bawls me out for saying that," I whisper to Jamie.

"She's just going through the middle-aged spread."

"Tellin' me. More like the middle-aged paunch."

We kick snow ahead of us as we head downtown. Jamie consults his list. "Granny wants a book, so that's easy. For Dad, I was thinking a scarf, but maybe a book. Something dealing with politics or the war. Maybe a book for Mother, too. Something on diets. Or would that be insulting?"

"Very. Don't do it."

"Maybe a book of poetry would be better."

"She doesn't read poetry."

"She could start."

"Are you getting something for Mary?"

"Of course."

The first night he was home, Jamie invited Mary to come over and listen to his Glen Miller recordings. She was still there when I came home from Ruthie's. Our parents were banished, I guessed, to their room. I plunked myself down on a chair, saying, "So what's new?"

Mary couldn't find much to talk about and, pretty soon, looked at her watch. She said, "I should go home because my mother will get mad if I stay out too late."

Jamie kept glaring at me, but I was able to ignore him. "I'll walk you home," he said, finally, and they went to put on their coats. He said, "I have a question for you, Mary." I was kind of lingering near the hall door and accidentally heard him. "When are you going to leave home and find yourself an apartment?"

"An apartment? Oh, well, I guess I won't," she said. "Not until I get married. There's no point."

"Oh." And that's when they went out, leaving me to wonder what would happen next.

"Maybe I'll give Mary an engagement ring," Jamie says as we head downtown.

"Waste of money," I say.

"I don't think so. I bet she wants proof that our friend-ship is going somewhere."

We come to Phillip's Jewelry Store, first, and look in the window at the gold and silver rings on display, their stones sparkling in a sudden burst of winter sunshine. We can't see any of the prices. I twist my head nearly upside down and glimpse a figure of $375.

"Oh." Jamie bites his lip. "A bit more than I'd bar-gained on."

"Don't look at me. I'm not turning over my savings to you."

"Actually, maybe she'd prefer a book." In the bookstore window is a copy of *The Boston Cooking-School Cook Book* by Fannie Farmer. "That cook book, for instance. If I give her that, she'll realize that one of these days I'm going to ask her to marry me."

"Not one of your better ideas."

We go inside while he mulls over the choices. "Diamond ring? Cook book? Hang on," he says, his eyes wide as if he's just had an epiphany.

"What, now?"

"Why would Mary Foley want to marry me, if she thinks I'm dying?"

I frown. I have no answer.

"I know what I have to do. I have to go straight to Woolworths and tell her the truth."

"The truth about what?"

"About the faith healer. That I've been cured."

He's out the door, the bell jingling, before I can say, "Hey, wait!"

Outside, sliding on a patch of ice, I yell, "Hey, wait!" But he's gone. I catch up to him just inside the department store, glaring at the cosmetics counter, near the back of the store. Mary's there, of course, looking beautiful, hair shining, eyebrows arched just so. She smiles winningly at a customer, someone familiar. That Armstrong guy! Roy Armstrong. We watch, from a distance, for a moment, as they carry on a hilarious conversation, both of them laughing like maniacs.

"What are they laughing about?" I whisper. "Nothing's that funny!"

Jamie's face looks like a blank page. He clutches the corner of a counter, as if it might try to get away.

"May I help you with something?" Mrs. Hulbert, the clerk, asks. She knows us because she's in Mother's church group. "I guess I'll look at the scarves." Jamie mumbles.

"Certainly." She shows him five scarves in five different colors, and he says he'll take them all. The Armstrong guy is still there chatting up a storm. When Mrs. Hulbert hands Jamie his change, she smiles at me and says, "And how is your mother keeping, dear?"

"Oh, she's fine," I say.

"I'm so happy for her."

That's nice, I think, but why?

We arrive home to the cinnamony smell of baking pies. And on the kitchen table, cookies are spread out on a piece of brown paper. Mother says, "Go ahead, try one. Two. You may each have two. They've just come out of the oven."

We take two each and breathe contented sighs because we're lucky enough to have a mother who bakes delicious cookies, and we know enough to appreciate it.

————

Christmas goes off as scheduled, with the usual good food and plenty of it. The presents we exchange are just what each of us wanted. Jamie and I went together on a gift for Mother, and when she opens it, she bursts into tears. That jars us both.

"It's so beautiful," she weeps. "Is it a garnet? That's my birthstone. How did you know that?"

"Mother," Jamie says, "calm down. It's only a necklace, not the crown jewels."

"Oh, my sweet, sweet, boy. Thank you so much, darling."

"It's from me, too," I say.

"Oh, yes, of course, thank you both."

Easy to see who's the favorite.

The phone rings in the afternoon, when we're lying around reading our new Christmas books. It's Mary Foley, who says a little too eagerly, "I'm afraid I've come down with a bad cold, so I won't be able to give Jamie his present." She coughs to demonstrate.

"I'll let him know." A corny little movie starring Roy Armstrong, flirting with Mary while she bats her eyes at him, plays over and over in my mind, and it's all I can do to remain civil. I'm thinking, I should just wrap up all those scarves Jamie bought in one big parcel and take them over to her. *Merry Christmas from Jamie,* I'd say. *These will keep your neck warm the rest of your short life.* Then I'd strangle her with them.

"Sorry about your cold," I say, although I'm not. I go upstairs and tell Jamie what she said.

"Good," he says.

"Good? Why good? Are you over her?"

He looks as if he's surprised himself. "Maybe I am. Maybe I'm just realizing that life's too short to pretend to be in love."

Two days after Christmas, one of Mary's brothers, Tim or Tom, drops by after lunch with a present for Jamie from Mary. I run upstairs to where he's studying, to tell him. He closes his book with a bang and mutters something under his breath. Grabbing one of the scarves from the back of the shelf in his cupboard, the red one, he finds tissue paper, hurriedly wraps it up, and licks three Christmas seals to stick it all together.

"You don't need to do this, you know," I say.

"It's a matter of pride."

I follow him down to the front hall, where Tim or Tom is waiting, and watch him hand over the scarf for Mary.

"Hope Mary gets over her cold soon," Jamie says.

Tim or Tom says, "She's not got a cold."

I frown. "She said she did on the telephone."

"Why did she say she has a cold, if she doesn't?" Jamie asks.

"I don't know. What she has is a new boyfriend. She asked me to tell you."

Jamie is stunned into silence, so I fill in. "Oh, yeah? Well, tell her the same goes for Jamie. In fact, he's the next thing to engaged. Hope you can come to the wedding."

Jamie glares at me as he closes the door behind Mary's brother. "Just once," he seethes, "just once, could you possibly mind your own business?"

"Sorry," I say. "I guess the way I said that, it sounded as if *you* had a new boyfriend."

"Whenever you butt in, you make me look like an incompetent idiot."

"Open the present," I say.

"Did you even hear what I said?"

"It's tattooed on my brain. Let's see what she gave you."

"I'm throwing it in the garbage."

"Don't you want to see what a girl who is about to dump her boyfriend would give him for Christmas? Let me open it." I peel back the tissue. It's a scarf, black and gray striped. It looks like something you'd wear to a funeral.

The day before New Year's Eve, our whole family is still around the kitchen table, after breakfast, drinking coffee. Jamie's going back to Toronto, but not until the afternoon. Even I am allowed half a cup, with plenty of cream and sugar.

The doorbell rings and Jamie goes to answer it. Mother pulls her dressing gown a little more securely across her front. *Dressing gown.* This is a breach of personal grooming that happens rarely, if ever. I am appalled. What has become of the straitlaced, prim and proper mother who bugs the life out of me, but who, nevertheless, is the one I'm used to, the one who preaches that proper etiquette means you come down in the morning fully dressed to greet the day? Sure, she's brushed her hair and put on lipstick. In fact, it looks suspiciously like mine, which is still lurking in a corner of the kitchen cupboard. On her, though, it looks a little more subdued, more like *Little Pink Lies.*

It's Will Cooper at the door. He keeps his coat on and follows Jamie into the kitchen, saying he can't stay. *What's he doing here?* I wonder. *Checking up on me, again?* I don't even rate a glance, however, as he says hello to the others.

"How are things at your place?" Jamie asks.

It takes Will a moment before he answers. "It's a bit eerie," he says. "We just got a letter from Arthur, written the day before his plane went down over Germany."

I have to translate Arthur into Coop, before I know who he means.

"A letter?" Jamie looks startled.

Dad motions Will over to an empty chair, but he shakes his head and leans against the sink.

"These things happen, I guess," Will says. "In a war, letters get lost. Maybe somebody found it and meant to mail it, but didn't for some reason. Who knows?"

"You're right," Jamie says. "I had a picture I kept meaning

to give back to a friend's widow, but I kept it a long time before I got up the nerve to face her."

"Will, it must have sent your parents into a tailspin," Granny says.

"Sure did. I thought my father was going to have a heart attack."

"What does the letter say?" Jamie asks.

"The usual. Mostly about flying. He mentions you. I copied it out to show you. You can keep it if you want."

Jamie takes the copy gratefully and goes into the dining room to read it.

In the kitchen, Will says, "He mostly just says that everyone on the flight crew was nervous about the next mission, but he wasn't. He never was superstitious. Bit like Dad."

Jamie comes back into the kitchen looking pale. His hand shakes when he picks up his coffee cup. "He writes the way he talks, doesn't he? He sure loves flying."

"Yup. He loved it, all right."

The change in tense is not lost on me. Will believes he's dead. Jamie doesn't. Will looks at his watch and says he has to leave. Jamie's rereading his copy of the letter, and so I walk with Will to the door.

He smiles. "Santa good to you?" A teasing, joking grin, but, I have to admit, a nice grin. Sort of.

"Nope. He only brings things to good little girls, and I am neither good nor little." I want to see him smile again, and he does. It seems to go on for three seconds longer than is absolutely necessary and causes me a little red-faced flutter. Do I look like some little juvenile? I rub my hand across my face because I probably have half my breakfast smeared across my cheek.

After Will goes, I ask Jamie if I can read the letter. It isn't long, so it doesn't take much time. The letter begins with something about the last parcel his mother sent, how he shared the food with the other crew members, and how they envy him the hand-knit socks.

Near the end, he wrote:

> Another bombing mission tonight. The other guys are sweating bullets and biting their nails till they bleed. They're spooked by this one, for some reason. I'm all smiles every time we take off. I wish my buddy Mac was here. He'd get a thrill out of being inside the belly of this giant bird as it takes flight. The earth just falls away, like old clothes. The roar is so loud, it's part of you. As the plane slices through clouds, you wonder if this time you'll get to touch the stars. Too bad Mac didn't choose the air force. Too bad we have to drop bombs, but we do.

It's a morning of callers. No sooner has Will left than there's a knock on the kitchen door. This time it's our next-door neighbor, Mrs. Hall.

Normally Mother would have bustled about—finding another cup, pouring coffee, apologizing that it wasn't very strong or was too strong—but she sits calmly while Granny gets the coffee. I've never seen her like this, so placid, oblivious to everything around her, sitting with her hands folded across her stomach. She looks as if she's swallowed something divine, like a whole chalice of communion wine.

Mrs. Hall waves an envelope at us. "A Christmas card, I think. Delivered to us by mistake," she says. "I meant to bring it a few days ago, but you know how it is. Busy, busy, busy. Happy New Year, everyone! Don't get up," she says as Dad pushes his chair back. "Sorry to disturb."

"Join us for a cup of coffee," Mother says, coming out of her reverie.

"Thank you, but I couldn't possibly. I can't stay."

Dad pulls an extra chair up to the table, anyway.

Granny says, "I made a big pot. It'll just go to waste."

Mrs. Hall sits down fussily, loosens her coat, and straightens her skirt over her knees. She pats Jamie's hand solicitously, grins at me, beams at Mother, and says, "You're looking radiant, my dear. When does this darling new baby make its grand entrance?"

No one says a word. It's as though everyone has stopped breathing. Mother's face moves from blank serenity to flushed embarrassment. Dad looks as if he's committed treason. Granny puts the breakfast frying pan into the sink with a clatter-bang.

"I hope," Mrs. Hall says, her finger to her lip, "that I haven't just let the cat out of the bag."

Mother suddenly takes repossession of her brain and says, "Certainly not. I'm sure Jamie and Rachel are well aware of . . . we just . . . haven't talked much about it. You know how it is, you like to wait a bit until you're sure of . . . everything." She smiles brightly. A smear of *my* lipstick has come off on one of her teeth.

Jamie looks hard at his watch, as if he were just learning to tell time. "You'll have to excuse me," he says. "I have some packing to do." He pushes his chair out from the table.

"Wait, son," Dad says, "I think your mother deserves a minute of your time."

He nearly sits down again but doesn't. He says brightly, glibly, "Congratulations, you two. I'm sure you'll be very happy with this fresh, new addition or edition, whichever the case may be." He leaves the table and hurries upstairs.

I follow him, but he closes his door in my face.

Letters not sent.

I left an unfinished letter to you a while back, telling you about the day we were bombed by our own planes. You know, I don't think we ever really got over that. I remember the way I felt after the disaster, as the drone of the Allied bombers drifted away. Stabbed in the back. Sucker punched.

Dragging my bloody leg, I hobbled away from Leeson's corpse. I had the picture of his wife in my pocket. My dead comrades were scattered like broken toys, carelessly left by a spoiled child. Then, I heard someone cry out. When I looked back, nothing moved except a cluster of wildflowers, petals still whole, drooping in the heat. I staggered back, listening. Again, an anxious cry that turned into a steady moan. My leg was killing me. All I could think of was getting back to what might be left of my platoon, to get relief from the pain.

I heard the moaning sound again and stopped. "Mother?" I heard someone call. I tried to keep going, one foot, drag the other, one foot. But then I stopped. I didn't want to, but I turned around.

Following the sound, I nearly stumbled over Herman Visser, a guy we used to call Herman-the-German. He had a gaping hole in his midsection that displayed blood and guts and I don't know what all, and there was a stench that made the bile come up in my throat. I took off my shirt and covered his wound.

Visser called out, "Nurse?"

I said, "It's Jamie."

He said, "Would you call my mother and ask her to come and get me?"

His icy blue eyes always used to send a chill through me because he was such a worrywart. I felt as if his anxiety would spread to me. But, this time, his eyes were swimming with tears, and I felt like crying myself.

"Mother!" he called. It came out almost a gasp. I didn't know what to do, so I put my hand on his forehead, like a mother checking for fever. He said, "Did she say she'd come?"

"Yes," I said.

The whole time, in the back of my mind, I wanted to yell at him to pull himself together, to get up, be a man, stop talking about his mother, for God's sake. But, after sitting with him for a while, in my undershirt, I kind of got caught up in the myth that Herman's mother would come and save him, that all our mothers would come and save all of us. I could just hear them! "Put down those guns right this minute before someone gets hurt," they'd say.

"Is she here yet?" he said.

"Almost," I said.

I saw Herman's eyes lose their luster and stare straight up. Something gurgled in his throat. I put my hand on his forehead again, cool in spite of the sun, and ran it down over his eyes hoping to close them, but they

*wouldn't close. I wondered if he had felt as
betrayed by the Allies as I did. I would never
find out.*

Jamie's pretty upset, that much is clear. I go back downstairs to see what other bombshells will be dropped around
the kitchen table. I'm still in a state of shocked embarrassment. How will I explain this to my friends? *Guess
what? My ancient Mother's having a baby!* God! Parents of
teenagers and grown-up sons just don't start having babies
again. *There should be some sort of law!* How can I face
Ruthie? I can just hear her. *Some people's parents! Snicker,
snicker.* Yeah, mine!

Mrs. Hall is on her way out when I come down. "Thank
you, my dears, for the coffee. Must run. I have a hair
appointment in fifteen minutes."

Right, I think. She'll have to rehearse her lines for the
ladies at the Crowning Glory Beauty Salon. I can imagine
what she'll say about Jamie and me. *And they didn't even
know! Those great, grown children hadn't even guessed.*

How would we know? Why would we even guess that
our parents would, would . . . I'm not thinking about this
anymore.

When Jamie comes down with his suitcase, Mother is
waiting for him at the foot of the stairs. "You're not going
this early, are you?"

"I need to get back. I'll get the earlier train."

"Jamie, you're upset about our news. I meant to tell you. I was waiting for the right time." He stands holding his head back and off to one side because she looks as though she's getting ready to plant a slobbery kiss right on his lips. "Don't you think it's exciting?" she asks.

"What?" He frowns.

"The baby, of course. A little brother or sister for you and Rachel." She smiles brightly.

I watch Jamie glance from her face to her belly and back to her face. "I wish this was a joke," he says.

"It's the farthest thing from a joke, son. Don't look so cross."

He brushes past her and goes out to the kitchen, where Dad is halfheartedly gathering up coffee cups. With muted anger, Jamie says through his teeth, "How could you let this happen?" Dad just stares into the sink.

Emptying coffee grounds from the percolator onto a newspaper, Granny says to Jamie, "If there was ever a time to grow up, lad, it's now." He's still staring at Dad.

Mother stands in the doorway between kitchen and back hall. "Jamie! Think of it. We'll all have a little one to cuddle and play with."

"Aren't we all just a little too old for this?"

Mother turns and goes weeping down the hall and up the stairs. Dad leaves the kitchen to follow her.

Jamie grabs his coat, picks up his suitcase, and opens the side door.

Granny says, "I thought you weren't going until later."

"I have to get back to study. I have a chemistry exam next week."

"There's no train for at least two hours."

"I'm sure there is."

"I'll drive you to the station. No need for you to walk."

"I want to walk."

"It's too cold to walk all the way to the station carrying a suitcase. Now wait right there while I get my coat and galoshes. Where are *your* galoshes? They should be on your feet."

I ran to get my coat, too. "I'll come along for the ride."

The three of us are crushed together in the truck. Granny drives like a maniac, tooting at anyone who threatens to get in her way. She glances past me at Jamie. "You're behaving like a child."

"So what? I guess that's what I am. A replaceable child. They can't even wait until I'm dead."

"Don't be such a self-centered ass." We nearly sideswipe a parked car.

I keep silent, my head swiveling between the two of them. I'm wondering, though, what's happened to his miraculous cure.

"Keep your eyes on the road, Granny," Jamie says. "You're going to cause a crash."

"Maybe it would knock a little sense into you. Do you ever consider other people's feelings?"

This is cruel, I think. Right now, I'm ready to hate Granny. I expect Jamie to say something biting or else open the door of the truck and leap out, but it's too late. We're pulling into the station parking area.

"Thanks for the ride," he says sullenly. He opens the door of the truck, letting in a malicious wind.

"Just so you know," Granny says before he can step down, "the baby wasn't planned. At your mother's age, you know, it was a surprise. It was an act of God."

"Oh, sure. Blame it on God. God and the virgin Dora."

There's half a second of absolute silence broken by Granny's cackling laughter. "All right, Mr. Smarty-pants, get out if you want, but shake hands first."

He looks past me into Granny's strong blue eyes, red-veined and a little watery at the moment. He takes her hand, and she holds on to his, nodding at him.

"You be good," she says, "if you can figure out how." She lets him go, and he puts a foot on the running board.

"What about me?" I say. I make a lunge for him and manage to plaster a kiss on his cheek.

"At least you're not wearing your war paint," he says.

Granny and I drive in silence back from the station until we're almost home.

"The world is going haywire," I say.

"It's always been haywire. But now we care."

"A baby, for God's sake!"

"A baby for all our sakes."

CHAPTER

17

"Granny, would you let me off at Hazel's corner?" I say. I can't face going home yet. I wish I could stay away forever.

Hazel answers the door when I ring the bell, looking troubled. "Hi," she says. "Anything wrong, Rachel?"

"With me?"

"You don't look very happy."

"Oh, I'm all right." I'm wondering what my face shows. "You're the one who doesn't look very happy," I say.

"I'll get over it, I guess. It's just that I'm packing. I have to go to live with my grandmother in Toronto for the rest of the school year."

"Why are you doing that? What about school?"

"It's my father's idea. It's really too hard to explain, but the point is, I'm going to enrol in a school there." Somewhere in the back of the house, I hear Hazel's father calling her. "I've got to go," she says. "I'll call you if I get back before that."

I barely have time to say a hurried good-bye before she closes the door.

There's nothing left to do except trundle on over to Ruthie's house. I expect her sisters will be hanging around. Ruthie said they were both taking time off before New Year's. I hope Ruthie and I can escape them to get some gab-time on our own.

Ruthie's house is alive with the sound of their new electric record player, as well as Ruthie and her sisters singing along to Sammy Kaye's "That's My Desire." Joan and Audrey are dancing cheek to cheek. I sit with them in the living room, but I'm not singing. At the end of the song, I elbow Ruthie. "Can we talk?"

"After. Let's hear this one first. We just got it. It's called 'I've Got a Crush on You.' It's Sarah Vaughan."

Blind with boredom, I stand at the window and look at nothing. Maybe I should just go home. The singer croons out the words, and the sisters join in. Some of the words are pretty silly, but some stick in my head. The song's about being in love, about not knowing how the other person feels. The singer yearns to share a little home, share her life, share everything she has with that special person. Ruthie and Joan are dancing now. "'I've got a crush on you,'" they croon softly. I no longer hear them.

I don't even see them. What I see, now, is the truth,

not the lies I've been telling myself. The truth is, I have a crush on Tommy. Not only that I see the possibility of dropping out of my present life and taking up a new one, I see my future.

Is it possible? Has there ever been a marriage between a teacher and a high school student? Would it be possible to escape to a little cottage I could share with Tommy? Would the world, including my parents, pardon my mush, because I have a crush on . . . ?

The music comes to an end. Ruthie grabs my arm and says, "C'mon. We can talk in my room."

"Is Mr. Tompkins really married, or did you make that up?" I ask once the door is shut, blocking out her nosy sisters.

"Joanie heard he was married, but then my sister hears a lot of things—some true, some not. She also heard that Hazel Carrington's mother is crazy and Mr. Tompkins feels sorry for Hazel and is counseling her during lunch period."

"What do you mean, counseling her?"

"You know. Chatting. Telling her not to worry. That sort of thing. She doesn't talk much about it, at least not to me. I'm surprised she hasn't told you. You know her better than I do."

"All she told me is, she's going to stay in Toronto with her grandmother, maybe until the end of the school year."

"Holy cow! Things must be pretty bad."

"Listen, here's something you don't know. My mother is going to have a baby."

"I knew that."

"How did *you* know? I just found out."

"My mother told me. Anyway, you must be pretty dense if you didn't notice how bulgy she's been getting. My mother said I couldn't talk about it until you did."

"Jamie and I thought she was just getting fat."

Ruthie shakes her head. "I can't believe you two! You're babes in the woods, both of you."

In my own defense and Jamie's, I say, "She always wears bulky sweaters and jackets. It isn't that obvious. Anyway, if your mother was putting on weight, would you automatically think she was pregnant?"

"My mother? Don't be ridiculous. She's old."

"Well, I think my mother is old, too, but look what happened."

To change the subject, Ruthie sings off-key "I've Got a Crush," while she rummages through the top drawer of her dresser.

"Rats! My sister stole my nail polish remover."

I press my forehead against the cold windowpane and watch some boys hang on to the rear bumper of a car going along the snowy street. They fall off into a snowbank at the corner and lie there laughing and punching each other. How immature!

When Ruthie stops crooning, I say, "Jamie's very upset about this baby."

"Probably just because he's so sick. I sure feel sorry for him. Maybe he'll never even see the kid. How long has he got?"

"What do you mean, 'how long has he got'?"

"You know. How many months? In the movies, doctors always tell cancer patients how long they've got to live."

"What he's got is called leukemia, and he will go on living forever, as long as they keep giving him blood transfusions." I know my voice is really loud, but it helps squeeze more truth out of what I'm saying.

"Okay, sorry, I didn't mean to say that. I take it back."

"It's all right." It really isn't all right. How can someone take back spoken words? I think of telling her about the faith healer, but I don't want her opinion on that subject.

"I have to go home," I say.

"Are you mad at me?"

"No." I am, but I'm not going to let on.

The Christmas holidays drone past. The temperature drops to what feels like forty below. And then, predictably, we have the January thaw at the beginning of February.

At school one morning, Mr. Tompkins calls me aside, in the hall, and says, "Please see me in my classroom after school." No explanation, no hint of what's on his mind.

I've been trying to avoid Tommy, kind of, since I heard that "I've Got a Crush" record, because all I can think about is being in love and wanting to marry him and escaping from home, forever. Because there isn't a hope that this will ever happen, I try not to attract his attention. In class, I keep my eyes on the page. It's torture to deny myself the glow he bestows on me, the sense that of all the girls in the school, he finds something in me to admire (now that Hazel has left), but in the interests of staying sane, I have to. He still has his after-school coterie of blushing girls, smelling faintly of perspiring armpits.

Avoiding Tommy-daydreams means I have more time to worry about what's happening at home, about my mother, who's old enough to have some gray in her hair and is, nevertheless, expecting a baby, and about the fact that both my parents are turning into certifiable lunatics. And in case that isn't enough, I worry about my brother's jealousy over the ghastly baby.

No one talks much anymore; Dad usually goes back to the drugstore after dinner, to work on the books; Mother sighs a lot and complains of backache. She listens to her favorite programs on the radio, in the living room, but turns them off partway through and sits in the rocking chair, staring into space. Every chance I get, I escape to my room to do homework. Mostly, I sit at my desk, doodling connected figure eights across the page, until they almost fall off the edge, onto my desk.

Dutifully, after my last class, I go to Tommy's class-room. He's alone. We sit in two front row seats opposite each other, our knees almost touching.

"You seem upset," he says, sounding as if I've let him down, somehow. "Is it because I haven't got back to you with the advice you asked me for?"

I keep my eyes on the toes of my scuffed-up saddle shoes. "Maybe a little."

"Well, I've finally had a chance to talk to my psychol-ogist friend about it. His advice is to leave well enough alone. Your brother's belief that he's cured may be helping him stay well. I'm sorry it took me so long to get back to you. I just didn't want to risk saying the wrong thing. I'm afraid you are upset with me."

"I'm not." My eyes will fill up if he doesn't stop sound-ing so kind and caring.

"Is he still doing well?"

"Yes." I can't look at him because I'm afraid that if I do, I'll throw myself into his arms, sobbing, *Save me, take me away from my disintegrating family*. He puts his finger under my chin and, against my better judgment, I let him tilt my head up to look into his eyes. I'm a goner.

He smiles his most endearing smile. "How is your play-writing going?"

My eczema is suddenly unbearable. I start scratching the insides of my arms through my sweater. This is where I should simply tell him I've killed the play and buried it.

I stumble over my words. "It's, uh, having a rest."

"When do I get to read it?"

"Pretty soon. I'm having trouble with the plot." On my tombstone, they will engrave *Rachel Liar McLaren. She meant well, but she had no backbone.*

He glances at his watch. "Look, I have to leave soon, but why don't I drive you home? We can talk about it on the way."

The word *no* springs to mind. I want to *say* no, understand I *must* say no, to preserve my ban on Tommy-dreams. To say *yes* would be downright stupid. "Okay," I say.

"Get your coat, then, and I'll meet you in the parking lot."

Sitting next to him in his Pontiac, I have never felt so adult. I sit up straight, cross my knees. I try to tuck my thick curls behind my ears, but they won't stay. They *sproing* out around my head like live snakes. My eyes slide sideways. I can barely raise them from the two inches of hairy wrist that show between his coat sleeve and gloves as he drives.

We pass a few students leaving the school; one of them is Will Cooper. I don't think he saw us, not that it matters. Mr. Tompkins says he knows where I live, yet, instead of taking the most direct route, he meanders down side streets and turns corners.

"Tell me about your play problems," he says.

My almost nonexistent play. My problems with it. I can't concentrate. "It's hard to explain, exactly." I turn to face him, memorizing his profile.

"Give me a hint."

"Well, I think I've got the beginning figured out." I look out the window when he turns along the street that leads to the park. "Actually, I don't live down this way." It's snowing lightly.

"I know. I thought we should find a quiet place to stop so we can talk. Is that all right?" His smile is apologetic and hopeful and boyish. I don't know why it should make me feel nervous.

"Don't look so worried," he says. "You've told me what's right with the play. Now tell me what's wrong."

"I should actually be getting home."

"Of course. In a minute. But, what about your play? I just thought we could talk a bit easier here than parked in front of your house." He looks directly, but sadly, into my eyes, making me feel as if I'm not holding up my end of the bargain. After all, he *is* kind enough to take an interest.

"Sorry," I say. "All right, so the beginning is there." *Just not in so many words,* I think, but don't say. "And I know how it should end. It's the middle that's giving me trouble. I don't know what to do with my people for a whole act."

"That's easy. You sit down with a pencil and paper and work it out like a mathematical equation." I stare at him.

"If A happens in act 1 and C is the conclusion, then steps must be taken to get from A through B to C. Any writing simply requires logic."

A solution. Just like that. Wow! Maybe he's a secret writer. If not, he should be, because he'd be good. It sounds so straightforward when he says it. So masculine. I can't stop looking into his compassionate eyes, glancing at the angle of his perfect jaw. "I'll try that." I'm not sure how to apply logic to a madwoman walking around with an ice pick up her sleeve, but if I tackle it again, I might find a way. I don't want him to know I've pretty well mothballed the project. No need to hurt his feelings.

I change the subject. "There's something else I've been wondering. Have you reached a decision about the school play?"

"Ahh! This is something I want to ask your opinion about."

"My opinion? What one are we doing?"

"I was thinking of Ibsen. There is apparently a school version of *A Doll's House* available."

"That sounds a bit juvenile."

He laughs at me. "Hardly. Have you never read it?"

I have to admit I'd never even heard of it.

"It's about a woman, a wife, asserting her independence." He takes off his gloves and turns toward me. He reaches out to tuck my curls back behind one ear. "You'd make a good Nora. Would you like to play the lead?"

"The lead?" I can hardly get the question out, I'm trembling so much. When his hand touches my cheek, I completely lose track of the conversation. Has he just offered me the lead role, just like that—no auditions, no read-through, nothing? "I can't act," I say.

We both notice a car drive into the park. He starts his car. "I'm sure you could act with a little coaching."

"Nope," I say. "I think you know what an onstage disaster I am."

"I would be more than happy to coach you."

For a moment, I relive last year's stage-terror. "I don't think so."

"Fine. It's up to you, I suppose."

Does his voice sound a little chilly, or is it my imagination?

As soon as we get close to my corner, he looks at his watch. "Mind if I drop you off here? I have to run. We'll talk about *A Doll's House* some other time." He takes my hand in his, for a moment. He looks as though he's going to say something else. Instead, he squeezes it and lets go, grinning boyishly. Light-headed, I get out of his car and watch him drive off.

It's starting to get dark. The streetlights come on. Looking up, I watch the snow filtering down through the golden glow of light and am reminded of Jamie and Mary under the same light. Almost a year ago, I made up my two-minute drama about them. Directed it. Commanded snow to fall. Made them kiss. It was my first awareness of the power I could beckon at will, and I rode it like a racehorse. But now it's gone. I am a living power failure. If Tommy says, *Follow me over a steep cliff,* I will close my eyes and, like a pea-brained lemming, take that mindless leap.

I stand, all by myself in the pool of light, as snowflakes melt in my hair and build up on my shoulders. No one applauds. I move sadly into the shadows and shuffle up our front walk. I hadn't even felt powerful enough to tell him about the trouble-making baby expected in late May.

CHAPTER

18

I don't know for sure whether the events in your life can make you physically sick or not, but I'm inclined to think they can. My problems are temporarily on hold because I'm in bed with the flu. It's the middle of March, the ides. It didn't do Caesar much good, either. It's my fifteenth birthday, but I'm too sick to care.

My mother says, "When would you like your birthday cake?"

"When I'm sixteen."

"You'll feel better before then."

I float feverishly in and out of dreams, not of Tommy, surprisingly, but of tents full of dingbats and dingbat healers and one in particular that cures Jamie and even gives him the power to fly. I begged him to take me flying with him, but he couldn't hear me, he was so busy flying higher and higher. I think once I did fly, but not very high. The fever subsides, finally, and I'm left with the feeling that Jamie really is cured. Somehow, the dingbat dreams have convinced me. I didn't dream once about Tommy.

I've just had a letter from Hazel. She says she's happy that she's gone to live with her grandmother, who is turning her into a spoiled brat. "I love being spoiled," she writes. "And the school I go to is nice. The teachers don't breathe down your neck the way they do in Middleborough (a certain teacher, anyway). I don't know if you know who I mean, but maybe you can guess. I didn't really understand my problems until I went away."

I should write her back. Physically, I feel better, so I could. Emotionally, I'm a mess, and this makes it difficult.

I try to write to Hazel, but no words come, because all I can think about is Tommy, visions of Tommy smiling at Hazel. I'm pretty sure Hazel had a crush on him, too. Maybe she's over it. I guess that's what she meant about not understanding her problems until she went away.

I sit at my desk chewing the end of my pen, wishing I could escape from him but wanting him close to me, wanting to feel his soft breath on my neck. I shiver and go back to bed, glad to have that cozy haven.

Next morning, Mother takes my temperature and pronounces it normal. "Back to school with you," she says. "You can't afford to miss any more classes so close to your spring exams."

"I can't go back to school."

"Of course you can. You're better."

"I just can't face it."

"Now you're being melodramatic. Why not?"

I shake my head and stare at the wall. Mother leaves but pauses at the door, and I sense her studying me. When I look, she leaves with a worried frown.

I mope my way back to school, dragging my feet. Spring made tentative inroads while I was lolling in bed. What's left of the snow continues to melt, turning into annoying puddles. Eventually, they'll dry up, leaving grit on the sidewalk that will blow into my eyes and mouth when the wind comes up, like a desert sandstorm.

Home, school, the whole town is cold and colorless. I feel numb and stupid. In each class, I'm given extra work to take home until, after a few days, I know it's hopeless. I can't possibly get it all into my head before the spring exams start. My inner elbow itch now covers my entire panic-stricken body.

After school, I lug my books home and go straight up to my room to study. I juggle French verbs with the origins of the French Revolution; I muddle algebra theorems with physics problems; I see bodies falling around me at a rate of thirty-two feet per second per second, shot at by French artillery as they shout something I can't translate. All the bodies look like Tommy. Nothing sticks in my head.

The next day, Ruthie offers to come home with me after school to help me study. "I'll ask you questions, and if you can't answer them, then you'll know what you need to study." I've done this for her a few times, so I agree that it might work.

When we get home, there's a note from Mother to say she's at her doctor's appointment. Up in my room, Ruthie lies on my bed and fires questions at me, while I slouch over my desk. I get nearly all the answers wrong, but we keep on until it's time for her to go home. "Your problem is," she says, on her way to the kitchen door, "you have too much on your mind."

"You're right about that."

"When you're madly in love, it knocks everything else out of your head."

"I'm not in love."

"*Ha*! That's the biggest lie you've ever told. I've seen the way you look at Tommy and drool."

"Drop it, will you? That's so stupid."

"And I've seen how he looks at you, like he could just eat you up."

I'm about to yell at her, but then I think the best way to get her to shut up about it is to play along. "Okay, the truth is, we're running away together. It's all planned."

"I'm sure."

"No, no. It's true. I have a bag all packed."

She laughs wickedly and says, "Wouldn't that scandalize

the world! I'll believe it if and when it actually happens."

She leaves, finally, and I close the door firmly behind her.

"Rachel!"

Mother's home. I didn't hear her come in. "Yes?"

"I'm in the dining room. Come here for a minute."

She's spreading out a fresh tablecloth. "I couldn't help hearing what you and Ruthie were talking about."

My cheeks burn. "I was just joking," I say.

"Rachel, I'd like you to tell me what's going on. This is serious."

"It's a joke. Ruthie and I make up stuff like this all the time."

She glares fiercely. "Hmm. Well, we'll talk about this later. Right now, you can set the table."

Dinner is an almost silent affair—pass this, pass that, please, thank you. When we finish, I say, "May I be excused to go and study?"

"Not so fast, young lady," Dad says. "I think you need to tell us about your boyfriend. Your mother is afraid your studies are being neglected."

"I haven't got a boyfriend. Ruthie and I were just kidding around."

Mother says levelly, "How do we know you're telling the truth, now? What you said to Ruth was very convincing."

"I guess you'll have to trust me." There is a moment of silence. I study the cookie crumbs left on my plate, my face on fire.

"The fact that you said you were running away with a boy is a very serious matter," my father says. "It would be wrong of any parent to ignore that because, often, where there's smoke, there's fire. And the way you're blushing causes me more concern. I think I should make some enquiries. Someone at your school might be able to provide details, if you won't come clean. The drama coach, for instance, may have noticed you with someone. What's his name? Tompkins?"

The silence is suffocating. "Stop!" I scream, when I get my breath. "This is crazy! I can't believe you'd do something as stupid as go to my school." My voice is shrill. It doesn't even sound like my voice. "Smoke," I say, derisively. "Fire! There's a fire, all right!" I'm shouting again. "And it's in my brain! If you go blabbing about this at school, I'll never speak to you again." I get up from the table, pound up the stairs, slam my bedroom door, and use every swearword I've ever heard.

A little later, one of them knocks and looks in, but I am in bed, pretending to be asleep. I do sleep, finally, but not very deeply. If only Jamie were here, he'd understand how ridiculous they're being. I desperately need to talk to him.

I wake up early to a gray morning, knowing exactly what I have to do. I tiptoe to prevent waking my mother. My father has already left for work. I put a few items in a shopping bag and empty my money sock into my coat pocket. Before setting out, I pack a sloppy peanut butter sandwich.

It isn't cold, in fact, crocuses are pushing hopefully through the brown earth in people's flower beds. Still, I shiver inside my coat, new, longer than last year's rag. I break into a trot to keep warm. To avoid kids walking to school, I zigzag my way to Station Street and run again before I change my mind.

"Yup," says the ticket agent, "there's a train for Toronto due in about one hour."

Out of breath, I say, "How much is a one-way?"

Standing in front of Union Station in Toronto, staring at tall buildings, noisy streetcars, and crowds of unfamiliar people, I have a change of heart. I can't do this. I think of Middleborough's familiar sights, my school, Ruthie hamming it up onstage, Will Cooper loping down the street, Woolworths' candy counter. And what about my mother's cooking? Even though I'm mad at her, I would almost go back just to have Sunday roast beef.

I turn around to face the station doors, ready to go back inside, but before I take a step, a cat stalks up to me, arches her scruffy back, and brushes against my legs. She's a scrawny little thing with longish fur, white with a gray streak down her nose. *Meow*, she says, following it with a question mark. When I crouch down to pat her, she tries to climb up onto my knee. My first new friend. I take courage.

I know I have to walk north from the station to get to Jamie's apartment. I have the address written down and show it to a few people as I walk up Yonge Street. Straight up to College, they tell me, then go left for a bit, then right. There's a fierce wind blowing, so I keep my head down and walk quickly.

I can't avoid thinking about my parents. They won't even know I'm gone until I don't show up for dinner. Mother will pace the floor and bite on her thumbnail, first one then the other. Dad will become silent, move from window to window, frowning. They'll think I lied about the boyfriend. Will they phone the police? Yikes! I wonder what Tommy will think when he hears I've run away. Even more, I wonder what he'll think if my father makes the "enquiries" he was threatening. At least they'll find out I was telling the truth about the boyfriend.

Of course, they'll be sick with worry. And, of course, they'll phone the police. A search party will go out. I feel hollow and mean. What a stupid idea this was!

The cat stays with me, so I whisper to her along the way that she's a good pal, that we'll get where we're going soon, and that maybe things will work out. I'm sure she's a stray. Like me. Wrong, I'm an escapee. It's a long walk and I'm tired, but I can't stop to rest.

I find his apartment house without much difficulty, a narrow, boxlike place in need of a coat of paint. The front steps sag, and the railing wobbles. Not exactly a palace, but if Jamie can live here, so can I. I'll get used to it.

Getting used to things is what living is all about, I'm beginning to notice. I'm thinking about Jamie now. I'm pretty sure he must be over the anti-baby thing. He wrote a letter of apology to our parents for his behavior just before New Year's. It was a tad formal, but that's Jamie. Mother said she understands how he must feel, but that he'll get used to the idea. I don't think either of us will ever really get used to having a whiny baby around, but then we'll only be there on visits. I walk inside and knock on the door of apartment one.

An hour after I get into his place, Jamie appears. I hear his footsteps coming along the hall and then his key in the already unlocked door. Once inside, his jaw drops. Curled up with a cat in my lap, in his one comfortable chair, the radio blaring, I greet him with a big happy grin.

No answering smile. "What the heck?"

"I ran away from home."

"You can't do that."

"Well, I did, didn't I?"

"Come with me," he says. "You can use my landlady's phone to tell *your* parents where you are."

"Already did."

He doesn't hear me in his rush to go clattering down the stairs to the landlady's apartment.

"I called them already," I say, a few steps behind him.

"What?" He's knocking on the door of apartment one.

"When I asked your landlady to let me into your apartment, she made me phone home first."

Velda, the landlady, is expecting us and opens the door right away. Tall and broad-shouldered, with a bosom jutting like a shelf, she makes me think of the house she lives in. She's built like it, square and solid, although not the least bit shabby, with her shiny dress and dangly earrings. She takes one look at Jamie's stormy face and blurts, "Sister is very lovely girl. You be nice brother to her."

"Oh, she's lovely all right. She just ran away from home. Our parents will be frantic."

"She phone home. I hear it all."

Jamie scowls at me and asks, "What did they say?"

"That I'm thoughtless and irresponsible. They were really mad, shouting, even." Velda, my witness, nods in agreement. "But then they calmed down. Dad was home for lunch. He said he'd come and get me as soon as he felt all right about leaving Mother, and I said I wanted to stay with you, so he said, 'Okay, I'll come tomorrow, and we'll talk about this.'"

"What did Mother say?"

"That I'm a burden to her. That she's in a delicate condition; that I have no heart; that she hopes I packed warm clothes. Let's see, what else? That I'll be the death of her. That's about it."

"Well, well, ancient history, now," Velda says. "Come

back for dinner, bring sister. A big feast tonight, plenty of food for all. Come at six. I open very good wine. My niece, Opal, enjoy to come, too. 'You come meet a nice young man for a change,' I tell her."

"Okay, we can come." I don't even look at Jamie for confirmation. I'm hungry. "Thanks," I remember to say.

Back in his apartment, Jamie clutches his head as if he's trying to hold his brain in place. His usually neat hair stands on end, making him look hopelessly deranged. The cat occupies the chair as if she's its rightful owner. She looks at Jamie archly, licks a paw, scratches an ear, and settles in for a nap.

"Why is there a cat here?" he says.

"I don't know. She followed me from the station."

"It probably belongs to somebody."

"Of course she does. She belongs to me, but I'm giving her to you. My compliments. Her name is Rose."

"I don't want a cat." He turfs Rose out of the chair and sits down. The cat jumps back up to settle in his lap.

"See? She loves you."

Hands on the chair arms, refusing to touch the cat, Jamie says, in his most put-upon voice, "Okay, okay, now tell me what happened. Why did you leave home?"

"*Your* parents don't trust me. Ruthie thinks I have a boyfriend and wouldn't believe me when I said I didn't, so I made up a story that I was running away with him.

Mother overheard and wouldn't believe that I just made it up." This was very close to the truth, without being one hundred percent true. "So I got mad and yelled at them. I really needed you to be on my side, but you weren't there."

"I don't get it."

"And I'm going to fail all my exams because I missed so much school when I was sick."

"Maybe you're sick in the head."

"And," I take a big breath, "I want to escape from . . . some of the teachers, from the way they keep breathing down my neck. If I could live with you and go to school in Toronto, like my friend Hazel, my problems would disappear. As soon as Hazel moved in with her grandmother, hers did."

He keeps his scowl in place, but I watch him stroking the cat's soft coat and think that if he could just do that for a while, he'd agree.

"You can't escape problems, you know. You have to confront them. How did you get here?"

"The train. Paid for from my savings. And then I asked people for directions."

"You talked to total strangers?"

"No, idiot, first we introduced ourselves and exchanged life histories."

He grunts, not amused. "Well, what am I supposed to do with you, now that you're here? We could go to the museum, I guess."

"Nope. First things first. Get your coat, we're going shopping."

Jamie accompanies me reluctantly, first to a hardware store, then to a grocery store. I manage to fast-talk him into buying a litter box and sand and six cans of cat food. "In one end and out the other," I say.

"Do you think you could be a little less explicit?"

"Might as well face facts."

We lug the stuff back to his apartment, where Rose mews us a brief greeting before curling up again. "Look what we bought for you, Rose," I say, "a brand-new toilet."

She responds by licking her chest.

Even though I'm starving, I feel we have to do things right. After all, we're in the big city. "We can't turn up for dinner at Velda's too early," I say. "We have to wait until at least five after six, to be fashionably late."

"There's not a lot of fashion going on at Velda's," Jamie says.

But at one minute past six, my stomach roars, *Time to go.*

Velda does not disappoint in the food department. The aroma of garlic and onions that seeped into Jamie's apartment all afternoon now greets us in her large kitchen. I've never seen so much food all at one time, except at a church banquet.

"Are other people coming?" I ask, gazing at the dishes and platters heaped high.

"My niece comes, after work, maybe."

Even for four, there is too much—two whole chickens swimming in gravy, half a baked ham, sausages, a steaming casserole that looks unappetizing but smells wonderful, a mountain of boiled potatoes, three dishes of vegetables whose names I've never even heard before.

Velda booms out her exuberant laugh. "All for my young cavalier and his lady-sister." She pinches Jamie's cheek and gives his head a shake. "We fatten you up nice, just like the witch in fairy tale. Sit, sit! Cold food no use."

We sit at Velda's enormous kitchen table. She carves off a chicken leg and some breast meat for us and begins to fork slabs of ham onto both our plates.

"No, no," Jamie says, "I can't possibly eat that much."

"What? You think my cooking is no good? Huh! In the old country, friends know how to eat. Look at you, James. Look at your waist, tiny like a girl's."

He puts small amounts of vegetables onto his plate to accompany the meat, but Velda scoops on more. "Oh!" She reaches for a bottle of wine on the sideboard behind her. "Most important of all." She pours a healthy tumbler of red wine for Jamie. "Taste it," she says.

He takes a sip and nods. "Not bad." She's about to pour one for me, but he puts his hand over my glass. "She's too young."

"Piff-puff!" Velda blows the remark away. "It's harmless. A drink for babies in old country."

Jamie seems to find the wine easier to enjoy than the

dinner. Velda pours him another glass. When he isn't looking, I take a large gulp from his glass. It tastes like medicine.

Just then a young woman bustles in—Velda's niece.
She throws off her coat, drapes it on a chair, and sits down
at the table. She's beautiful, with red hair ornately piled
on top of her head. Her eyes are a heavenly blue, set off by
the longest, thickest eyelashes I've ever seen. Her name is
Opal. Jamie stands up to shake her hand and says, "James
McLaren. Pleased to make your acquaintance."

I stare hard at him, because what he says sounds like
Pleased to mash your potatoes.

Opal helps herself to gobs of meat, potatoes, vegetables— in short, everything edible—douses it all with
salt and pepper, and forks it down as if it's her personal
last supper. Velda pours more wine. It really is a delicious
meal, I think, as I take another slug of Jamie's wine. Velda
tells us more about the old country, about how her family
was rich until bad men robbed them of all their wealth. I
could listen to her stories all night.

"Where do you work, Opal?" Jamie asks.

She holds up her finger for him to wait. It takes her a
moment to swallow her mouthful. Velda answers for her.
"Like a nurse only different."

"In a hospital?"

"She works for private," Velda says.

"I was in a hospital," Jamie says.

"You are sick?" Velda asks.

"Nope, not anymore. I'm all better."

"He's been faith healed." I try to sound convincing.

They smile, surprised. Opal asks, "What did you have?"

"I was just down a pint or two of blood," he says, looking darkly at me. A warning. "But the doctor topped me up, and now I'm right as rain."

Velda and Opal drink to his continued good health. Jamie stands up, glass raised high. He thanks them and tries to toast their good health, but he loses his balance. Falling back into his chair, he says something like, "Words cannot express," and sits smiling, like a sultan in his harem. At least he refuses more wine.

We barely get finished the dessert pastries, when Jamie staggers to his feet and pulls back my chair. "Time we were going, Ladies. Delightful evening, but it's my sister's bedtime. Most enjoyable dinner."

I think he sounds pompous, but I guess it's the effect of the wine.

"What? So early?" Velda says. "Why not let sister stay with me? No problem, I keep an eye on her. You have no proper space up there. She can sleep in extra bed in my place, all cozy and nice."

Jamie says, "She can have my bed, and I'll sleep on the floor." He pushes me ahead of him out the door.

Velda stands in the doorway, folded arms propped on her shelf, shaking her head. "No, no, no! Bad for your health. Why did God give us beds, I ask? Not so we can sleep on floors." Opal appears beside her. Velda looks over her shoulder. "Or Opal will take her in."

"Nope," Opal says. "I'm a working girl. I need my beauty sleep."

Jamie is dragging me up the stairs by the arm. "Thanks, anyway. We'll be fine."

I twist around and call, "Thanks for dinner. It was really delicious!"

Inside his apartment, I complain loudly that he's being an obnoxious bore, that we could have stayed a little longer, that there was a plate of chocolate cake we didn't even get to. Rose meows, agreeing with me.

Jamie ignores us both. He hands me the bag I brought and hustles me into the bathroom to get ready for bed. His bedroom, initially an alcove in some earlier, grander part of the house's existence, has no door.

In my pajamas, now, I watch him throw back the covers, brush out a few toast crumbs, and grab one of the two pillows and the extra blanket from the foot of his bed. In a moment, I patter across and climb into bed. "Where are you going to sleep?"

"On the chair, if Rose will allow me."

I watch him turn out the main light and feel his way back to the chair. I can make out his silhouette slouched there, pillow behind his back, his legs stretched out in front. He flips the blanket over them.

In a few minutes, he says, "Are you asleep?"

"Yes."

"Why did you have to bring up that thing about being faith healed?"

"I don't know. Something to say."

"Well, it's nobody's business."

"I know. But I was just wondering something."

"What?" He sounds wary.

"Now that you're cured, why did you blame Mother for replacing you with a new baby?"

"Go to sleep, Rachel."

"I was just wondering."

He puts his head back and pretends to be asleep, snoring like a large motor in need of repairs. He slings his long legs over one arm of the chair. The next time I look, he's propped them on another chair. I watch the cat, on the prowl, leap onto his shoulder to purr in his ear and lick his stubbly cheek with her raspy tongue. Eventually my busy day catches up to me, and I sleep.

I awake to spring sunlight and my brother softly snoring. He has moved in beside me on top of the blanket and is curled up like a snail. A moment later, he's awake and staring into my eyes as if he can't remember who I am.

I say, "Doesn't this remind you of when I was little and used to cry in the night when I had a bad dream and you came and lay down beside me and told me nursery rhymes to make them go away? Tell me one."

"Don't be ridiculous."

"Come on."

After a moment, he says, "The only one I can think of is 'Humpty Dumpty sat on a wall. Humpty Dumpty had a great fall . . .'"

I sit up. "Don't say that one. I hate it!"

"What's wrong with it?"

"He dies!"

"For Pete's sake, he's just an egg. C'mon, get up. We'll go out somewhere to have breakfast. You can have a dead egg."

The coffee tastes like wet sawdust, and my leathery fried eggs have been dead for weeks. I watch Jamie nibbling on toast as if he's trying to avoid swallowing. My spirits are so low, they drag on the floor. I will soon have to face my father. I don't want to go back home. Leaning on my elbows, I say, "I need to talk to you about something important."

"I'm all ears."

"I want to come and live here with you. I mean, I can go to school here as easily as in Middleborough. You could find a nicer place, big enough for two."

"Don't be insane."

"Look, school is awful. If I could move in with you and go to a different one, I could escape."

"Escape from what?"

"I don't mean escape. I just need a breather, a chance to think about the way my life is going."

"It *is* about some boy, isn't it?"

"More or less."

"Don't do it."

"Don't do what?"

"Whatever temptation is causing your problems with schoolwork, don't give in. Don't do it."

I want to tell him how I feel about Mr. Tompkins, but the disturbed look on his face changes my mind. He'd be shocked. He wouldn't understand. Even I don't understand how I can be both attracted and repelled by the same person. I long for Tommy, day and night, and hate myself for it, day and night. I need out.

"We'd better go back. Dad will be here to pick you up pretty soon."

"I know, but why can't I stay with you?"

"Because you need someone to keep a close eye on you, to guide you, and I can't always do that. Mother and Dad have to do that."

"Mother and Dad are in a world of their own, with no idea what it's like to be me. All they think about is their future little bundle of joy. I want to move out. If I stay at home, I'll end up as a convenient babysitter." I let out a

big anguished sigh. "I hate my life so much. I wish everything could go back to the way it was."

He puts down his half-drunk coffee and gazes sadly out
the window. "Wouldn't that be nice!" He pays the bill and
we leave.

The sun does its best to warm us in spite of a raw spring
wind as we trudge back to the apartment.

"Maybe it will be born dead," Jamie says.

Shocked, I pull him to a halt. "That's a horrible thing
to say."

"I'm a horrible guy."

"Is that what you hope, that the baby dies?"

He strides ahead, and I have to run to catch up. "No,
it's not what I hope."

Dad's car is in front of Velda's house. Inside Jamie's apartment, he stands looking out the window at the sad backyard, with its overflowing garbage cans, motorcycle parts, washtub heaped with what looks like the rest of the motorcycle, and clothesline on which hang ladies' fancy and colorful undergarments. He turns and shakes his head at us, with a deep sigh of disappointment.

"Rachel, why did you do this to your mother?"

I stoop to pick up the cat. "I didn't do anything to anybody. I needed to talk to Jamie. You may not have noticed, but he doesn't have a telephone."

He frowns at Jamie. "Why don't you simply have a phone installed? They're not that expensive."

"I don't want to."

One arm propping the other, Dad presses his fingers into

his forehead. "Could you turn a light on in here? It's dark."

Jamie flicks the light switch. "Would you like to sit down?" He indicates the one comfortable chair now covered with cat hairs. Dad doesn't seem to notice them and sits, willingly enough. I spoon cat food into a dish for Rose. Jamie perches on a rickety wooden stool.

Dad looks as if he's about to say something but, instead, shakes his head. After a moment, he says, "It's pretty hard, you know. These are difficult times."

"Yes," Jamie says.

"Sometimes it's hard to know what to do."

Jamie says, "Yes." There is another stretch of silence. Then Jamie says, "Rachel says she was just kidding about running away with some boy. She wants you to trust her."

Dad nods sadly. "Perhaps I was being a little overly protective."

"A little!" I say. "You were threatening to make my whole life unbearable."

"I'm sorry." He leans over his knees, head in his hands.

"You can't go snooping around, quizzing my friends and the teachers."

Jamie makes that throat-clearing sound that Granny does, when it's time for someone to step in and change the general mood. "Don't rub it in, Rachel. Dad's sorry. Isn't that enough?"

Dad sits back, leaning his head against the chair-back, and gives me a weary look.

I keep it up. "It's spying, that's what it is. You might as well lock me in my room and throw away the key." I stand directly in front of him so I can burn him with the heat of my anger.

"Rachel, what else can I say? Your mother and I have a lot on our minds right now."

I realize it's over. Fathers don't apologize, usually. I'm used to a world where fathers know everything, and daughters just accept it. "Okay," I say. He nods.

Nobody can think of what to say next. Rose prowls back and forth, flicking her tail across my ankles. I scoop her up and plunk her in Dad's lap. "This is Jamie's cat. How do you like her?"

Tentatively, he pats her, but she jumps down, preferring to keep contact with my ankles. "I didn't know you had a cat, son."

"Neither did I until *your* daughter introduced us." The atmosphere is lighter now, by several degrees.

Dad stands up. "Well, Rachel, you'd better gather your belongings. I don't like to leave your mother for too long."

I consider rebelling but decide that, if Jamie won't take me in, there isn't much point. While I throw my few items back into my bag, I hear Dad ask Jamie how university life suits him.

"A bit tiring."

"Are you feeling all right, son?"

"Yes, I'm fine."

"You look rather pale." I watch him peer closely, as if he'd like to study Jamie under a microscope. For the first time since I arrived on his doorstep, I notice how haggard Jamie looks, as if he's been off somewhere, fighting a war. And losing.

At home again, life does not change dramatically. I study, write my spring term exams, and actually pass them. My brain must be like a dark little attic. Lots of stuff in it, but you can't tell what's there until you pull the string on the lightbulb. Somehow it got pulled, just in time.

Mother is about the same, except that she keeps asking me if I'm hungry or warm enough or tired.

A letter arrives for Jamie, with "Please forward" on the envelope. As I'm hunting in Dad's desk for a bigger envelope to put it in, to readdress it, the phone rings. Dad hurries along the hall to answer it.

"Yes, Doctor Latham," I hear him say. "Yes, I see. Yes, by all means." It isn't a lengthy call, but I can barely contain my curiosity.

"They'd like to try blood transfusions, again," is all Dad says. "Get Jamie back into remission. He's agreed to go into hospital."

"Has something happened?" Mother asks.

"I don't know. I think this is what occurs from time to time."

I feel an instant chill. Upstairs, sitting at my desk, wrapped in a blanket, I stare at my math homework, believing I'm solving problems. I could be working in Egyptian hieroglyphics, for all I know.

Jamie's stay in the Toronto hospital is longer this time or, at least, seems longer. He phones us, from time to time, to bemoan the fact that he's missing so many classes.

The following Sunday, a bleak day that threatens rain, we drive to Toronto to visit him. I am first through his door.

"What's the occasion?" he says. He quickly puts a stack of handwritten papers he's been leafing through into the top drawer of his bedside table.

Mother and Dad fill the doorway. He says, "My whole family! I must be about to croak." I grimace. Has the faith-healing myth worn off?

Mother looks pained when he says that. She leans over to kiss him, her swollen belly pressing against his chest, making it hard for him to breathe. He could be asphyxiated right now, I think, killed by his unborn sibling.

"We brought you a treat," Mother says. She hands him a box of Laura Secord chocolates. He opens the box and passes it around. Mother declines, but whispers, "Save some to offer the nurses. They're always so nice to you."

"Where's Rose?" I ask.

"Velda's looking after her."

Mother busies herself folding Jamie's bathrobe and

stacking newspapers in a neat pile. "Who?" she asks. I translate for her, even though I've already told her about the cat.

Jamie and Dad talk about the work he's missed and about his final exams. "They've got to let me out in time to write them. I wish I had my books. I need to study."

"Don't push yourself too hard," Dad says. "They might give you your year, based on your marks to date."

"I don't want to take that chance. I want to make sure I get back in, next fall."

"I think you should talk to your professors or the dean and tell them about your situation," Mother says.

Jamie closes his eyes. "What exactly is the *situation* I'm supposed to tell them about?" He opens them. "That I am burdened with a cat named Rose? That I might be dead by next fall? That my mother is busy baking another little gingerbread man to take my place?"

I stop breathing. Both parents look as if they're being sucked backwards, into an abyss. Their faces are bloodless. How can someone as sensitive as Jamie be so heartless? He suddenly puts his fist to his mouth and bites down hard on his knuckle, as if he thinks physical pain will wipe out the emotional pain he's inflicting on all of us, but on Mother most of all. My brother, the jerk.

It's as though I can see myself, in slow motion, pick up the glass of water from beside his bed. In quick-time, now, I throw its contents in his face. He looks as shocked as if

I've turned a fire hose on him. He wipes the water from his eyes with the sleeve of his pajamas.

Mother's hands cover her face, but tears escape down her cheeks, anyway. Dad puts his arm around her and helps her out of the room. Comforting her, he takes out his washed and ironed hankie and wipes her tears. Then he rubs a knuckle past the corner of his own eye as they head down the hall toward the waiting room.

While I'm deciding whether to stay and say something to Jamie or leave with Mother and Dad, he says, "Go. I need to be alone. The world will be well rid of the likes of me."

We fumble our way out of the hospital, like three blind mice, turning this way and that, until we find the right door. A different kind of family might stay, go back, ask for an explanation, an apology, comfort. We don't seem to know how to be that kind of family. There doesn't seem much point in staying.

Mother stops crying and looks through the rain-spotted side window of the car. Through the windshield, the view is of gray streets lined with ghostly trees and colorless buildings, half-hidden in a weeping fog that the wipers can't obliterate.

On the seat beside me lies an envelope addressed to James McLaren. "Cripes!" I say. Mother doesn't even flinch at the word, deafened either by the drumming rain or her grief. "Dad, stop the car! We have to go back."

"We're not going back."

"I forgot to give Jamie the letter."

"What letter?"

"Somebody sent him a letter with 'Please forward' on it. I brought it to give to him, only I forgot. I want to go back."

Dad wheels into a side street and pulls up to the curb. He looks at Mother, whose expression gives away nothing. "What do you think, Dora, should we go back?"

"I don't care."

We sit together in silence for a moment. "Please, Dad." I wave the letter at him. He turns in the driveway of an apartment building and heads back the way we came. The rain is coming down steadily, now, as he pulls in close to the entrance.

"In you go," he says. "I don't think your mother wants to get out in this downpour." He looks at Mother, who is busy studying the path of raindrops down the windshield. "And come right back. Don't dillydally."

When I get to Jamie's floor, I go straight to his room. The door is closed, so I knock. I can hear voices, none of them Jamie's. I open the door and peek in.

A nurse catches sight of me and quickly slips through, closing the door behind her. "James can't have visitors just now," she says.

"Why not?"

"He's lost a bit of blood, and we're . . . involved with treatments."

"Did he cut himself?"

"No, nothing like that. A nosebleed. A rather severe one."

Fear presses heavily on my chest, making it hard for me to breathe. "Well, is he all right? He's my brother, you know. Can't I even see him? I have a letter for him."

"I'm sorry. He can't have visitors just now. I'll see that he gets the letter, once he's feeling better." She holds out her hand. Reluctantly, I put the letter into it.

"But what about my parents? Shouldn't they see him?"

"No need. He's going to be fine." When the nurse opens the door to go back in, I crane my neck to see what's going on, but she shuts it too quickly.

I trudge back down the stairs, not bothering with the elevator. The big question is, should I tell my parents about the nosebleed or not? Not. But then, surely they have a right to know. Tell. They will worry. Tell them tomorrow, once they've calmed down. And that's my final decision. Possibly.

CHAPTER

20

Letters not sent.

Rachel, oh, Rachel. My one ally! And you dumped water on me. If I stop clenching my teeth and my fists, I will drown in tears. I will howl. I'm not sure what the date is today, but some days have gone by since that awful one. I tried to catch up to you and Mother and Dad after you left. I got out of the stupid bed and struggled into my bathrobe. My arms got stuck in the sleeves because I was trying to hurry. Hunted for my slippers. Found them. The more I hurried, the slower I got. I wanted to apologize. Needed to apologize.

These letters are supposed to be about the war, and here I am writing about wanting to tell my mother that I didn't mean it, that I love her, no matter what. I've never had this kind of remorse before. Right now I feel as if my whole life is a battleground, so I guess I'm justified in writing about this.

By the time I got to the waiting room, it was empty, and you were not at the elevators, so I went down the stairs thinking it would be faster, all the time planning what I would say and whether I had to actually tell Mother I loved her because wouldn't she sort of already know? Do people actually go around saying "I love you" to their mothers? Probably not Coop.

Right now, though, as I write, I can't help thinking about the war and about this guy Visser, lying there bleeding all over the ground after the Allies bombed us, guts spilled out everywhere, calling for his mother. He would have told her. I'm sure of it.

I had to rest against the stair railing until my heart rate slowed down, even though I had one more flight to go. And then I got thinking about Dad. I mean, I love him, too. It goes without saying, doesn't it? But I can hardly put my arms around my father and tell him I love him. He'd think I was daft. I thought maybe I would put one arm around him, the way I did when I got home from the war. But the words "I love you"?

I wondered if there might be some other more
manly expression. These were my thoughts as I
rushed down to the main floor and looked around.
But you'd gone.

   I looked through the glass in the doors that
lead to the parking lot and thought I saw Dad's
car backing out of a parking space. I went outside and waved and called, but the wind carried my
voice up into the trees, and I just stood there,
in the rain, under a sky the color of gun barrels.

   I saw you drive away. I saw your faces looking forward to what lay ahead. All my energy
seeped from my muscles, then, and the fog somehow drifted into my brain. I even wished someone
would come along and carry me back up to bed.
I wished I could curl up under the covers and
cease to exist.

   The wind was blowing hard, and I had to strug-
gle with the heavy door. Luckily someone coming
out opened it for me. I waited for the elevator,
like everyone else. I squeezed on board, like
everyone else. Glancing at the others, I knew
that no matter how hard I tried to imitate them,
I was doomed to fail. I know I'm a loner, more
so since the war, since Coop dropped bombs on
me and then went missing in action. It occurred
to me that I spend a lot of time trying to not

share my life with anybody. Well, except for you, I guess.

I noticed people staring at me, openmouthed. I put my hand to my face and brought it away covered in blood. I tried to soak it up with my sleeve, but blood kept pouring from my nose. Someone said, "Oh, God, let me out of here!" It was the last thing I remember hearing before sliding to the floor of the elevator, bleeding all over people's shoes.

At home again, life drones on. It's mostly rainy and windy, but March is on its way out. There is a flurry of excitement when, a few days after our disastrous visit, Jamie phones to apologize. There are tears and handkerchiefs and what amounts to verbal shoulder pattings on the phone. There is a certain amount of gruff harrumphing from Dad and various sounds of forgiveness from Mother. Afterwards, Mother goes upstairs to lie down, and Dad goes back to work.

Granny has heard the entire story. "A sound spanking might have worked wonders on that lad," she says.

But I need more than his apology. I want to sneak off and visit him again, to find out the true state of his mind. I long to know if he still believes he's been cured by the faith healer. And, I confess, I'm dying to find out who his letter is from.

As it turns out, I don't have to sneak off. School is closed for a teachers' conference on Friday, and Dad has to go to a meeting of pharmacists in Toronto. I'm going with him. Mother has a bundle of freshly laundered clothes for us to take to Jamie.

After a brief visit, Dad leaves for his meeting, giving me two whole hours with Jamie. He looks much better. There's pink in his cheeks and life in his eyes. His hair is a little shaggy.

"Want me to cut your hair for you?" I ask helpfully.

He shrinks back and swipes it out it out of his eyes. "Get away from my head!"

"So who was your letter from?"

He rolls his eyes and calls me nosy, but, finally, he gives in, almost proudly. "They didn't give it to me until yesterday. When I saw the handwriting on the inside envelope, I yelled right out loud. They thought I was having a relapse and started fluttering around, trying to calm me down. They even threatened me with a needle. Look," he says, "I'll show you the envelope."

I guess I didn't pay much attention to the handwriting when it came, but looking at it now makes me shiver. "Huh?" I say. "Wait a minute. Is that from Coop?" I remember the way Coop tended to swoop the tail end of the last letter up to cross a *t* or dot an *i*. And there it is. I make a grab for it, to see it up close, but Jamie pulls it back.

"I was sure it was," he says. "I could just see him in my mind, the way he used to write something and then scratch it out and bite the end of his pen while he tried to think of a better word. I had to really concentrate before it sank in that the letter was from Coop's sister Ellie."

"But she writes just like Coop."

"She must have copied his style."

"Doubt it. More likely he copied hers. What does she have to say?"

"Not much. She's in training to be a nurse at the Hospital for Sick Children, here in Toronto. She wonders if we could have coffee on her day off, usually a Thursday. She's a bit homesick. She gave me her address and phone number."

"So, are you going to?"

"Probably. I've written back. It will be nice to have someone not related to me to think about."

This sounds insulting, but I let it pass. "When are they going to let you out of this joint?"

"Soon. I can't wait to close the door on this place of needles and blood. Can't wait to get back to my apartment and crack the books again. I'm even looking forward to communing with old Rose and being covered with cat hairs. And I'm going to see about trying my exams, later. You know, I'm positive that, in spite of this latest relapse, the faith healer's shake-up that night in the tent must have worked. I feel tip-top right now." He lies back against his pillows, beaming. And I beam along with him. And then there's a brisk *rat-a-tat-tat* on his door.

I frown at the intrusion, as Velda's head appears around the door, followed by the hefty rest of her. "So," she says, swinging her purse back and forth at her side, as if she needs to be in perpetual motion, "I find you, at last, after I worry myself sick. Lucky thing I scribble down your papa's phone number."

"Is there something wrong with Rose?" Jamie asks.

"Oosh!" she says, fluttering her hand as if brushing away a fly. "You have no idea."

"What happened?"

She looks so hot and flustered that I motion her into the chair, while I lean against the window. "What happened, you ask? What happened with you, my friend? One little note to say you go away for some days, please look after cat. I look after that cat like she's my baby, and the thanks I get? She throws up on my good carpet, straight from Turkey, very high-class. Carpet, not cat."

"I'm sorry, Velda. Poor old Rose. I'll make it up to you. Get the carpet cleaned, and I'll pay for it."

"That's a small matter. The large matter is, no more house. Sold to a developer to build fancy new apartments. No more job for me."

"I thought you owned the building."

"No. Only hired to look after it."

Jamie's only comment is, "Hmm."

"What! You say nothing? 'Hum' is all you know? I feed you, care for your cat, treat you like the Lord God, and you say 'hum' only?"

"I'm sorry, Velda," Jamie says. "It must be a blow. What will you do?"

"What can I do? My son in Edmonton might love to have me visit, maybe stay. His wife, maybe not. She acts too good to walk on the same street with me."

"So, what about my apartment, my lease?"

"Now is the time for hum. Now we shrug shoulders. Talk to the owners. Look for a new place."

"But I need time to study."

"Hmm!" she says, now. She shrugs her shoulders.

After she's gone, Jamie says, "I'll get my stuff home on the train. I can study at home and go back for the exams."

"Dad can come for you in the car. Don't forget there's Rose."

"I'll bring her with me on the train."

"But, she's a cat."

"Oh. I hadn't noticed."

"But . . ."

"No buts. And no butting in. Let me handle this my own way." He signals me to zipper my mouth, so I do.

My brother loves school. I do not. Physically, being at school is fine. It means I can escape the sounds of worry at home, an unceasing drone in my head that makes concentrating difficult.

The drama club keeps me going, even though the principal has vetoed *The Doll's House*. Too long and difficult, he says, and we're too late getting started. It's already the beginning of April, nearly Easter.

"Have a look at this," Mr. Tompkins says. The play is a lighthearted comedy called *Rabbit Stew*. He passes out mimeographed copies. Nearly all the members of the drama club get a chuckle out of it as they read it. It's a silly, slapstick piece, and I despise it. Not a dramatic heartbeat in its entire ninety minutes.

As everyone heads for home, I gather up the copies to hand back to Mr. Tompkins. "My offer to be your acting coach still stands," he says, "if you want to play the lead."

"No, thank you," I mumble. It's all I can do to keep from shuddering at the nightmare thought of ever going on stage again. Acting in a play I have no respect for would make it even worse.

I must be looking distressed because Mr. Tompkins beckons me to a rickety chair backstage. Sitting opposite me on a stool, he says, "You don't seem to be yourself, Rachel." He reaches over and touches my shoulder. "I know you're worried about your brother. We could set up some counseling sessions for you, if you like. One on one. Just you and me. It would give you a chance to talk about your feelings."

"My feelings?" I have a momentary, fuzzy memory of a puzzling expression I once saw on Hazel Carrington's face, when Tommy reminded her of a lunchtime meeting they were to have. I wasn't sure what it was about, but I think, now, it must have been the counseling sessions Ruthie told me about. Hazel's look was respectful enough, but it seemed tinged with panic.

He smiles at me in such a gentle way, though, I can't imagine why Hazel would be afraid. Kindness shows in his eyes. It's the way they droop at the outer corners, helplessly, boyishly. He's the closest thing to an ideal lover I can imagine. Better than anything I could even dream. I wish I could see inside his mind. I wonder what he thinks of me. . . .

He shoots his wrist out of his cuff to look at his watch. "We can discuss this later, if you like," he says. "I have a meeting. Just tell me when you'd like to start."

Bones of his wrist. Black hairs. I could press my lips against them.

"Start?" *Start what?*

"The counseling sessions. If you won't let me teach you some acting skills, at least let me help you with your personal life. Are you okay with that?"

I want to say, *Oh, sure, anytime.* Instead, I say, "I think I'm okay for the time being." *Now, why would I do that? Maybe I don't trust myself.*

He gives me a sorrowful look, as if his heart is breaking,

but nods. He reaches out and pats my shoulder. He slides his hand down my arm, in a comforting way, and squeezes my hand. But, I don't feel comforted. I feel like throwing myself into his arms. He hurries away, and I slowly pick up my books.

Walking home from school by myself, I count dandelions, which are beginning to dot the lawns. Thunder in the distance threatens an immediate April shower.

Ruthie is still in the drama club, but she's started hanging around with an older crowd, now. "Come on, join in," she says. "The stuff they talk about! I tell you! Quite the education!"

"What?" I ask. "The crooked seams in their nylon stockings? Their next Toni Home Permanent?"

"Much more. You'd be amazed how far they go with their boyfriends. It's an education."

Maybe I *should* join in. I could use a little advanced education.

Next day, Mr. Tompkins stops me in the hall. "Would you consider helping me direct the play?" He catches me off guard. I just assumed I would do makeup again and prompt.

"Help direct?" I'm not sure whether to take him seriously.

"Be assistant director, in other words."

I'm flattered all over again. The play is not that bad. I didn't actually gag when I read it a second time. It's lighthearted fun, I tell myself. Not everything needs to be a matter of life, death, and passionate love.

"Yes," I say, "I would love to."

We choose the cast quickly and start rehearsing. We want to stage the play at the beginning of June. Ruthie has the lead, partly because of my casting advice, but also because she's becoming a convincing actress. The busier she becomes with the play, the more she drifts away from the older girls. Once again, we walk home together after rehearsal.

"You know, you were right," Ruthie says to me one day. "You have to get inside your character's skin and feel what she's feeling."

"Did I say that?" We're dawdling along, although I know I should be hurrying home. Granny has moved in with us to help out, and I'm supposed to be helping her.

"You said something like it. Or maybe I was the one who said it. Anyway, it works. I'm getting pretty good at acting, don't you think?"

I assume Ruthie is gloating and decide not to comment. A split second later, I see our positions reversed. If I had an acting role, I would definitely want a pat on the back. As if by magic, I'm inside Ruthie's skin. Heartily, I say, "Yup, you really are!"

"I thought so. I keep dreaming about Hollywood, real honest-to-god, sound-asleep dreams. I think that means something, don't you? I mean, I think I should seriously consider acting as a career, when I finish school."

The inside of Ruthie's skin is beginning to feel a bit tight and itchy. But, as a good friend should, I let her warble on. My mind wanders to the way Tommy's eyes crinkle when he smiles and his rich, deep voice when he speaks my name. We part at our usual corner, and very quickly, I'm back inside my own skin.

Tommy often asks me to stay after rehearsal, in the empty auditorium, to discuss certain scenes and what props we need. Once he put his arm across my shoulders. "You're an excellent assistant, you know." The heat of his arm seared through my sweater, and the sensation stayed with me for the rest of the day and on into the night.

Will Cooper sometimes comes after rehearsal to talk about sets. He and one of his friends volunteered to build a fence as well as something to look like the back porch of a house. I have to admit I resent the intrusion. I don't feel as special, as sought out, as I do when I'm alone with Tommy. When Will stays, all three of us leave together, and Will insists on walking me partway home. "How's Jamie?" he often asks. "When's he coming home?"

"Soon. He has to move out of his apartment, so he's going to come home to study and then go back to write his exams. I guess he'll stay with one of his classmates when he goes back."

It's early May, three weeks before the play goes on. My mother is about the size of an elephant, but the baby still isn't ready to be born. It's waiting in the wings, waiting for its cue to step out onto the stage.

Late one afternoon, long after everyone else has left the auditorium, Tommy and I are hashing out how to allow Ruthie's character to slam the back porch door without the entire wall quaking and threatening to fall. Will is supposed to be with us, but he's at home, sick with a cold. What we need to do is get stronger bracing behind the wall, but the space is so narrow that it poses a problem.

"This will be difficult," Tommy says.

"Don't worry. When Will gets back, he'll figure it out. He's good at solving problems."

Tommy looks at me with narrowed eyes. "Yes, I guess he is. What kind of problems do you talk about when he walks you home?"

"My brother, mostly." Tommy smiles, in his understanding way, and starts turning out the stage lights. It's very late. I know I should head home to help Granny get dinner ready.

We turn out the rest of the lights and make our way to the main door of the auditorium. In the near darkness, I stumble against a chair. Mr. Tompkins says whoops and grabs my arm to keep me from falling. He holds it gently, tucking me close to him, until we reach the door.

"You know, I really appreciate your help with this play. It's a tricky one, but it's going pretty well, don't you think?" He is groping for the door handle, but not finding it.

I feel so faint, being this close to him, I can't even answer. It's as if I'm in a dream, or maybe a play, a love story. He bends his head over me, and almost automatically, my face goes up to meet his. Shatteringly, the lights go on.

"Oh," says the janitor, from the stage. "Thought you'd all gone home."

"We're just leaving," Mr. Tompkins says. He opens the door and ushers me out, ahead of him. In the corridor, there are other people—teachers.

"Tompkins," someone says. "You missed the meeting."

Mr. Tompkins slams his hand against his forehead. "This blasted play completely knocked it out of my head. You'll have to fill me in." He catches up to the other teachers without so much as a glance in my direction.

Inside me, something bigger than a balloon deflates. Something the size of a heart shatters.

Walking home alone, the sun sinking behind indigo clouds, I know what I need. I have to know exactly where I stand with Tommy and how much, if anything, I mean to him. I need to see him alone, without fear of being disturbed. *Yeah, sure.* Nothing like asking for the impossible.

CHAPTER

21

Early the next evening, I hear a car door slam in front of our house. When I look out, there's Jamie and a taxi driver, hauling cardboard cartons of books from the taxi and depositing them on the front steps. I'm outside to help, in a flash. No chance to hug him because he says, "Hey, kiddo, grab a box."

We finish just as the front door opens cautiously, revealing Mother's startled eyes, peering into the dusk. "Jamie?" The overhead light goes on, and Dad appears behind her. "It's Jamie," she says, with more relief than surprise. "Your father and I have been frantic with worry!"

I can tell by the way Jamie clenches and unclenches his jaw that he's trying to prevent her getting on his nerves, even before he walks into the house. He greets her lightheartedly. "Hi, Mother." Soon Granny's there, too. Mother tries to put her arms around him, but her girth gets in the way.

"We put in a long-distance call to Velda's," she says, "but the phone has been disconnected. We've been just frantic."

Ignoring her, he hands a box to Dad, who sets it down in the front hall. I rush around checking the boxes. "What about Rose? Where is she?"

"She escaped."

"You didn't bring her?"

"Of course I brought her. Somehow she got out of her carton in the baggage car and disappeared."

"We can't just leave her there," I say. "I'm going down to the station. Did you even look for her? Did you call her?"

"She's not a dog."

"What's that got to do with it? I'm sure she knows her name. I'm going to look for her."

"You're not going to walk all the way to the station at this hour of the night," my mother says.

"I'll drive her," Granny says.

"Mother," Dad says to Granny, "stop courting martyr-dom. I'll drive her."

Jamie: "I'll drive her, for Pete's sake."

Mother: "You'll do no such thing. You're not well enough."

Jamie: "Pass me the keys, Dad."

"Oh, dear." Mother frowns, putting a hand on her abdomen. "Oh, dear." With a look of panic, Dad leads her indoors.

"Get in the truck, Rachel," Granny says. "I'm driving."

She goes into the house to fetch her keys, quite happily leaving Dad to deal with his wife's *oh, dears*, not to mention the sea of boxes and pieces of luggage in the front hall. She backs out of the driveway, at high speed, with Jamie and me squashed in beside her. "All this fuss over a stray cat!" she says.

"Turn on your headlights, Granny," Jamie says.

"Aren't they on?"

"She's not a stray. She's Jamie's pride and joy."

"Cripes, Granny. That was a stop sign."

"Fuss, fuss, fuss! There was no one coming."

We drive along peacefully for a time, in relative safety, until Jamie speaks as if he's just thought of something. But, clearly, it's been on his mind for a while. "Granny, I was wondering if you'd mind if I moved out to the farm. I could keep an eye on things while you're staying here."

I answer for her, with a firm "No, you may not!"

"Did I ask you?"

"We need you at home." My voice sounds bossy, even to me. One of my worst fears: I'm turning into my mother.

"Well, dear," Granny says calmly, now that we've turned onto Station Street and there are no more stop signs to miss. "I'd like to be able to let you do that, but I've got a young couple living there right now. They're renting for the time being, but I think they'll likely want to buy the farm come fall. And it's time I sold. I'm either too old or too lazy to run the place the way I used to. I can't decide which."

Jamie peers past me to clearly see her face. "You can't just sell the farm, Granny. You need that place. And I need that place. It's part of all of us."

I know what he means. I felt the same way, when she first told us she was renting it. We used to go with Dad, almost every summer weekend of our childhood, to help with the chores.

"It would be like an amputation to sell the farm to some stranger," he says, his voice catching. He turns his head away. In a quieter voice, he says, "I thought it would be a good place for me to get my strength back to normal."

"I'm sorry, love. The opportunity arose, and I took it."

"So, who's living there, now?"

"Prepare yourself," I say.

"It's that old girlfriend of yours, Mary Foley. Armstrong, she is now—a good Protestant name, not one her mother approves of, though, apparently."

"Mary Foley got married?"

"Had to," I pipe up.

"What do you mean, she had to? As in, actually, you know, had to?"

"Precisely," I say. "Not as if she could hide it in this town."

"To Roy Armstrong?"

"Well, I don't hold it against them," Granny says. "He's a hard worker. If they're going to have babies anyway, they might as well get a good start on it and not wait until they're on the verge of old age." She gives a little cough and clears her throat. No one feels like commenting.

Jamie's quiet. I wonder if he's jealous. After all, Roy Armstrong succeeded where he failed. "Well," he growls, "got to hand it to old Roy. I don't know how he managed to get past the Blessed Mother, both blessed mothers."

After a minute, Granny says, "Mrs. Pool over on Maple Avenue is wanting to let the upstairs of her house come fall, and I think I'll take her up on it. I've no need of a big house anymore. I can rattle my bones around a small place just as easily."

"Why don't you just stay on living with us?" I ask.

"Oh, I'll stay long enough to wear out my welcome. Your mother'll be worn to a frazzle with the new baby, so I'll help out there. As long as I'm needed, I'll stick around. But, the minute I become irrelevant, that's the minute it's time to go."

"Don't say that, Granny," Jamie says.

"We'll always need you," I say.

"When I'm a useless, toothless, mindless old hag, you'll be saying, *Off to the bone yard with her*."

"We will not. Don't talk like that. You're scaring me."

It is no easy matter to extricate the cat from the baggage car. We get to the station a mere ten minutes before the train is to leave. Destination: Montreal. My winning ways and my threats of suicide if the stationmaster doesn't let me into the baggage car save the day. I call Rose gently, persuasively, and at last lure her to me, gathering her in my arms as best I can. Stiff-legged, claws out, Rose is not yet ready to let down her guard. Quickly, I hand her over to Jamie, loose cat hair flying, and she snuggles right into his chest, purring.

"Hmmph!" I say.

"Well," Jamie says, "well, now." He sounds like Dad. "I think she kind of likes me."

Our cat-rescuing party returns to find an empty house and a note on the kitchen table from Dad: "We are going to the hospital. Dora thinks the baby is on its way. I'll get back when I can."

"This can't be good," Granny says. "The baby's not due for another two weeks." Jamie's eyes meet mine. We are both remembering what Jamie said as we were walking away from the breakfast restaurant in Toronto.

Rose sets off on a sightseeing roam around the house. "Put her sandbox somewhere and show it to her," Granny says. "If that cat moves its bowels on my bed, someone's head will roll. I mean it."

Dad arrives just as we're all thinking of heading for bed. "False alarm," he says. "However, they want to keep Dora there to monitor her."

"That will be hard on her," Granny says, "with Jamie just arrived and the, ah, joy of having a cat in the house."

"The baby could come anytime, they think, so they talked her into staying." He beams a smile at each of us as if he wants approval. It looks a bit forced to me. Jamie probably thinks he looks sheepish. Granny's eyes are full of pity. She probably sees a man at his wit's end.

It strikes me, suddenly, that Dad has a lot of gray in his hair and deep lines in his face. *Looks almost old enough to be a grandfather,* I think. He turns off the downstairs lights, and we all troop up to bed. Granny moves spryly on ahead, to get into and out of the bathroom before there's a lineup.

Glancing into my parents' bedroom before I go into my own, I can't help thinking about the bassinet, sitting on the cedar chest, at the foot of their bed. It looks pretty small. Judging by the size of Mother, the baby's going to be a great lump of a thing. It'll never fit in that flimsy affair. The old crib, once Jamie's and then mine, is in pieces, leaning against the wall in the upstairs hall. Waiting. No room at the inn, for the time being. Granny has the guest room and is here to stay for the foreseeable future. And neither Jamie nor I intend to share our rooms. Why should we? We both feel the same way about this small intruder. Some new kid who'll try to take over.

I hear Jamie sneeze and hope he isn't catching a cold.

The next morning at breakfast, Granny says, "I don't like the sound of your voice, James McLaren. Are you coming down with a cold?"

"Nope."

When I get home from school, Jamie is just getting up from a long afternoon nap. He comes out of his room, still rubbing his eyes. "I had the weirdest dream," he says. He follows me into my room while I dump my armload of books on my desk.

"About what?"

"The war, my usual dream source. I could actually hear the enemy's artillery. I could feel the shock waves as bombs burst, and I thought I saw spectacular fireworks as planes fell spinning from the sky. I even dreamt about Herman Visser's mother, for some reason. She was making her way among the dead and the dying, buttoning their coats, winding scarves around their necks, pulling on mittens. Crazy stuff. And she was wearing a coat with fox furs around the collar, whose heads were alive. Their pointy jaws kept snapping at me. I was lying in the mud beside Herman, who was dying, and I couldn't help thinking that I was dying, too. I kept trying to open my eyes, but I couldn't."

"What a nightmare! Don't think about it anymore. Do you want me to recite nursery rhymes for you to help you get over it?"

"Don't worry. I'm over it." He still sounds a little hoarse, but he looks fine. His cheeks are pink.

At dinner, Granny says, "We'll just leave the dishes until later, and we'll all go and visit your mother in the maternity ward."

"Sorry," I say. "I have too much homework. Can't possibly go."

But Granny says, "If you insist upon staying late after school, then your homework has to be put off until later, too. Those are the consequences. Your mother must be lonesome in the hospital waiting for the baby. We will all go and make sure she's comfortable."

"And how am I supposed to study for exams?"

"By letting your famous Mr. Tompkins direct the play alone for a few weeks."

Oops. I must stop blathering so much, at home, about assisting Mr. Tompkins. "Oh, for Pete's sake," I grumble and push my chair back from the table.

I kiss my mother, then lean against the wall of her hospital room, with dark thoughts and a dark expression. My arms itch like crazy, but I don't want to draw attention to this fact. I try to scratch them without being obvious. Granny, chatting pleasantly, hands Mother a couple of new magazines that she brought, and I watch Mother glance at them without interest. Jamie stands just inside the door, looking uncomfortable. Dad sits in the chair, but then offers it to Granny.

"Nice flowers," I say, just to say something. "Where did they come from?"

"Mrs. Hall brought them," Mother says wearily.

"I wish I'd thought to bring some," Dad says.

"I've got plenty," Mother says. "Not worth spending the money. They'll just die."

"How are you feeling?" Granny asks quickly.

"My back's killing me."

"Well, let me see if I can do something to help. I'll go and ask a nurse for another pillow, if you like."

"No, don't bother. Nothing helps." She turns the pages of a magazine without looking at them.

I need to brighten the gloom. "Don't forget we're putting on the play soon. It'll be the first weekend in June. I guess you'll be out of here by then."

"Of course," Mother says. She attempts a smile.

"Um," I say, trying again. "What are we going to call the baby? I mean, have you thought up any names?"

"Names?" Mother says, as if this is a brand-new idea. "I guess we'll just have to wait and see."

Granny busies herself with the flowers, checking the water level, picking off drooping leaves. She chatters to fill in blank spaces in the almost nonexistent conversation. "It's a pity tulips don't last longer in a vase. It seems a shame to pick them. But they're lovely, aren't they?"

I fold my arms and dig my thumbs into the folds at my elbows for a furtive scratch.

"They smell rancid," Mother says. Granny takes them into the bathroom to change the water.

Jamie sneezes into his pocket handkerchief.

Mother looks at him closely. "Your eyes are a little dull, Jamie," she says. "Are you catching a cold?"

"Nope."

"When you go home, I want you to gargle with hot salt water."

I catch his quick, agitated glance at the ceiling. "Okay," he says.

"And Rachel . . . use plenty of ointment on your arms, tonight, and wrap them well with bandages so you won't scratch in your sleep."

If we were in the middle of the war and bombs were dropping on our house, she'd still be nattering away at us about life's minor problems. She'd probably tell us to make our beds and tidy our rooms before they're blown to bits. What she looks like, right now, is a large helium-filled blimp, waiting to explode.

We don't stay long. I don't think she wants us to.

22

By the next morning, Jamie definitely has a cold. Granny orders him back to bed. "And stay there until I say you can get up."

So, that's where he is when I get home from school. I go into his room to tell him how badly the play is going. "It's supposed to be a comedy, but it's about as funny as a sinking ship, all hands on board. Mr. Tompkins has to yell at everybody to get them to perk up."

"Does that work?"

I have to stop to think. "Not really. It should. He's a wonderful director. It's them, really, the actors. They haven't a clue about comedy."

"Can't you perk them up? You're the assistant, aren't you?"

Before I can tell him that "assistant director" seems to be merely another name for prompter, Granny comes puffing up the stairs and into Jamie's room, her eyes aglow.

"Your father called. The baby has arrived safe and sound, and your mother's fine, too—a boy, seven pounds, seven ounces, dark hair and plenty of it."

"What's his name?"

"So far it's just *the baby*. Your parents can't agree on a name."

It's a week before Dad brings home Mother and a squawky little runt cocooned in a blanket, wrapped tight as a butcher's sausage.

Jamie's cold lingers. Everyone thinks it best if he stays in his room and keeps his germs to himself. I go in to him every day to bring him up-to-date on all the details. "She's not nursing the baby herself because she doesn't think her milk is any good."

"Please," Jamie says, "spare me the details." He puts his nose back in the book he's reading.

"Her milk's dried up."

"Out," Jamie yells, fanning me away with the book.

"*Hee-hee-hee!* The baby has mustard-colored poop."

"Rachel, I'm serious."

I back away toward the door with one last detail. "I changed his diaper, and he peed straight up into the air and got me on the forehead."

Jamie hurls the book at me, but I escape being hit and

close the door quietly behind me. Accidently waking the baby is a crime worthy of the death penalty in this house.

For once in my life, I try to do the intelligent thing. Monday morning, I tell Mr. Tompkins that I now have a baby brother, and he laughs because it seems so bizarre.

"Your mother must have been a child bride," he says.

"I don't know about that. All I know is, I have to go straight home after school to help out."

"And leave me to cope with the play alone?" He looks at me with a little boy pout that almost makes me want to put *my* arms around *him*.

"Oh, well . . . maybe I can stay, just for a little while. I can probably manage half an hour."

He tucks a curl behind my ear, grinning like a devil. "I have a favor to ask," he says. He rests his hand on my shoulder, burning it to a cinder. "The high school in Henley Falls put on *Rabbit Stew* last year and will lend us some props and costumes. They have a great rocking chair—better than the junky one we have." He bit his lip. "Could you do me a big favor?"

"Sure." *Doesn't he know I would do anything for him?*

"I've borrowed a pickup truck. Will you drive over with me next Saturday to help me load the stuff? Can you do that? If we leave fairly early in the morning, we'll be back by noon . . . or we could go somewhere for lunch."

This is beginning to sound like a date. "I, um, don't know if they'll let me."

"Who?"

"My parents."

"Oh, well . . . I could probably get someone else."

"But, maybe."

"I'm not sure which costumes to borrow. It's really you I need." His expression is tragic, a prince about to lose his princedom, unless I come to his rescue.

Of course, I say yes. How I'll square it at home is another question.

The baby is turning into a serious problem. He cries for part of the day and most of the night, with only brief pauses in between. Mother doesn't have the strength to look after him and spends her days in bed, recovering from his birth. She lies in semidarkness with the blinds down, not reading, not sleeping. I picture her drifting away out to sea in a little boat.

Each day when I get home from school, Granny and I share baby duties. Sometimes Dad takes the baby and walks up and down the living room with him. He seems to have more success than anyone else at getting him to settle down. Now that Mother is staying in bed, Jamie thinks it's about time he was over his cold. He gets up, even though he's still coughing. Doctor Melvin makes a house call and orders Jamie back to bed until further notice. He tells

Mother to get up and look after her baby. Each ignores his advice.

Jamie stays in bed in the mornings, getting up in the early afternoons to lie on the couch in the living room. That's where I usually find him when I return from school.

"How's the baby?" I say.

"How would I know?"

"Haven't you even seen him yet?"

"No, not yet. I still have a bit of a cold, so I go back to my room whenever he's likely to make an appearance."

Every day, we have the same exchange of words, until finally he gets annoyed. "I have no interest in seeing a baby. Squalling babies bore me."

"He's our little brother. And he doesn't even have a name."

"So call him Irony."

He makes me so mad!

Dad returns home for lunch every day, and lately, so do I. I'm getting tired of packing the same dry old peanut butter sandwiches for myself. I notice that the first thing Dad does at noon is make his rounds, looking in on Jamie, on Mother, on the baby, in that order. By the time he gets home, Granny has already carried trays up to Mother and Jamie. He brings them back down after they've eaten.

"It's hard to get used to the idea that I have two sons," Dad says to me one day at lunchtime.

"It's hard to get used to my mother spending her life in bed," I say. "Why doesn't she get up?"

"Doctor Melvin believes it's a state of mind that some women fall into after giving birth. A depression of spirits. He thinks she'll snap out of it soon enough, if we show patience and gently try to cheer her up."

I sit down at the table, and Granny puts a bowl of soup in front of me. I break up crackers over the soup and stir them in. Canned soup. Granny never used to serve canned soup.

"Good," Dad says, spooning down a hearty mouthful.

"It's out of a can," Granny says.

"Still, it's quite nice, isn't it, Rachel?"

"Um, sure."

The baby is crying again. Dad puts his soup bowl in the sink and runs water into it. "I'll get him," he says.

Granny's beginning to look ancient. Her gray hair, usually caught up in a knot at the back of her head, hangs in straggles over her ears. She looks up from her soup bowl and nods.

I hear Dad go upstairs and into the baby's room. It's at the back of the house, above the kitchen, formerly the sewing room. To convert it, he shoved the sewing machine against one wall and moved the ironing board down to the kitchen. He also padded the sewing table with towels for a change table and put up some shelves. Mother knit a few things for the baby before she became so apathetic and sick, fortunately, otherwise he'd be pretty chilly.

I have a hard time thinking of her as sick. A cold makes you sick, or the flu. Or leukemia. Even Jamie with his cold has more energy than she does. In fact, once he's completely over it, I'm hoping he'll be just like his old prewar self. I'm beginning to think that the faith healer really cured him, or maybe the doctors made a mistake. It could happen. Either way, he looks pretty healthy.

"I can't believe Mother's actually sick," I say, when Dad comes back down, cradling the baby. I want to say, *She's just being lazy*, but I bite my tongue.

"Having too much to cope with can make you sick," he says. "Besides the baby, Jamie is a constant worry for her."

"You know what? Jamie's going to be fine." I'm on the point of telling him about the faith healer, but the baby starts to wail again. Dad puts him up over his shoulder and walks up and down while the baby shrieks in his ear. And then the little darling burps up a big gob of milky vomit down Dad's back.

The next day, again just after lunch, Mrs. Hall drops by with a gift for the baby, a sweater and bonnet. Granny bought a few smocked nighties for him at the church bazaar, and various friends and neighbors have brought over other little items. The kid's building quite a wardrobe. Mrs. Hall says, "Is there anything I can do to help out?"

"Not a thing," Granny says. She gives her a bright smile as she clears away the lunch dishes. Typical of our family.

We don't ask for help; we don't like to impose on people; we like to appear self-sufficient.

"Well, I haven't seen Dora outside with the baby, yet. I was wondering, is she all right?"

"She's getting her strength back. It takes time," Granny says.

"And the baby?"

"Beautiful, but a little colicky."

Upstairs, the baby screeches his lungs out. I go up to the poor little red-faced creature, beating the air with his tightly clenched fists, his legs drawn up to his belly as he fills the air with outrage and his diaper with something else. He stops howling when I pick him up to change him. By the time I take him downstairs, Mrs. Hall has gone.

"Hand him over," Granny says. She's warmed a bottle for him.

Upstairs, I clean my teeth and try to get a brush through my hair. I put ointment on the scaly insides of my arms. Soon I hear Granny take the baby into Mother's room.

Before leaving for school, I go in to see Mother. She's lying on her side, with the baby asleep on the bed beside her. She looks bored and a little angry, and, for a brief moment, it goes through my mind that she doesn't appear to like the baby very much.

"Want me to put him in his bassinet?" I ask. Because, what if she forgets about him and rolls on top of him? The small bassinet continues to sit on the cedar chest, at the end of the bed, in the hope that, if the baby spends part of his day near her, Mother will pick him up from time to time and comfort him. No one knows if this ever occurs.

She looks at him, biting her lip. "He's so fragile, isn't he? I hope nothing happens to him."

"He'll be all right," I say. He stays asleep while I pick him up and carefully place him in his little nest.

Next, I pop into Jamie's room. He's dressed and sitting at his desk, sealing an envelope. "I was just leaving," he says.

"Where are you going?"

"Post office."

The letter, I notice, is addressed to Ellie Cooper. "How come you're writing to Ellie?"

"Just for something to do, Miss Nosy."

I examine his face. "Are you in love with Ellie, now?"

"Don't be ridiculous."

Instead of going downstairs, though, he lies on top of his bed, heaving a big sigh. "I'll just have a little rest first."

"I'll mail it on my way to school, if you like." Of course, he'll say no, but he surprises me.

"It's got a stamp, so you can just stick it in the box at the corner. Thanks," he says, almost as an afterthought.

Granny comes into his room. "Hustle, now," she says to me, "You don't want to be late." She glances at Jamie. "Are you all right?"

"Never better."

"I don't like your color."

"What an insulting thing to say."

"Why don't you go in and talk to your mother? Have a peek at the baby. He looks just like you."

"That's not what Rachel said."

"What did I say?"

"You said he looks like a Martian."

"Go in and pick him up," Granny says. "It would do you the world of good."

"If I did, I'd drop him for sure. I can't be trusted."

"Oh, Jamie!" she says, "You're a trial to my patience."

It's Friday. I still haven't said anything to my parents about Henley Falls. Tomorrow is the day I'm to drive there with Mr. Tompkins. Walking home, I remember how I used to look forward to the weekend. Not anymore. All I can see ahead is work and more work, and my only company, my sad little excuse for a family. I need the trip to Henley Falls.

I hurl myself into the house a little after four-thirty, banging the door behind me without a thought for the sleeping baby. I dump my schoolbooks on the back stairs and storm into the kitchen, confronted by the usual scene: brimming laundry basket, bottles boiling on the stove, stacks of folded diapers and nighties, and Granny looking about a hundred years old.

I sit at the table across from her. "I'm never going to have a baby," I say. "I'm never even getting married!"

"You'll change your tune when you get to a certain age."

"Not if having babies turns you into a hopeless vegetable. I'm serious. This is slave labor we're doing here. Why can't that woman get off her bed and down here to help out?"

"Now, now, she would if she could. You don't understand what she's going through."

"What *she's* going through! What about me? What about you? Does anyone care what *we're* going through? I have no friends. Even if Ruthie wasn't completely involved in the play, she still wouldn't have time for me. She says I'm no fun. I never get to do anything useful with the play because I always have to leave to look after the little monster." I'm scratching like a madwoman. "It's hopeless, just hopeless."

Rose rubs up against my ankles, purring. I don't care; I feel like kicking her. Of course, I don't. I sit, picking at a chip of paint on the corner of the table, until Granny says, "Stop taking out your frustration on the furniture. And stop scratching. I'm going to trim those nails of yours right back to the quick if this keeps up."

Now is not the best time to ask permission to go to Henley Falls. But, I have to go; it's as simple as that. My one chance to find out where I stand with Tommy! I'll have him all to myself for a whole morning. There's only one way to do it. Lie. My lipstick is lurking in the corner of a kitchen cupboard. If I go, I will definitely wear it.

Granny says, "Just think how your little brother will appreciate you someday."

"Who? That little eating-puking-peeing-pooping-crying machine? The kid doesn't have a clue. He's not even cute. He looks like something that accidently fell off the moon. He doesn't even have a name."

"Give him a chance. Every kid has some redeeming features. Look at you."

"Look at *me*! What's that supposed to mean?"

"It means you're a doll, kiddo. Now, come and help me take these baby things upstairs."

As we pile clean diapers and baby clothes on the shelves in the baby's room, a decision makes itself. Taking a breath, I say, "I have to help with the sets for the play tomorrow. We're starting early in the morning, so I'll be home by noon." *Or a little after, if we go out for lunch. Or never, if we take off for Mexico.* "Is that all right?" There are certain elements of truth there.

"Fine with me. Better just mention it to your mother."

"She won't care."

"She's your mother."

As predicted, she doesn't seem to care.

I'm up early Saturday morning, just as it becomes light. Wide-awake after a toss-and-turn night, I study the clothes in my closet. My first choice is a new dress I'm saving for summer, cut low front and back, with narrow shoulder straps and a little bolero jacket I can take off if I want. My mother hates it, but she let me get it anyway. It's the most sophisticated thing I own. I'm about to slip it from its hanger, but I stop. It looks like a costume. It looks as if I'm trying to be somebody I'm not.

No, that's crazy. I hold it in front of me and look down, but the feeling of unreality stays with me. Yes, it's a costume. I hang it back up.

It isn't exactly summer yet, anyway, only the middle of May. I'm shivering in the breeze coming through my partly open window. Goose bumps. How romantic! I close the window, trying not to slam it, and unwind the bandages from my scaly arms. What a mess! Better to hide them under the long sleeves of my angora sweater. It's so fuzzy and clean, I wear it only for special occasions. Skirt and sweater—like something I'd wear to school. I brush my hair and tuck one side behind my ear with a barrette. The other side I let drape half over my eye to give me an air of mystery. *Lipstick. Don't forget.*

Scene after approaching scene unfolds in my hectic imagination. We'll kiss. That's a given. We were so close to it, in the darkened auditorium, before we were surprised by the janitor. We'll have to pull off the road, of course. And naturally, we'll discuss our age difference. Sure, I'm just fifteen, but I'll turn sixteen in, what? Less than ten months. We can easily keep our affair secret until then, and after that, I can do what I like. We'll decide age doesn't matter, because it really doesn't. We'll make plans for the future. Time spreads endlessly before me filled with Tommy, his smile, his wonderfully soulful eyes that promise me a heavenly new life.

I regret telling Granny that I'll never marry. What I meant was, I'll never marry a mere boy. I'm holding out for a god.

What if, halfway there, Tommy says, *Let's just run away and never come back?* It's the sort of daring thing he *would* say. I take a huge breath. I'd do it. I really would, in the snap of a finger. It's the sort of thing you could write a play about. Or, a big fat book. I take a fistful of money from my savings, just in case. My hands shake with excitement as I carefully fold the money, mostly ones and twos, and put it in the pocket of my skirt.

No one else is up, thankfully. I hear little mewing noises and hope it's the cat. It isn't. Rose is licking her paws, on the end of my bed.

It's baby brother, unfortunately, telling *me*, since I'm the only one up, that if he doesn't get fed pretty soon, his mewing will turn into ear-splitting howls. And that'll rouse the entire family. Maybe even the neighbors. The last thing I want is to have the romance I'm staging in my head interrupted by my father's early morning yawns and throat-clearings. After that, I'd have to listen to Granny's disapproving remarks about my mysterious hairstyle. Add to that questions about why I'm wearing my best sweater just to work on sets, and any whiff of romance gets tossed right into the garbage pail. I head into the baby's room.

There he is, in his little flannel nightie and booties, wriggling, flailing, kicking, turning his face to the side and opening his mouth like a baby bird, looking for worms.

I should leave now, I think, before he gets into full voice. I'm to meet Tommy at the school, but it's way too early. And chilly.

But, so what?

Although, what if someone sees me lurking in front of the school? They'll know it's a tryst, a love affair. Maybe even an elopement. They might try to stop me.

The baby has such tiny, perfect hands. I can't help myself. I reach into his crib and put my finger into the curl of his palm, and he hangs on to it. He's strong. He doesn't want to let go. They should call him Samson, after the guy in the Bible story, and never cut his hair. I give in and pick him up.

Downstairs, I make him a bottle. The mere thought of food gives me butterflies. While the milk is warming, I bounce the baby, trying to keep him quiet. *Lipstick!* I try to put it on without a mirror. *Oops!* I must look like a freak.

To make sure the baby doesn't wake everybody, I take him outside to the front veranda, where we sit in one of the wicker chairs, facing the street. He sucks eagerly at the bottle, and I hold him closely, the way Granny taught me. He puts one tiny hand on top of mine.

The refreshing scent of lilacs wafts on a warm breeze. It's going to be a gorgeous day for our trip. I imagine getting up beside Tommy in the borrowed truck. He'll reach out to take my hand. Maybe kiss it. We'll drive a few miles out of town, and then he'll say, *Do you mind if I stop for a moment?* I feel a tiny, electric prick of fear, when I think of him pulling the truck off the road. I don't know why, unless it means that, by then, I'll be powerless to change my mind.

I decide to change the script. We'll keep driving. If he wants to kiss me, and I hope he will, he can wait until we get to the Henley Falls high school. It will be every bit as sweet, every bit as exciting.

If this were a romance involving two fictitious people, however, I would definitely pull them off the road, where they could give full vent to their passion. Steamy kisses behind steamed-up windows, hands exploring—

Exploring what?

This is real life. The hero is a teacher. Teachers, in real life, do not make love to students. *Do they?* There must be a rule against it. Not even in the fiction pages of *Ladies' Home Journal* would this happen.

But, wait. *Why not?* There's always a first time. For a hazy moment, I'm back into my romance. Tommy's jaw, the shadow of a beard, hair on the backs of his wrists, his eager hands.

A slight rumbling sound means the baby just filled his diaper. How romantic!

I pat his back to burp him, and he obliges, spitting up milk down the front of my sweater.

Suddenly, I'm shivering. The personal romance I've been concocting makes me feel a little sick. My watch tells me I should be at the school, by now. Mr. Tompkins will wonder where I am. Still, I sit on the veranda. I'll go in a minute, as soon as my skin stops feeling hot and prickly, as if I'm drifting toward danger.

Just as the baby falls asleep, a red truck drives slowly past our house with Tommy at the wheel. He must have seen me on the veranda because, in a few moments, he comes back, going the other way. He stops. My insides quivering, I stand up and start down the veranda steps. His dark eyes are filled with love for me and me alone! I see this clearly. He looks puzzled, but he's smiling. His hair, slanting across his forehead, makes me sigh. I want to touch it. I'm hooked, as I knew I would be the minute I saw him, again. I am drawn like a fish into a net. I picture myself drifting toward him, floating. He reaches for me. Our lips touch.

"I thought you were coming with me." He has his head out the window.

"I am, I . . ." I'm aware, now, of the bundle in my arms. No longer asleep, my baby brother opens his mouth and howls. I jiggle him, trying to soothe him before my entire family wakes up and runs out of the house to find out what's going on. Maybe they'll think I'm just showing off my new brother to my teacher. I hold him up to the truck window, and the baby promptly vents his opinion by throwing up what looks like a gallon of curdled milk, right through the open window. It lands on the shoulder of Tommy's open-necked shirt. Some might have gone down inside.

I am mortified. "I'm so sorry! He does this all the time. I should have . . . here, use this." I extricate a vomity baby blanket and try to shove it through the window to Mr. Tompkins, who backs away in horror. Looking as if he might be the next to throw up, he swipes at his shirt with his clean pocket handkerchief.

I use a corner of the blanket to wipe my brother's chin, then sling it back over my shoulder. The angora's a mess now, anyway. Holding the baby in the crook of my arm, I make soothing noises to him.

Mr. Tompkins looks as sour as he now smells. "Well, are you coming or not?"

The baby finds my finger and holds on with all his might.

I have to say *something*. "I—I can't go." It sounds like a wail. Next, I'll be crying, bawling.

Looking straight ahead, Tommy continues to scowl. "May I ask why not?"

I want to scratch my arms, but my hands are full. I need to answer. "Um." *Think*. "My, um, brother won't let me." I have to bite my lip to keep back a shriek of manic laughter.

Mr. Tompkins gives me a disgusted glance. "Fine. You might at least have let me know in advance. Your friend Ruth would have been happy to help out."

"Ruthie?"

Mr. Tompkins rolls up the window and drives off, leaving nothing but exhaust fumes and emptiness. The sensation lasts only a moment, because almost immediately, I know I'm light as air.

I fly inside with the baby and take him up to his crib. He's probably going to cry, but I hope I can get back to my room before anyone else hears him and gets up. I just make it. Quickly, I take off my smelly clothes, pitch them into the back of the closet to deal with later, and change into my Saturday grubbies—shapeless slacks and an old plaid shirt of Jamie's.

Opening my door a crack, I peek out. The coast is clear. I hurry down the stairs and grab an apple from a bowl on the kitchen table because I'm starving. Quickly, I scrawl a note to say I fed the baby and escape outside. My plan is to walk up to the school, hang around for a little while, then come home and say something like, *It didn't take as long as we thought it would. Lots of people there to help.* Or something. A smear of lipstick comes off onto the apple as I bite into it.

I don't really need my made-up alibi because no one comments on my early return from the school. Dad's gone back to work, and Granny's sipping her coffee with the newspaper open in front of her. Everyone else is upstairs. "It's quiet around here for a change," I say.

"Blessedly quiet. I might even get to finish reading the paper."

"Don't do anything rash."

I'm in the middle of buttering some toast, when I hear the dull thud and then silence. Granny and I put down what we're doing and frown at each other. Then we hear Mother's shriek.

CHAPTER

23

The baby? White with panic, Granny races out of the kitchen, with me so close behind I'm nearly on top of her. I don't know what to expect—the baby, like a broken doll, lifeless on the floor?

In the hall, I look up to see Mother staring down in horror over the banister, moaning into her hands, "Oh, no, oh, no!" The back of my neck tingles as hair stands up like hackles. I scream. On the stairs, near the bottom, Jamie lies crumpled.

I practically fly to him, crying, screaming, trying to pick him up. Granny keeps yelling at me to leave him, not to try to lift him. I look up the stairs just as Mother, running down, trips on the hem of her nightgown. I throw myself across Jamie to protect him, afraid she'll land on top of us. She catches hold of the banister and seems to glide the rest of the way down.

Mother is transformed. It's as if the screaming and panic slashed the curtain she'd drawn across her mind. Suddenly she takes charge. "Give him some air," she says, tugging me away. Together we manage to get him into a more comfortable position. His eyes are closed, as if he's sound asleep.

I sit on the hall floor whimpering, chewing my knuckles. "He's going to be all right, isn't he? Isn't he!" It's not a question. I squeeze past Mother and put my ear next to Jamie's chest, but all I hear is my own heart thumping madly.

Granny phones the ambulance, then Dad at the store. They both reach the house at the same time.

While men come in with a stretcher, my parents cling together, as if they've just found each other after a long search. As the men skillfully move Jamie onto the stretcher, I notice how drawn my father's face is, how deeply lined, his eyes hallow, dark with pain. He looks breakable. He's always been the backbone of the family, but now, I see that, like the rest of us, he isn't indestructible. He rubs the back of his hand across his eyes and says, "I'll follow the ambulance in the car."

I'm not sure how long the baby's been wailing. Granny has her arms around me, comforting me. "He's going to be fine, just fine. You've got to stop crying." I'm not even aware that I'm crying.

Over Granny's shoulder, I catch a glimpse of Mother, alone on the stairs, left out. Upstairs, the little alien howls his heart out. It's as though Mother realizes that there are only two people left to comfort each other. She hurries up the stairs.

Sometime later, looking distractedly out the living room window, I'm aware of Mother behind me, dressed, cradling the baby in her arms. "Rachel," she says softly, "can you look after him for a while?"

"Sure."

"Iris," she says to Granny, "would you be kind enough to drive me to the hospital?"

"Certainly."

I feel ridiculous now, remembering my fear that the baby might have been dropped over the banister. A bit like my image of Hazel Carrington's mother, wandering around with an ice pick up her sleeve, looking for someone to murder. That's what comes of having an overly active imagination.

I hold my sleeping brother in the crook of my arm, watching through the window as Mother and Granny drive off in the truck. I can't help puzzling over the change in Mother. She makes me think of an abandoned sailboat, becalmed for weeks. Now, with the wind at her back, she's able to sail bravely forward. But, to where? That's the question we all face. Maybe she'll be a lifeboat coming to our rescue, because that's what we need right now—me, my brother, brothers I mean, my dad—something, anyway, to keep us all from floundering, drowning.

———

Tubes, bottles, the antiseptic smell of the hospital, and Jamie only half-awake. That's what greets Granny and me when we visit Jamie the next day, Sunday. Afterwards, on the way home, Granny says, "I meant to ask you before, but so much has happened that it slipped my mind. Who was in that truck that pulled up in front of the house, early yesterday morning? I happened to look out the window and thought I saw you talking to someone."

"Oh, that," I begin. I feel little stabs of panic under my skin. I can make something up. Or—bizarre thought—I can confess everything and face the consequences. I am suddenly exhausted. I think of that stupid little tube of aptly named lipstick and all the troubles I've been trying to avoid with my colorful lies. I have a momentary picture of myself taking an ice pick from up my sleeve, skewering that red stick, and pitching the whole thing off the edge of the world. Granny's looking at me, instead of the road, and narrowly misses sideswiping a parked car.

"It's a long story, Granny. Maybe you should park the truck first." And so, once we get home and into the house, it all comes out. Mother has just made a pot of tea and put out a plate of Granny's homemade cookies. We all sit down at the kitchen table. The baby is asleep upstairs. "Um," I begin as soon as we sit down. "I have a confession."

"Eat first, sing later," Granny says. My parents look at us curiously.

"How's Jamie doing, now?" Dad asks.

"Still a bit dopey, but he's doing fine."

Granny prods me to finish my cookie, but I'm not hungry.

I push my chair back from the table, in case I have to make a quick getaway, and sit with my arms folded in front of me, like armor. I have to clear my throat once or twice, but I tell them everything in a level voice, at first, including the near kiss in the auditorium. Finally, tearfully, haltingly, I admit that I have been so much in love with Mr. Tompkins that I wanted to run away with him, would have, in fact, if it had come to that. Every sordid detail comes out, before I weep into my hands. I'm not crying about Mr. Tompkins, though. My grief is for the end of love. Every sweet, remembered morsel of how I once felt has gone sour, putrefied, and slithered right down the drain.

Mother puts her arms around me, rocking slightly. Dad hands me his handkerchief. A minute or so later, we calm down.

"The man should be horsewhipped," Granny says. "He's been setting you up."

"At least you had the brains not to go with him yesterday," Mother says.

"I think this would be of some interest to, not only the principal, but the school board," Dad says. "Do you know of any other girls who might be . . . involved with him?"

"I wasn't involved; I was in love." I don't want to talk about this anymore.

"I think you know what I mean."

I remember the look of near panic I sometimes saw on Hazel's face, when she looked up to see Mr. Tompkins' eyes on her, in English class. I wonder if the reason she's gone away to live with her grandmother has something to do with Mr. Tompkins' unwanted attention. And then, there's Ruthie. She's been a Tommy fan, right from the start. I remember Mr. Tompkins suggesting that Ruthie would have gone with him to Henley Falls. How did he know that?

I have to face a moment of truth. What would be the honorable thing to do? Should I involve Ruthie and Hazel or allow them their privacy? "There might be others," I say, "but they might not want the gossip."

Granny says, "If you saw a hungry wolf slinking into town, would you warn your neighbors?"

"Well, sure . . . but that's different."

"A predator is a predator."

Tears are running down my face again. "There's a possibility that Hazel Carrington is involved in some way. And maybe . . ." I'm losing my voice, so I whisper, "Maybe Ruthie. I don't know for sure. I'd have to ask her."

Mother hugs me again.

Dad says, "There-there."

"But, if I *am* the only one," I say, "Ruthie will be mad as hops if she thinks I'm trying to mix her up in this." I put my hands over my face and howl again. And then the baby wakes up and howls, too. Oddly, this has a calming effect on *me*.

By the time we all get a grip on our emotions, things move pretty quickly. I phone Ruthie and tell her everything, all the stuff that happened at school, all the stuff after school, my near elopement, even though that part, at least, was only my wishful thinking.

After she squeals *Good Lord* and *You're kidding* a few times, Ruthie confesses that Mr. Tompkins has been flirting with her, too. "Not only that," she says, "he actually sneaked into the girls' dressing room, while I was alone, trying on a costume. I was wearing only my slip, and he just stood there, staring at me. I thought I would die. He told me I had the figure of a goddess."

"A goddess?" Now it's my turn for *Good Lord* and *You're kidding*. "What a horrid man!" I screech. I'm also thinking, *a goddess? Is he blind?*

"And listen to this," Ruthie says, "my sister, Joan, who always hears the gossip, said that Hazel Carrington left town because Tompkins kept trying to put his arms around her while he was counseling her. He said she needed to be caressed to get over the trauma of having an alcoholic mother. Caressed! So what do you think of that?"

"Alcoholic mother?"

"Yes, very sad. She's away somewhere getting treatment."

"Oh." My madwoman in the attic with the lethal ice pick just got tossed out the window for a second time.

"Listen," I say, "Tommy is a creep, the worst kind of creep there is. Tell your parents about him spying on you. Tell them to phone my parents."

In her usual blunt way, Ruthie asks, "So are you still in love with him?"

"No, I hate him. Actually I hate myself because I loved the attention so much."

"I know what you mean. I was completely flattered that he liked me."

"Now, I could almost throw up. I must be such a despicable person," I say. "I loved being with him. I really did. It was like being in a romantic movie that you never want to end. But, now, now that it has ended, all I have is me, looking foolish, hating myself."

"You'll get over it. I'm already over it, sort of."

"I wish I could simply shed my skin and get rid of that part of me that needed him to touch me. I wish I could just peel it off and throw it on the floor."

"I wonder if Hazel is over it."

"Of course then I'd have to get out the vacuum cleaner and Hoover it up before my mother saw it. And it would probably jam up the works, and then I'd be in trouble for breaking the Hoover."

"Rachel?"

"What?"

"You have an insane imagination."

———

This is what it's like to live in a small place like Middleborough. Time has a will of its own. Events can occur, sometimes, with the speed of lightning. I hear my father making phone calls and hear him say, a little later, that he's going to a meeting at the school.

On Monday morning, Mr. Tompkins is not at school. The halls and classrooms are abuzz with rumors and half-truths and complete untruths. Ruthie and I make a pact that we won't add a thing. We practice shrugging our shoulders.

In English class, there's a substitute teacher who looks way older than Tommy. She's a short, lively, butterball of a woman, with a voice like a sergeant major and red hair that won't stay pinned up in a bun. Her name is Mrs. Borke. Life at school descends into the mundane.

I drag myself to drama that afternoon to witness the rehearsal of the hopeless play. Mrs. Borke is, of course, the new director. She watches the actors run lifelessly through their roles, hands on her hips, hair straggling around her ears. When it's over, no one says a word. It seems that Mr. Tompkins has stolen the play's very life and taken it away with him, wherever he is.

"Well, now," says Mrs. Borke, at the end. "Wasn't that a pathetic little offering!" She marches up and down the stage. "This play is supposed to be a comedy," she roars. "I didn't feel like cracking a smile, not even once." She peers around at cast and crew through her round-rimmed spectacles. "It's supposed to be a thigh-slapper! You have to play to the audience. Tickle them. Make 'em laugh till they cry."

She turns to Ruthie's first speech in her copy of the script. She throws out lines in a hearty, comical voice, prances across the stage, throws herself into a chair, crosses her legs, and gives the male lead a broad come-hither look. I don't know what everyone else thinks, but I'm thinking, *She's not really a teacher! She's a human being.* It isn't long before she has us all laughing. A little more work, a little more laughter, and the play is reborn.

Even better, she says to me, "It's time you started earning your keep as assistant director. I need you to be solely in charge for the first thirty minutes three days a week. I'm doing catch-up lessons with some of the fifth form students."

"Okay," I say. My arms aren't even itchy. I walk home, grinning all the way.

CHAPTER

24

Soon Jamie's tubes and bottles disappear, but his recovery is slow, at least it seems slow to me. The days go by like weeks of darkness. And, then, the sun comes out. Granny and I are sitting with him in his hospital room. He wakes up, rubs his eyes, and says, "What happened to my watch?"

Both Granny and I spring to attention. "Your watch?" I say. "You were so sleepy, you didn't really need a watch."

"The nurses put it with your clothes," Granny says.

"Of course I need it. What were they thinking? That I was finished with time?"

I rummage through his narrow closet and find it on the high shelf. After it's set and wound, I buckle it on his wrist. He winces when I move his arm. "I feel as if I have toothaches in all my bones," he says. Granny says she'll find the nurse.

The next day, I go with Mother to visit him. He's cranked up to an almost sitting position. His eyes widen when he sees her. "You're better!" he says.

"Almost. I'll be tip-top as soon as we get you home again." Thinner now, she bends over and kisses him without any trouble. She smiles at him, like the mother we've always known.

"What happened? How did you get better so fast? Whatever it is, how about getting some for me? I'm sick of being sick."

A few days later, when I come home from school, Mother and Granny are in the kitchen folding diapers. "Go up and look in Jamie's room," Mother says.

I don't even bother to put my books down. Looking a little pale, a little thin, but there in the flesh is my big brother. "Apparently, I'm a mystery to the medical world," he says. "I'm not strictly adhering to the textbook's description of my illness. In spite of my diagnosis, I'm thriving. I'm supposed to stay in bed for a day or two, but soon I'll be doing push-ups and running around the block six or eight times before breakfast."

I deposit my books on his desk. "Maybe you should start a little slower. How about stargazing? How about fishing?"

"Good idea. Good way to get back to normal. Where's my fishing rod, by the way? Is it here or at the farm? I wouldn't want old Armstrong to get hold of it."

"I'll find it."

I want to raise the issue of the faith healer, but I'm afraid to. Even though he's a fake, Jamie must still believe in him. That's why he keeps bouncing back. Maybe the important word is *faith*, Jamie's faith in his own ability to heal.

We both hear the doorbell. A minute later, Ellie Cooper is standing in the doorway saying, "Knock, knock, knock. May I come in?"

Jamie sits up higher on his pillows and says, "Please do." Suddenly, he has color in his cheeks. Ellie Cooper looks less like Coop's shy sister, now, and more like a pretty young woman who is finding her way in the world. She says hi to me, then directs all her attention to Jamie.

"I got your letter. I had no idea you'd had an accident until your grandmother told my mother. What happened?"

"Something stupid. I fell down the stairs and sort of knocked myself out."

I watch him smile at her as if he can barely take his eyes away. I'm beginning to feel like an outsider.

"Really? I heard you fainted."

"Don't believe everything you hear."

He doesn't seem to have any trouble lying, and he doesn't need anything but his bare lips to do it.

Ellie looks happy. "The good news is, you're feeling better."

"By the minute!" He's grinning so broadly, I'm afraid his lips will crack.

"Well, I have to go and do my homework, now," I say. They don't seem heartbroken by this news. I'm not sure they even heard me. I'm moving toward the door but not going through it.

"I'm sorry we didn't get to go out for coffee," Jamie says.

"Maybe we will when you're better." Ellie pulls the desk chair a little closer to his bed and sits down, resting her chin on her knuckles.

"How's nursing?" he asks.

"I like it, but they're very strict with new students, and they work us to death, but still, it's what I want to do. I like working with children. We have a two-week break right now."

"See you around, then," I say, backing out reluctantly. Ellie nods, and Jamie ignores me. And, then, I go back in because I forgot to take my books.

"I guess there's still no word about Coop," he says.

"No, nothing at all. We haven't lost hope, really, but we *are* getting back to normal. My dad isn't as hard to live with."

I go into my own room but leave the door open. Pretty soon, I hear Ellie say she has to leave. Jamie makes her promise to come back. I go and stand in the doorway, not to spy on them really, just to be friendly. I like Ellie. Well, all right, I'm also a spy.

He's still smiling broadly. "Come back tomorrow," he says.

She's laughing. "Are you sure? Don't you need time to recuperate?"

"I'll improve faster if you visit me." He looks a little embarrassed and says, "I hope that doesn't sound too pathetic. It's hard to be suave about making a date with a girl while you're lying in bed, wearing striped pajamas, and looking like the ghost of Christmas past." He stretches out a hand to her, and she takes it.

"I'll come tomorrow." She has the same big open smile as Coop.

Mrs. Hall drops in on Saturday morning, and Granny pours her a cup of coffee. "I want to know," she says to me, "whether I can get tickets for the play at the door, or are they likely to be sold out?"

"At the door will be fine," I say. "The school play is never sold out. Unfortunately."

"Good to know. Now, tell me," she says, changing the subject, "what are you calling the baby?"

My parents look blankly at each other. I pipe up, "His first name is The, second name, Baby." If Jamie had been downstairs, he'd have laughed. Nobody else does.

"It's getting serious," Dad says. "I've got the birth registration papers on my desk waiting to be filled in and sent, but we keep putting it off."

"You know," Mother says to Mrs. Hall, "I can talk about this now, but I wasn't very well for a while, which made it hard to think of a name. Names are so important. I hate to admit this, but it needs to be said. Back then, when I was in the depths of my own personal black cave, I thought that if he went without a name, then perhaps he didn't really exist, and that if he didn't exist, Jamie wouldn't feel he was being shoved aside. That's how sick I was."

Dad pats her hand. "You're better now, and that's the main thing. It's good to have you back."

Just then, as if to prove he exists, The Baby, upstairs in his crib, begins to grumble. We leave him for a bit, to see if he'll go back to sleep.

"This naming business is becoming pressing," Dad says. "After all, he's three weeks old. How about John, after my father?"

"Mmm," Mother says. "James has always been my favorite name for a boy. Hard to think of another. And, well, your father *was* a little frightening."

"Call him Walter, after your father," Dad says.

"Mmm," she replies. "Bit stuffy."

"How about Baby X? It suits him," I call, on my way up to fetch him down. "Gives him an aura of mystery." He's managed to set up quite a little howl by this time. And why not? Poor nameless, little nobody.

This time, it takes longer for Jamie's strength to return. He gets up and dressed every day, but has to lie down again to rest. Mostly, he lies on top of his bed. Sometimes he sits at his desk, writing in that curious booklet tied up with string. He puts it away whenever he has company. Ellie, still on her vacation, visits him when I'm at school, and when I get home, I spend time with him.

"There's something I want to do," he says, after he's been home a few days, "but I'm not sure how to do it. Look at my corkboard. Empty, except for that faded school pennant. No timetables, no group pictures, no snapshots. It's kind of depressing. It looks as if I'm just marking time, waiting for the rest of my life to happen. Judging by my empty desk, maybe it already has."

"Hmm!" I say, which, I admit, isn't very helpful. It reminds me of our last conversation with Velda. Jamie got a letter from her a while ago, telling him she's decided to stay in Edmonton, in spite of her son's wife. "She doesn't want me to stay," Velda wrote, "but I tell her to go sit on a tack."

I'm standing in front of Jamie's desk, mulling over what to do with the corkboard to liven things up and thinking, *I'm not scratching.* My arms aren't even itchy.

"And look at this," Jamie says, "the only thing on my desk is the magnifying glass you gave me for my eighteenth birthday."

"Did you ever use it?"

"I can't remember."

"Not even to start a fire?"

He shakes his head with a resigned look. "Afraid not."

I say firmly, "You have a huge chunk of life left, and you know it."

"Do I?"

"Rachel!" Downstairs my mother is bellowing. "You should be studying. Your exams are coming up."

"Okay, okay!" I stomp loudly across the hall to my room, shut my door firmly, open it quietly, and tiptoe back to Jamie's room. He's still staring at his empty corkboard but frowns when I turn up again.

"Go," he says.

"Make me."

He lies down on his bed, his arm across his forehead. His sigh sounds like he's giving up.

"Look," I say, "you're forgetting the faith healer."

"No, I'm not. I'm ignoring him. He was a fraud."

I swallow and say, "Oh?"

"It was in the Toronto papers, months ago."

"So all this time you've known, and you didn't say a word?"

"I didn't want to spoil it for you."

"For me! But I knew." And then I tell him that I saw the faith healer treat the same guy twice, with the same miraculous results.

"Aren't we the suckers!" he says, as we smile ruefully at each other.

Just then, Mother sticks her head around his door and screeches at me for not being in my room, studying. I think it's safe to say, she's entirely back to normal. I leave Jamie's room without solving his corkboard problem. But, I'm getting ideas.

It isn't until the next day when, home from school, I start providing him with a lifetime of memories. The first thing I do is bring him the picture from my room of Coop and him, together with their fishing rods and their meager catch. "Here's a memory for you. That's what you need in here."

Next, I explore the back of his closet, spreading my finds out on his desk. There are snapshots, clippings from school yearbooks, sports articles from the newspaper, and a lucky fish lure that Coop gave him, the time he had his tonsils out. I discover the map of the night skies and put it on his desk. Under some books, I find a picture he took, with the camera he got for his eighteenth birthday, of the sprawling old climbing tree, down by the swale.

His fishing rod comes in from the garage, next. It's mounted like a trophy on the wall above the corkboard, using picture-hanging nails.

He picks up and studies each item I bring him. He even looks at some of them through the magnifying glass. Some he leaves on his desk; the rest he thumbtacks to his corkboard. From a desk drawer, he takes out the war clippings Dad saved for him. He looks through them and reads out the place names to me, with awe in his voice, and pain: "Normandy, Falaise, Chambois, Antwerp. I was there," he says. "I was part of it all."

"We didn't want you to go."

"I know. But I wanted to. I had to. And I suffered, sure, but we all did. I watched friends die, worried I'd be next. Fear was always out there, raging around and among us like a flooding river, black as blood. Yet, somehow, we carried on. Maybe we had something to believe in, even if it was only luck." He puts the newspapers down. "I think I'm beginning to realize what its like to be a human being in the world."

The play is ready for performance, one only this year. When Ellie comes over, I happen to go into Jamie's room just as he's inviting her to go with him. "I'd love to go," she says, "provided I can drive us in my father's car."

"I'm capable of driving," Jamie says.

"I don't know about that, Jamie." I always like to get my two cents' worth in. "When I wanted you to teach me to drive, you said the steering wheel took strong muscles for a sharp turn. And, what about the gears? You always say they're stiff."

"I exaggerated."

Ellie says, "You're missing the point. I just got my license and need the practice before I go back to Toronto, where I'll probably forget how." Jamie gallantly agrees. I think he's secretly relieved.

The night of the performance, I'm in the wings prompting, and from there I'm able to glimpse Jamie and Ellie. He looks tired but happy. The best part about the whole play is watching Jamie laugh, something I haven't seen him do for a long time. He and Ellie both laugh in all the right places, look at each other, and laugh some more. Will is in the wings, too, waiting to change the sets for the next act. I beckon him closer to get a glimpse of Jamie and Ellie. We give each other conspiratorial little smiles.

I'm tired by the time the play is finished and don't stay long at the cast party. Will comes up beside me while I'm getting ready to leave. "I'm leaving now, too," he says. "I'll walk you home."

"Oh, good," I say. "Ruthie wants to stay to the bitter end." I smile at him. "Nice to have someone to walk with." *Nice that it's Will Cooper*, I think, but don't say. The Coopers' Ford is still in front of our house when we get there. "Why don't you come in?" I ask.

"Oh, I don't know. I thought you were tired."

"I'm not the least bit tired," I say. And, suddenly, I'm not.

Will follows me inside to what is the closest thing to a party our family has witnessed in a long, long time. Dad opens soft drinks, while Granny pops popcorn, until it burns the bottom of the pot. Upstairs, the baby begins to wail, sad to be left out, I guess. Mother is already warming a bottle for him.

Ellie says, "It must be fun to have a baby in the house. I wish we had one."

Mother says, "He's just a little darling."

"He has changed our lives," Dad says happily.

In more ways than one, I think.

Mother wraps the warm bottle in a towel and says good night, taking it upstairs with her, and soon Dad follows, with a fistful of popcorn to munch on his way upstairs.

Granny puts the pot to soak. Before she goes up, she says, "Now don't you younger set stay up too late. Jamie needs his beauty rest."

We rehash the play, eat popcorn, and laugh at some of the antics of the actors, especially Ruthie's. She's a good comic actress, we all agree.

Ellie glances over at Jamie, who slouches low in a chair, looking exhausted, legs straight out in front of him. "Come on, little brother," she says to Will, "time to go."

She kisses Jamie on the cheek, but he quickly grabs her by the shoulders and pulls her toward him for a real kiss. If Coop were here, he'd have hooted and howled *Hubba-hubba* and teased the life out of both of them, but he isn't. Ellie goes out to start the car.

"I'll be along in a minute," Will calls. At the door, he smiles down at me. "Now that my rival has been banished, I think I have the nerve to ask you out. Can I phone you, sometime?"

I feel my face turn red. Will has seen me, often enough, looking up adoringly at Mr. Tompkins, to guess the way I used to feel about him. "Don't remind me of that phase of my life. I want to forget it."

He takes my hands and gives me a gentle shake. "I'm just teasing. Sorry. I guess I shouldn't have."

"It's all right. I'm sort of over it." When I look up, he's smiling, and I remember how much I've always liked the way he smiles. So I tell him. *Dumb thing to say.*

He looks a little puzzled. "Does that mean yes, I can phone you?"

"Oh. Yes, of course."

Ellie softly calls her brother from the open car window, not wanting to waken the entire neighborhood. He leaps, like a pole-vaulter, down the steps, turning once to look back before he gallops to the car. I like his energy. Maybe it's him I like.

CHAPTER

25

It takes me a long time to fall asleep. I have the dream-like feeling that I'm just beginning to find my way, after being lost, somehow, between the pages of a very long, very difficult book. Not one I can even begin to understand. Maybe I never will. I would be happy simply to close the cover and put it away on some shelf at the back of my mind, but it's not that easy.

I can faintly hear my parents. Standing still, I listen. "The baby will grow up in a far different world." I think that's what my mother says.

"Indeed, he will," Dad says. "He's a child for modern times."

"He's a darling," Mother says.

"Tonight, in the kitchen," Dad says, "with the kids, and the popcorn, and everything lighthearted, I had the curious feeling that the lights were gradually becoming brighter. Or else, everything was taking on intense color, as if we've all been putting up with a kind of tarnished existence. Life goes on," he says, "whether we poor humans will it to or not."

Time to stop eavesdropping, I think. This is not a conversation meant for me. I head for the bathroom, where I meet Granny coming out with a hot water bottle. "Oh, these aching joints," she whispers. "They give me no peace, even after such a delightful evening."

"It was fun," I agree.

"The reason I'm having trouble falling asleep, tonight," she says, "is because I keep seeing Jamie's girlfriend, that nice Ellie Cooper, looking at him as if he's the only person in the world. That's a rare thing, you know? I'm happy for your brother, happy he's able to pack so much into his life."

"Yup, me, too. She's one in a million."

"Night-night, then." Granny gives me a tired smile, shuffles into her room, a little stooped, the hot water bottle slung by a string over her back.

On my way to bed, I notice that Jamie's desk light is still on. Sometimes, he falls asleep with it on. By now, I feel tired enough to fall asleep myself and flop into bed, pulling the blankets up around my ears.

————

Letters not sent.

A moment ago, I was lying on top of my bed, not sure whether I had been asleep. I think I was drifting in that half-life between waking and dreaming, when time seems to stop, although the hands of the clock keep up their usual rounds. In that gentle country between sleep and aware-ness, I was able to believe war existed only in some book I'd read, and so did my illness. I was fine, and Coop was fine, and as soon as we untangled our fishing lines, we would head for the river.

And, then, I thought I was back in France, lying in a field, and Coop found me and pulled me up into an airplane, where we drank beer and laughed out loud as we flew far above the world. Below us, planes were bombing their own soldiers, soldiers were shooting children, children were shooting children. But up we flew, escaping into the night-filled sky, where we seemed to float on a sea of stars.

Something woke me. At first I wasn't sure what, but as I lay there, I soon recognized the wail of a train as it steamed closer. Funny, I thought. Trains don't usually stop here in the middle of the night. I started to shiver, even

though I had all my clothes on. My desk lamp was
still on. I looked at my watch and saw that it
was 3:20. I remembered there had been something
I wanted to do. I'd meant to just lie down for a
moment or two while I got up a head of steam. I
hadn't intended to drift into sleep.

I got up and sat at my desk and pulled out
this old pile of papers I've been working on for
so long. The string tying it together is beginning to fray. I leafed through the letters I
hadn't sent to you, Rachel, and smiled at some.
Others brought pain. I turned to the last one I
wrote overseas. Here it is.

About two minutes ago, I found out that I'm going
home. Home! I hardly know what that means. I
feel like laughing and crying at the same time.
I want to think it will be just like it was when
I left, that nothing will have changed. I want
everything to go on as if the war never happened,
but my common sense tells me this is a vain hope.
Too many have died. Too much has happened.

Just now, off in the back of the house, I heard
the baby whimpering, getting started on his
nightly howl. I was still shivering and pulled
on a sweater. I listened for someone to get out

*of bed and go to him, do whatever it is they do
to keep him from waking the whole household, but
nothing happened.*

*The baby switched into a higher gear. I
thought Granny usually got up in the night with
him because she was usually awake anyway. Not
this time, apparently.*

*Maybe I'll go. I'm thinking on paper now. And
do what? I find that half-crying, half-moaning
thing the baby does really hard on the nerves. I
hope I don't faint because I feel a little funny
right now. I guess I'll be all right if I hang
on to things.*

I roll over in bed and wake with a start. Turning on my
bed lamp, I see that it's 3:20. I don't know what woke me,
but I lie here listening. I think I hear the wail of a train,
but that can't be. It's only the wind. I roll onto my other
side but can't get back to sleep. A few moments later, I
hear footsteps. Jamie's? They're heading down the stairs,
but wait. They're veering off, going back to the sewing
room, I mean the baby's bedroom.

Hardly. Why would he go back there, when he has so
successfully avoided contact with the baby up to now?
He's probably going downstairs for a bite to eat. I get up
and put on my bathrobe and slippers because the baby is
beginning his nightly whimper. It usually turns into the

kind of cry that makes you think he will be heartbroken if no one comes to pick him up. Granny usually gets up, but maybe she's taken a sleeping pill. Big-hearted me! All right, all right, I'm coming.

When I get to the baby's room, there's Jamie, in the middle of the room, lit by moonlight flooding through the window, making it almost as bright as day. Perhaps this is what wakened the baby. I watch Jamie watching the wee thing as he scrunches up his face to bellow while he tries to stuff his fist into his mouth.

Suddenly, Jamie is aware of me in the doorway. "Is he really our brother?" he says.

"No, he dropped in from some other galaxy and decided to stay." I want to comment on Jamie's actually showing an interest in the kid, but I'm afraid of spoiling the moment.

"I don't think he looks like any of us," Jamie says.

"Don't be silly, he's the dead-spit of you. You need to see him in daylight. Want the experience of changing him?"

"Good God, no!"

After I do all the dirty work, I hand him to Jamie, who nearly drops him. "I didn't think he'd be so heavy," he says. I steer them to the rocking chair and show him how to bundle the baby up close, leaving the blanket a little loose at the top for him to get his hands free. "He likes that," I say.

"There's something I want to do," Jamie says. "I want to take him outside and show him the stars." This doesn't seem strange to me, on a starry night like this. I go down the back stairs first, and Jamie follows, holding the baby close to him in one arm and clutching the banister with his other hand. In the glow through the window, the kitchen is transformed. You can almost hear the moon calling us, begging us to come out.

In the backyard, the baby snuffles at his fist and makes tiny attempts to cry. "Hush, little baby," Jamie says. We watch him blink at the moon and then reach out. "You can't have the moon," Jamie says.

When the Martians come to call, this is the scene I'll describe—me and my two brothers under a starry sky. At this very moment, I know I'm happy. This is what it's like to be human.

"Ah," the baby says, "ah-ah-ah."

Jamie smiles down at him. "I think he's trying to say something to me."

"The stars look really close tonight, don't they?" I say.

"You can't have all those stars, little guy. Me and Coop have first dibs." Jamie is silent for a moment. "I know what I'm going to do," he says finally. The baby is nearly asleep in his arms.

"What?"

"You'll find out."

Jamie is shivering. "Can you carry the baby for me?"

"Hand him over."

Cradling him, I follow Jamie back inside. I'm right behind him as he struggles up the stairs to his own bedroom.

We're both tiptoeing, both afraid to speak. It must be the motion that lulls the baby back to sleep. Gently, Jamie takes him and puts him on his bed, up near the pillow, all snugly tucked up in his baby blanket.

Jamie's shivering like mad, now. He has to sit on the side of his bed to catch his breath. I hand him a jacket from his closet, but he ignores me. All I can do is stand in the doorway, quietly watching. He manages to push himself upright again to go and sit at his desk, where he tears a sheet of paper from a pad of foolscap. Slowly, painstakingly, he writes something in large letters, so no one will miss it, and props it against the lucky fishing lure Coop gave him so long ago.

I am intensely curious but wait, hoping Jamie will explain in good time.

He goes back to his bed, manages to kick off his shoes and slip under the covers without waking the baby. He sighs deeply. "I feel better," he whispers so quietly I can hardly hear him, "in spite of being cold as a block of ice. This little guy makes me feel good, you know? He's going to go far. Way into the future."

Another sigh leaves his body, as if he's releasing something he's held inside too long. He turns on his side to face the baby and pulls him close. The baby's soft, sweet breath warms his face and Jamie snuggles in, his arm around the top of the baby's head, knees drawn up close to his feet.

I creep closer, softly, and lie down on top of the covers, on the other side of our little brother. "You're still shivering," I whisper, turning to face Jamie.

"A little bit."

I put my arm over his arm. "Look, we've made a nest for Baby X."

"Not Baby X any longer."

I lift my head to look at him, but his eyes are closed. "What do you mean?"

He doesn't explain right away. Instead he says, "'Rub-a-dub-dub.'"

It takes me a minute to think what he means. "'Three men in a tub'? How about, two brothers and a sister in a bed? Or, here's one. How about this? 'Wynken, Blynken and Nod one night Sailed off in a wooden shoe'? You used to know that one. What comes next?"

He doesn't say anything. I wonder if he's drifting off. In a moment he whispers, ". . . 'The little stars were the herring fish That lived in that beautiful sea. . . .' Can't remember the rest. Funny, the blanket's warm, but the cold is deep inside me. I'm a bit drifty. Need to tell you something before I drift out too far."

"What?"

"I named the baby."

"What did you say?"

"The baby," he says. "I named him."

"Just like that? You suddenly gave him a name?"

"Shh!" He whispers, "His name is Cooper James McLaren. I wrote it down."

I am silent for a moment. "It's good," I say quietly. "It fits him. He'll grow up just fine with that name."

"You'll have to keep an eye on him."

"I guess somebody has to. God knows, his parents can't be relied on."

"He'll like the climbing tree down near the swale. You have to take him. Show him how to get a good foothold on those lower branches." Jamie smiles in the moonlight coming through his window. "And don't forget to show him the Milky Way."

"I remember how it goes now," I say.

"Mmm?"

"'All night long their nets they threw
To the stars in the twinkling foam—
Then down from the skies came the wooden shoe,
Bringing the fishermen home;
'T was all so pretty a sail it seemed
As if it could not be,
And some folks thought 't was a dream they'd dreamed
Of sailing the beautiful sea—
But I shall name you the fishermen three:
    Wynken,

Blynken,
And Nod.'"

Each breath seems like a sigh as it leaves Jamie, a contented sigh.

"Don't," I whisper.

"Mmm?"

"Don't leave us."

"Okay," I think I hear him say.

Softly, in the moonlit night, Cooper James breathes
peacefully beside me.

THE END

ALSO BY JULIE JOHNSTON

Hero of Lesser Causes
Adam and Eve and Pinch-Me
The Only Outcast
In Spite of Killer Bees
Susanna's Quill
A Very Fine Line